surveillance

surveillance

RILEY CHANCE

CP
BOOKS

ISBN 978-1-99-115459-0 (Paperback – printed)
ISBN 978-1-99-115607-5 (EPub)
ISBN 978-1-99-115608-2 (Kindle)
ISBN 978-1-9911906-2-8 (Paperback – print-on-demand)

Published by Copy Press Books, Nelson, New Zealand 2022
Copy Press Books, 141 Pascoe Street, Nelson, New Zealand

Typesetting and cover design by Suzanne North, The CopyPress
Proofreading by Stephanie McConchie, Focus Proofreading & Editing
Copy editing and literary input – Geoff Walker & Sue Reidy

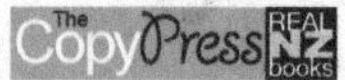

Designed and distributed in New Zealand by
The CopyPress, Nelson, New Zealand.
www.copypress.co.nz

Imagine having the ability to track every citizen. Pandemics controlled, terrorists thwarted, and crimes solved. A utopian society . . . for those with nothing to hide.

Grace Marks, Journalist

PROLOGUE

The road ahead kinked gently right, the small town's sole impact on the state highway. Grace let her old, reliable but in-need-of-a-service radiant-red Ford Mondeo coast up the small rise before Tokomaru, the small town with the gentle kink near Palmerston North and home. She glanced at the dashboard: it was almost seven o'clock.

'Whatever will be, will be . . .'

She sang along to the song Spotify had selected for her. She had Googled Doris Day recently when researching a story, clearly security cameras weren't the only devices monitoring people day and night.

Grace buzzed down the window, letting the warm evening air rush over her. Tokomaru had never looked so good. She was in a rare mood because she had a story, and not just any story, a scoop. For a semi-salaried journalist that was the equivalent of finding an oasis in the desert. It wouldn't change her life, but success equalled money and money kept the financial wolves kennelled.

'The future's not ours to see . . .'

As her car took the kink, Grace rolled her shoulders and clicked her neck. She had been up since half five and was too mentally drained to put the polish on her story tonight, not that it needed much. It was Saturday tomorrow, and as getting up before her teenage children surfaced was no contest, she could finish the story in peace. Once she had filed it, along with the document that had caused all the trouble, she would feel safe.

'Que sera, sera . . .'

The headlights of the car behind her blazed brightly as the driver failed to observe the reduced speed limit. With the light blinding in her rear-view mirrors, the car raced up behind her and sat on her bumper.

'What will be . . . Fucking dickheads,' Grace muttered. Kiwis were mostly good drivers but there were a few morons with a death wish.

Leaving the town limits, she slowly increased her speed. The car following stayed glued to her bumper. Now pissed off, she took her foot off the accelerator as she took the next corner, a gentle left-hand bend. With a sudden mix of insight and alarm, she realised it wasn't a typical moron tailgater. And at that instant the car behind rammed into her.

Grace instinctively braked. The combined forces jolted her forwards, the seatbelt saving her from damage. In the rear-view mirror she could see Tom and Jerry, the two thugs masquerading as agents who had tried to warn her off the story. Bathed in the red of her brake lights, the scene was hellish. The agents with predator-wide eyes and excited leers.

There wasn't time for rational decision making. When they dropped back a few metres, Grace accelerated, but her car was no match for whatever they were driving. It ploughed into her for a second time.

'Fuck you!' she yelled.

Speeding up wasn't going to work. Stopping was likely to be a death sentence.

With no plan in mind, she slowed as they approached another left-hand bend, bracing herself. This time the blow was less severe, but well-aimed. The car hit her left back panel and, as the thug who was driving accelerated hard, the back of Grace's car started to slide to the right.

Time slowed. Grace saw her speed was eighty and, unhelpfully given the circumstances, that she needed petrol. There were no headlights from oncoming vehicles – that was good. They had the road to themselves – that was bad. And ironically there were no security cameras to capture the action.

She felt the car sliding out of control. A rally driver would have counter steered and taken their foot off the brake. Grace wasn't a rally driver. Her instinct was to steer left and brake.

Physics took over, Grace swore quietly. As Doris sang sweetly on, she closed her eyes.

How could a story that had started so innocuously end up like this?

PART 1

CHAPTER 1

Grace wrinkled her nose at the paused newsreader on the television. She looked towards her partner Sean, who was working diligently at the dining table. She huffed quietly.

After what felt like a gym session designed for elite athletes, Grace was lolling on her couch, wine in hand, watching the news. She was still wearing her damp gym gear of leggings under a pair of shorts – because nobody needed to see a relief map of her backside – and her favourite grey hoodie. She enjoyed her frequent gym visits. They gave her time to think and countered her fondness for food and alcohol. Although she had passed the dreaded five zero, a few years ago too, on a good day she could pass for forty.

'I *said* it's strange.' This time she said it louder.

Sean, a family court lawyer, looked up briefly and grunted his agreement before carrying on reading a legal document. Grace glared at the top of his head. She didn't want to disturb him, but she did want to talk about the story on the news, a story she herself was kicking around.

The lounge door opened before she could press Sean further, in walked her children looking serious. Joined by Roxy, Sean's golden retriever, the small deputation stood in front of Grace.

'When's dinner, we're starving,' said her daughter. Still at high school, Sophie was a slightly rebellious teenager, her long hair constantly changing colour as her way of asserting her adultness. Grace's son

Kane, eighteen and two years older than his sister, added his weight to his sister's demand by nodding solemnly. Having started university, after years of a strict uniform code that included short back and sides haircuts, he was enjoying all the freedoms university brought. Roxy stood smiling, happy to be part of the team.

'How are the assignments and homework going?' asked Grace.

Her children shuffled their feet before saying, 'Fine,' in unison.

'Poor darlings, education wasn't as stressful in my day. When I came in, I heard a burst of gunfire and one of you yell, "Die you motherfuckers". I assumed you were rehearsing a modern adaptation of a Shakespearian tragedy.'

Sophie scowled. Kane rolled his eyes. Roxy smiled, while Grace chuckled at her own joke.

'Okay,' said Grace, holding up her arms in surrender. 'Let's do takeaways. I can't be arsed cooking now. Order enough for four but keep it healthyish. Do you want my card?'

'I'll text you the amount and you can transfer it,' said her son.

'Healthy *and* reasonable,' she called out as they left conspiratorially happy.

'I can pay if you like,' said Sean.

'I'm not that broke.'

'I know but—'

'But nothing,' she interrupted, sounding slightly whiney. She frowned as she scratched Roxy's head. 'Sorry, I didn't mean to bite. It's just that . . . it makes me feel like I can't cope as an adult. I'm eighteen again, bailed out by my parents.'

'Fair enough,' said Sean.

'Getting takeaways is bad enough. That makes me feel like I'm failing as a parent,' Grace said more to herself than Sean. 'But how can you be a parent, breadwinner, domestic goddess and have a life?'

'You're doing awesome, Grace, and all by yourself for the last decade. They're two cool kids.'

'Yeah, I'm awesome,' she said flatly, staring into her wine.

'You are. You've raised two great kids *and* reinvented yourself as a successful investigative journalist.'

'True. That term though, "reinvented": there's an overused word that needs banning. It's a bullshit way of saying you found a way to survive for a little longer in the capitalist hunger games. And successful? I don't know if the retainer I'm on could be classed as success.'

'After what your story did to expose the tax system,' said Sean, 'NewsNZ's offer did seem a little frugal.'

She laughed. 'That's an understatement.'

Grace was a journalist for NewsNZ, the recently created state-owned enterprise which ran in conjunction with RadioNZ and TelevisionNZ. It was the government's response to the steep decline in the traditional media's revenue caused by the dual evils of the pandemic and multi-nationals such as Facebook and Google devouring advertising spend.

'Still,' said Grace, 'if the government hadn't reinvented the media we'd all be at the mercy of fake news and social media's advertising algorithms. And I'd still be consulting, stroking the egos of morons and narcissists.'

Sean chuckled before going back to his work.

Grace finished her wine as the frozen news item recaptured her attention. She played the item again.

The impeccably dressed newsreader took up the story. 'Boy racers, graffiti and gangs of youths are terrorising residents in suburbs in metropolitan areas across Aotearoa New Zealand. Covering the story for One News is Ryan Boswell.'

The shot changed to a car, its back tyres spinning up a cloud of choking smoke as it did a doughnut before accelerating away. Boswell voiced over the action. 'This scene, recorded last night in Hamilton, is typical of scenes playing out in suburbs across Aotearoa New Zealand.'

The shot changed to a dimly-lit recording of two people in the distance crouched in front of a fence. Off camera a voice yells, 'Get the bleep out of it.' The graffiti artists run as the image staggers towards the fence revealing they have tagged it with the popular street slogan *Anarquay*. The amateur cameraperson yells at them, the words before and after the word 'little' are bleeped out.

The next shot is of a blurry female figure sitting on a park bench as Boswell continues. 'This individual, who didn't want to be identified, lives in the area.'

The blurred image, recognisable as the face of an elderly woman, says, 'They're driving us mad with their cars and letting off fireworks at all times of the night. If you confront them, the language is atrocious. We're sick to death of them. It's about time the police locked them up.'

The shot changed to Boswell standing on a street corner. 'Police say they have noticed a marked increase in the number of complaints of minor vandalism, graffiti, boy racers and people complaining of being hassled in the street. The police say the majority of the incidences are minor in nature and that they don't have the resources to identify the individuals responsible. Residents I've spoken to want security cameras installed to catch the offenders.'

Grace sighed. 'Just what we need, more security cameras.'

The item finished with more interviews interspersed with shots of cars doing burnouts and more images of graffiti on fences.

She pressed pause, her nose again wrinkling. On the surface it was an inconsequential story concerning a rise in minor disturbances. She had initially put it down to the economy and it had sat at the bottom of her pile of possible stories to chase. Unfortunately for her it wasn't a big pile, so she did a little digging.

She levered herself up, stretched and walked behind Sean, draping her arms over his shoulders. She whispered seductively, 'In fact, I'd say it's *very* strange.'

He sighed. 'What's strange?'

She stood up. 'Boy racers, people being hassled in the street, fireworks at all hours, minor vandalism like car wing mirrors being smashed, graffiti. That sort of thing. It doesn't make sense.'

He put the document he was reading back in a bundle and retied it with the legal sector's traditional pink ribbon.

'Don't let me disturb you,' said Grace.

Giving her a yeah, right look, he loosened his tie. 'Do things like that usually make sense?'

'They usually make sense to someone.' In her previous life as a business consultant, when she encountered strange behaviour, it didn't take long to work out what was happening. When nurses were visiting the same patient three times in a day, when a single visit would suffice, it was due to management counting the number of visits as a measure of productivity. Grace explained to an angry group of mainly suited, older white men that it wasn't the nurse's fault if the system was stupid. They didn't invite her back. It wasn't the first time that honesty had contributed to Grace's challenging financial position.

'Okay, and it's on the rise?' asked Sean.

'But the point is, it usually isn't,' she said, sitting on the armrest of the couch.

'Sorry?' said Sean, going into the kitchen, Roxy following hopefully behind.

'It's reported more *because* it's in the news. Dog attacks are the classic. A dog mauls a child, and it makes the news. For the next few weeks dog attacks are newsworthy. Everyone's talking about a spate of attacks, but it's fiction. Dogs haven't suddenly turned on us.'

'Right. Street disturbances aren't on the rise then?'

'That's what's strange,' she said, sipping her wine. 'They really are. Over the past weeks they've risen significantly.'

Sean scratched his stubble. 'You've lost me. Now it's strange what the news is reporting *is* happening.'

'I know it seems upside down, but yes. These minor incidents have risen dramatically.'

'Are you sure?' he asked, slumping into Grace's old, uncomfortable couch.

Grace flicked a shrug. 'CT sent me the stats along with possible contacts I could follow up.' CT, Corin Tait, was a police detective and Grace's main contact in the police. Complicating matters, she had dated him before she met Sean.

'Are you *still* in touch with him?'

'Only professionally.'

Sean gave her a look.

'You know there's nothing to worry about. Besides, you see Glenda every day at work. What's the difference?'

'The difference is . . .' He started his sentence with a confidence that seemed to evaporate.

Grace raised her eyebrows playfully. 'Were you going to say that you can be trusted and I can't?'

'No, I was going to say *I* can be trusted and *Corin* can't.'

Grace pouted. 'Isn't that the same thing?'

After a moment Sean conceded, 'Yes, you're right. There's no difference but it feels different.'

'Like I'm cheating?'

He looked at her. 'No, I know you're not.'

Grace put a hand on his leg. 'Of course I'm not. Like Glenda, he's a former lover, now a friend. You and Glenda were closer than us. You told me you contemplated marriage.'

His face reddened.

Grace changed the conversation. 'Do you want to see the numbers?'

'Sure. Show me *Corin's* numbers.' He said his name like an unhappy child.

Grace went to retrieve her laptop. When her back was to him, she allowed herself a generous smirk.

'You better have wiped that grin off your face by the time you turn around.'

They both laughed and were soon looking at a graph of police statistics.

'Wow,' he said. 'A four-fold increase in a month. They must be counting differently, or they've changed the categories.'

She shook her head. 'That was my first question. Nothing's changed in the collection, no new computer system and they've checked the data. It's exactly what it looks like, a rapid increase in minor public disturbances.'

'Is it everywhere?'

'Hmm, good question.'

She clicked on different menus until the data was displayed by location. They both leaned closer to inspect the refreshed table.

Grace spoke first. 'Weird. What do you think?'

'Weird,' he echoed. 'The increase is in Auckland, Hamilton, here, Wellington and Dunedin.'

'Students?' she asked. 'They're university cities.'

'It doesn't sound like students,' said Sean. 'They like drinking and having a good time, not burnouts, vandalising property and hassling people. Besides, what about the students in Christchurch? Their stats haven't changed.'

'You're right, it's not students.' Grace sat on the floor and stretched. 'God my arse is sore. Tuck jumps should come with a health warning.'

Sean chuckled, watching her discomfort. 'There must be a link,' he said. 'A change of this magnitude can't be random, can it? And if it was a stupid social media meme, like drenching yourself with ice water or Momo, we'd see it across New Zealand. What do the police think?'

'That's just it,' she said. 'CT contacted me, not the other way around. He wanted to know if the media had heard anything.'

'And now you're curious.'

'I haven't anything much else on the go. My domestic violence story should be good but that's waiting for the court case.'

'Do you reckon this story will be big?' he asked.

'It looks to me like it's tied to the economic squeeze or an internet thing. In other words, a disorganised coincidence. But . . .' She left the sentence hanging.

He frowned. 'Not a coincidence?'

'And that makes it organised.'

Sean smirked more than smiled. 'You *are* looking for a juicy story.'

She chuckled.

'What are you going to do?'

A knock on the front door interrupted their conversation.

'Eat dinner,' said Grace, leaping athletically off the floor. 'Tomorrow I'm going to put that tired old Sherlock Holmes quote to use. "Once you have eliminated the impossible, whatever remains, no matter how improbable, must be the truth". I'm going to interview some of those involved. Start eliminating the impossibilities.'

CHAPTER 2

Grace parked outside a pair of two-storey semi-detached houses in Cannon's Creek, Porirua. They were state houses, the 1930s square timber design commonplace in inner city suburbs across New Zealand. She had driven past similar houses, but this was one of the addresses her police contact had given her. Although the street appeared quiet, Grace was wary. She knew this was a tough neighbourhood; her ex-husband grew up here.

The twin houses were in good repair though they conveyed polar opposite impressions. The first house had a well-kept lawn and a garden featuring small fruit trees. The second house, the one Grace was interested in, featured an array of modified cars and stacks of empty RTD bottles. Two youths, who looked to Grace about seventeen, sat vaping on the front step. They were keeping a wary eye on her car while trying to look cool and uninterested.

Sitting with Grace was her hairdresser, Zack. Apart from being Grace's stylist and somehow related to Sean, Zack was an aspiring actor. It was his day off and she had borrowed him to give her street credibility. He looked like a well-groomed version of the two youths sitting on the front step. He was to play the part of a trainee journalist and wore a tidy hoodie and borrowed baggy jeans from his flatmate. He refused to wear a cap telling her it would flatten his hair irreversibly.

Under his breath Zack said, 'Bloody hell, Ace.' Only her partner Sean called her Grace, everyone else used the nickname she had acquired at school – for her feeble tennis serve.

'It'll be fine,' she assured him. 'As we planned, you're a keen streetwise kid learning the ropes. Leave the talking to me.'

Zack looked at her. 'Acting I can do, but if there's any trouble, I'm running for the hills.'

'It'll be fine. We're just here to get their side of the story. You ready?'

'Yo blood!'

'Is that how they're going to talk?'

'How the fuck should I know?' he said. 'I'm treating this as improv.'

Grace choked back a laugh. 'Classic. You don't need to say much, if anything. Remember, we want them to do the talking. We already know what we know.'

'I'm good.'

Getting out of the car, Grace smoothed down her skirt. She had chosen the consultant look for the encounter – black skirt and jacket, white shirt and black ballet pumps. Net curtains moved, blinds quivered and faces appeared and disappeared from neighbouring windows as they walked towards the house.

'How many security cameras can you see, Zack?'

Zack looked around. 'I can't see any. Why? Are we in danger?'

'No,' said Grace. 'It's how to tell how affluent a suburb is. More cameras, more money, more shit to protect.'

When they reached the front gate, the two boys retreated inside. Grace shrugged to Zack as they walked up the path and knocked on the door. She could hear an urgent, whispered conversation behind the front door, then feet clumping up a set of stairs. Seconds later, an unsmiling Māori woman opened the door. Standing on the top step, she stared down at them. In stark contrast to the impression the house gave, she was immaculately dressed in real estate agent attire. Grace thought she looked in her thirties, but with dyed auburn hair she could easily be mid-forties.

She looked warily at each of them in turn, her arms folded across her chest. 'Can I help you?'

'I hope so. I'm Grace Marks, a journalist with NewsNZ. This is my trainee, Zack.'

'Kia ora,' said Zack.

The woman angled her head. 'Grace Marks? Were you the one that made the rich pay tax?'

'I was.' Grace smiled to encourage the conversation, though she didn't need to act. She enjoyed it when people recognised her as 'the one who made the rich pay tax'.

'I'm Rita,' the woman said, her face softening. 'I'm guessing it's not about that.'

'No. It's about the increase in neighbourhood disturbances.' Rita's wariness returned so Grace continued quickly. She only had one or two sentences in which to make her case. 'I'm trying to get the other side of the story. The media are jumping on young people, they don't seem interested in what's really happening.'

Rita's face remained etched with suspicion. 'Why here?'

Grace seldom lied but sometimes it was necessary. She could hardly say their details came from the police; the door would slam shut. 'I asked around at the shops, it's how we journalists roll. This address came up, that's all.'

Rita scowled. 'Who told you to come here?'

To Grace's surprise Zack answered in a respectful tone. 'We don't ask for names. People don't like giving out their name.'

'My whanau isn't in trouble?'

'Not from us,' said Grace. 'We want to hear their side of the story.'

Rita unfolded her arms. 'You won't use their names?'

'That's their call. If they, or you, don't want them named, we won't.'

'Okay. It seems harmless.' Rita stepped back letting them enter her clean, tidy house. As if reading Grace's mind, Rita said, 'I go hoarse hassling them about the cars and bottles. It makes the whare look stink.'

'Who owns the cars?' asked Grace. 'I mean, there are so many.'

'I know. Corey, my eldest, he's a mechanic and this has become his DIY yard. He and his mates buy wrecks and sell the parts online. They do okay, as well as me some weeks. The boys will move out one day and I'll grow roses,' she said with a chuckle.

They followed her into the kitchen. As she passed the foot of the stairs, Rita used a well-practised parental yell. 'Corey, Liam. Get down here.' In the kitchen her voice returned to real estate agent volume. 'They won't be long, have a seat.'

Grace and Zack sat down. Grace opened a notebook. Zack did the same.

'Fancy a hot drink?'

'Thank you, if it's no trouble.'

'I was about to put the kettle on. I've an open home in an hour so there's time. It's not going to take longer, is it?'

'No, twenty minutes at the outside,' said Grace. 'Black coffee for me, no sugar.'

'The same please,' said Zack. His usual trim soy latte would be out of character and unlikely.

As Rita busied herself making the hot drinks, Grace heard the trudge of reluctant feet grow louder until two sullen shapes slouched into the kitchen, plonking themselves at the table. Dressed in low-slung jeans and hoodies splattered with American basketball logos, they were older than Grace first thought, early twenties.

Corey, recognisable by his mechanic's grimy hands, spoke. 'What's this about? We haven't done anything.'

Grace was about to speak but Rita beat her. 'Relax, it's fine. No one's in trouble, they're journalists.'

Rita joined them at the table. 'This one's Corey, he's the apprentice mechanic. That one's Liam. He's studying hospitality, though there's not much work around here because of Covid. You don't mind if I listen in?' She raised her eyebrows, making it clear it was a rhetorical question.

'Not at all.' Grace introduced herself and Zack, explaining why they were there. Importantly, she stressed, anything they said wouldn't leave the room. Corey and Liam sat impassively, the odd eyebrow flash showed they understood, but they remained guarded.

'You got any questions before we kick off?' asked Zack, his voice now sounding like theirs.

Grace mentally grinned. Zack was doing great.

Corey and Liam glanced at each other and shook their heads.

'Right,' said Grace. 'First off, how tough is life around here for you and your friends?'

After a substantial pause, Corey spoke. 'Yeah, pretty tough. Most of our mates are on the dole or they're training like Liam. Or they've gone.'

Grace kept quiet. Zack did the same.

Corey looked at Liam, who added, 'The training's good but there ain't no jobs. It's like an interesting version of the dole.'

Rita's face softened as she put a hand on Liam's arm. 'It'll pick up, son.'

'Yeah, maybe,' said Liam. 'If we get rid of Covid. Even you're struggling, Mum, now the property market has turned to shit.'

Rita's eyes widened. 'Language. You're right though. Selling houses is hard mahi now. I have to work my butt off to make ends meet.'

'It's a tough market,' said Grace.

'It's dreadful. I'm reselling the houses I sold in the last few years but now for the bank. I feel like I'm betraying the owners, but if it wasn't me, it would be another agent.' She sat up straight. 'But you're not here about the woes of the real estate industry.'

Grace smiled. 'No, but it's interesting. The media covers the financial aspects of the property market forgetting foreclosure statistics are a measure of human misery. I may come back in the future.' She turned back to Corey and Liam. 'As I said, I'm interested in the other side of the increase in street disturbances.'

Corey and Liam remained silent.

She pressed on. 'What's happening around here?'

'Nothing around here,' Corey said.

'Why not around here?' Corey's answer was too quick.

Corey looked at the table. 'The events are organised for Wellington, not here. We wouldn't do that . . . not around here. This is our hood.'

'Organised?' said Rita. 'Sorry, Grace, you're asking the questions.'

'It's the exact question I was going to ask.'

Liam picked up the story. 'Yeah. If they're organising an invasion, we get texted the location and head over. Have a little fun before the cops shut it down. We aren't hurting anyone.'

'Right. I take it an invasion is a gathering?' asked Grace.

'Yeah, invade the aves.'

In response to her puzzled look, Zack leaned over. 'The avenues. You know, the streets.'

'Right, the aves. Got it. Why?'

Corey and Liam shrugged.

'Boredom mainly,' said Liam, 'but the money helps.'

Grace, Rita and Zack exchanged glances.

'What money?' asked Grace.

'One hundred a car, as long as you burn enough rubber,' said Corey.

She was struggling to follow this lurch in their story. Were these boys being paid to burn up streets? 'Who gives you the money?'

Corey glanced at Liam. 'It's not a secret. There's an aves invasion coordinator on Facebook. You let him know you're in, you get the text. Afterwards, we park up in a line and a masked-up dude gives us the cash.'

'Do you know the dude?' asked Grace.

Corey again glanced at Liam, 'No.'

'Do you get involved in any other stuff? Fireworks?'

They shook their heads, this time without conferring.

'Any of your friends?'

Another dual headshake.

Grace waited but, although she sensed they knew more, it was all Corey and Liam were going to divulge. She asked additional questions about how the pandemic was affecting them, answers she didn't need and wasn't going to use, but it paid to keep the illusion solid. As a journalist, it was useful to develop lasting relationships with everyone you came across. They finished their coffee, thanked them and left.

When they were back in the car, Grace said, 'Great work Zack, you were perfect.'

Zack beamed. Grace could see his acting dream had received a boost.

As they drove away, she asked, 'First impressions, Zack?'

'How can anyone tolerate so much dirt under their nails,' he said, looking at his hands.

She laughed. 'I mean the aves invasions.'

'Boy racers paid to burn up the streets? It's hard to believe. I mean, why? They'd do it for nothing. Can't see why anyone would want to pay them.'

Grace considered his question as he went back to cleaning his already clean fingernails.

'You'd only pay them,' she said slowly, 'if you wanted them to turn up where and when you wanted. But your question's the right one. Why?'

She felt a tingle that told her that this was a story worth chasing.

CHAPTER 3

Looking around, Grace spotted Corin sitting at a table near the back of the café. He was hard to miss, sharply dressed in a dark blue suit, police-issue blue shirt and black and white striped tie. He made a point of looking at his watch as she joined him.

'Good of you to make it, Ace. I've ordered coffee. I know you're not fussy, so I ordered you an Americano.'

'Thanks Detective Tait, you're looking sharp. I'm not late, am I?'

'You're always late, Ace. It's being a journo and not having a real job.'

As she sat, she checked the time on her phone. 'Two minutes? Come on, that's not late.'

'On time is black and white, not grey. You're the type who expects planes to wait because traffic was heavy.'

She bowed her head. 'I'm sorry, I feel duly chastened.'

'I'm only yanking your chain. I expected you'd be five minutes late, at a minimum. Like you were for dinner last week.'

She shrugged. 'Traffic was heavy.'

They both smirked.

'I enjoyed dinner,' he said. 'It was nice to go out without the complication of trying to get you into bed.'

'It was fun,' agreed Grace. 'And you *did* try to get me into bed.'

He chuckled. 'I had to test the water. Did you tell your special person you were out with me?'

She winced. 'No, I said I ate room service.'

'You lied?'

'A white lie,' said Grace. 'The problem with platonic get-togethers is they don't sound platonic. I'm taking my ex out to dinner sounds exactly like I'm shagging my ex for old times' sake.'

'True. I always pegged you as loyal. You didn't disappoint.'

'Shall we get down to business? Street disturbances?'

Their coffees arrived, the interruption giving her the time she needed to get the unhelpful thought of shagging Corin out of her head.

'The increase in street disturbances has plateaued,' he said, 'but it's triple the normal rate. And it's minor shit – menacing people in the street, lewd comments, boy racers, late night fireworks, gangs of youths prowling but not breaking the law. That sort of stuff.'

Grace nodded. 'Activities that make people call the police, but not serious enough for arrests.'

'Correct. The media are having a field day covering angry citizens venting, demanding we act. Even if we doubled the size of the force, we'd catch fuck all of them and we'd be issuing warnings. Most of it isn't close to category one. What have you dug up?'

'A few bits and pieces. Listening to you, it could be material. I interviewed a couple of boy racers from Cannon's Creek.'

'On the phone?'

'Hardly. I can't imagine boy racers chatting freely over the phone. I paid them a visit.'

Corin raised his eyebrows. 'The last of the real journos went to Cannibal Creek. Didn't your ex grow up there? What's he doing now?'

'Probably screwing a different research assistant.'

'Sorry.'

Grace shrugged. 'I couldn't care less, it's his life. As long as he keeps paying his share of the children's costs, I prefer him on the other side of the planet.'

'Fair enough. What did you learn in Cannon's Creek?'

'I found out there's a closed group on Facebook used to organise times and places for aves invasions.'

'They've been doing that for a while.'

'But when did they start paying them to turn up?'

Corin's eyes widened. 'Paying them? Who? And how much?'

'No idea who, not yet. As for how much, they said a hundred if they turn up and lose enough rubber.' She watched as his detective brain incorporated her information into what he knew but hadn't told her. 'I've developed a phrase for it, you know, for my story.'

'Go on,' he said.

'Organised minor crime.'

'Not bad,' he said, drumming his fingers on the table. It was a habit she recognised; it meant his brain was in overdrive.

He stopped drumming. 'Let's make an assumption.'

'Okay.'

He spoke deliberately. 'If the boy racers are organised . . . and paid, let's assume the other disturbances are too.'

She nodded slowly. 'It's a logical assumption. It also ties in with the types of crime. I mean, if you're getting paid to be a suburban irritation, you don't want to get arrested and taken off the payroll.'

'If the assumption holds,' said Corin, 'they're being paid to make the streets unsafe—'

'Or seem unsafe,' she interrupted. 'So, *cui bono*?'

Corin rolled his eyes. 'Only halfwit authors say *cui bono*. How many in the police do you imagine go around speaking Latin?'

Grace smirked. 'Fair enough. *Who benefits* from seemingly unsafe streets?'

'Not the police, that's for sure. It's a huge waste of our time.'

'Maybe it's keeping you distracted.'

'From what?'

'Criminal gangs,' she suggested. 'Maybe drug importers.'

They contemplated the scenario before simultaneously shaking their heads.

'I agree,' she said. 'It's too far-fetched. Maybe if we were in a movie.'

Corin drummed his fingers. 'What do people do when they don't feel safe?'

'Apart from calling the police, I don't know, buy a dog.'

He stopped drumming and stared at her. 'You've cracked it. Doberman breeders are behind this.'

'I was joking,' said Grace with an exaggerated eye-roll.

'Really? It's hard to tell with you. Most of the time you're insightful, other times you'd struggle to navigate your way through a revolving door.'

'What bit attracted you?' she asked.

'Bit of both. Back to the question.'

She leaned forward. 'Security firms.'

'Yeah, security firms. That was my thought too.'

'Yes, but no,' said Grace. 'Times are hard enough. Security firms must be super busy. And it's a hell of a risk, isn't it? Sowing civil unrest as a marketing strategy.'

Corin rubbed his chin. 'They're in the frame but, as you say, it'd be stupid. One drunken comment or boast and you'd go from running a successful business to behind bars. The individual actions may be trivial, but organising civil unrest isn't.'

'Yeah,' she said. 'Security firms benefit, but they can't be behind this.'

Corin's police brain and Grace's journalistic brain juggled the pieces, each trying to make sense of a picture that currently resembled a drunk surrealist's first draft.

'If we assume organised,' she said, 'that means not a lone wolf.

There've been individuals who've used their wealth to corner markets, but this is hardly a Soros-type play.'

'Agreed. That also eliminates a single security firm. The increase in crime helps everyone. And the likelihood New Zealand security firms have formed a cartel without anyone noticing is less than fuck all.'

'That would be a massive turn-up. Be a good story though.'

He gave her a you've-got-to-be-joking look.

After a short pause, Grace said, 'I'll say it, but I know you're thinking it too.'

He nodded. 'It sounds mad. Like we're a couple of conspiracy nongs who think Covid doesn't exist.'

'And the Government are microchipping us,' she said. 'But if it's organised, and paying boy racers indicates part of it is, and it's not the security firms or a gang of crims, it could be bigger than Texas.'

He sniffed. 'The words "state sponsored" do spring to mind.'

'But which state?' said Grace. 'And why?'

CHAPTER 4

'What the fuck are those Yanks up to?'

Will Manilow, the CEO of Erebus Optics, put down the phone and rested his chin on his hand. He had said the question aloud, although he was alone in his third-floor office, staring out over Wellington's busy, upmarket The Terrace.

After sipping his lukewarm and bitter coffee, he pushed it away and rubbed his temples. It was his fourth coffee of the morning but, if anything, it was making his hangover worse. He pressed a button on his desk phone which resembled a racing car's dashboard. The new American owners had upgraded the company's technology in line with the equipment they used. It was ridiculously over the top for what they needed.

'Yes?' The uninterested voice of his executive assistant Mandy drifted into the room.

He leaned unnecessarily closer to the phone. 'Mandy, can you nip out and buy a couple of sausage rolls? Take the money out of petty cash.'

After a pause she said, 'Fine.'

'Thanks Mandy . . .' He was about to say, 'you're a treasure', but she had already disconnected.

Blowing out a long, groggy breath, he woke up his computer. The January operational meeting was due to start in five minutes; it would take an hour, give or take. When he owned the company he had made everyone take the whole of January off to enjoy the sun. The Americans didn't want to slow down, not even for Christmas, but he had given everyone three weeks leave. Bugger their stretch goals.

Will leaned back heavily in his chair, closing his eyes. It was only the first week after the Christmas break, he should be feeling revitalised, not like roadkill. The pressure he was under from the American owners of what used to be his company was relentless. Their focus was on breakneck growth at the expense of profitability. He agreed with their strategy in principle, profits would eventually come with market share, but getting the company's cashflow in order was surely a priority. They insisted on a growth-first approach, assuring him money wasn't a problem. Their latest edict on sales incentives for street-facing cameras was an example of this single-minded focus.

He checked the time, swore and started the meeting. He detested online meetings, preferring the face-to-face days when, for the first ten minutes, everyone told stories and laughed. Yes, it was an excuse to have good coffee and morning tea. Yes, the stories were seldom politically correct, but they were civilised. Online meetings made sense during lockdowns but they had become business as usual. He found them disheartening, it was like sitting in the grandstand at the cricket watching it rain. If this was the future, it was time to declare. Three years, that's all he had left on his contract.

A mechanical but recognisably female voice said, 'This meeting is being recorded.'

It was the policy of Erebus Group, an American controlled conglomerate who owned the company, to record meetings rather than take minutes. They claimed it was easier, more accurate and saved resources. That was all true, but it meant everyone performed for the camera. Everyone said what they were expected to say. Business pre-technology and pre-pandemic relied on talking to people, how else did you find out what was going on? Now everyone played the part of the dedicated, enthusiastic, unquestioning employee. The only time you found out anything real was over a drink, and those occasions had become increasingly rare.

His office door opened semi-violently and an unsmiling Mandy marched into the room. She had stopped knocking politely when her three-month trial period finished. She also dressed more casually, but always attractively. Will considered her a looker and he didn't mind what she wore. They had few visitors, and her days could be quiet and boring. He monitored her internet traffic, another Erebus Group policy, and employment websites featured heavily. Those and fifty-shades-of-grey inspired semi-porn sites, which must serve as a distraction.

'Perfect timing, Mandy,' he said, trying to look perky.

Handing over a greasy brown paper bag, she forced a smile.

'How does my diary look this afternoon?'

'You mean *after* your regular lunch across the road?' Mandy carried on without waiting for him to answer. 'Starting at two, you've six half-hour online interviews back-to-back for the branch manager role in New Plymouth.'

Will groaned. 'Is that today?'

'Are you still planning to go to New Plymouth for the final interviews?'

He nodded. 'Getting a decent feel for a person is hopeless online.'

'I'll tentatively block out a day.'

The door shut behind her seconds later.

Making sure the sticky note was still covering his webcam, he devoured half the first sausage roll in a single bite. 'That's so good,' he said quietly, enjoying the instantaneous surge of healing pleasure. 'How could a food that tastes so good be bad for you?'

'Will? Is that you?' A voice from his computer startled him. He had forgotten to mute himself.

He finished the rest of the sausage roll quickly, talking awkwardly between swallows. 'Hi Keith, I'll be a few seconds. The others aren't online yet.' As he said this, two boxes containing faces appeared on his screen. He wiped his face and scrunched the brown bag shut. He would eat the second sausage roll after the meeting.

As people logged on there were the usual hellos and polite small talk. How was the golf tournament? Who went where over the Christmas break? How has everyone coped with Covid? It sounded forced, which wasn't surprising. They hadn't yet had the opportunity to meet as a team, to get to know each other. What they needed, he thought, was a strategy retreat. A few nights away for team bonding.

Will adjusted his tie and removed the sticky note. 'Hi team. Sorry Christmas is over and we're back down the mines. I hope you managed to get a bit of a break. Let's not muck around. A quick whip around the regions, then I'll bring you up to speed with the latest thinking from across the Pacific.'

Everyone knew this was the politically correct way of saying the latest dictates from the oligarch Americans who contracted an organisation to watch their recorded meetings and report anything out of the ordinary.

'Let's start at the bottom and work our way up.'

Janine, the Dunedin branch manager started giving her report as Will started mentally drifting out of the meeting. He had already seen the reports and his mind wandered forward three years. He would resign the instant his five-year contract ended, sell his mansion on the hill and buy a small lifestyle block where he could hear the ocean.

Who knows, he may have a special person in his life by then, though his current lifestyle made it unlikely. Not only was he getting fatter, from too much alcohol and too little exercise, but his wardrobe had deteriorated tragically. His business clothes were tidy, sharp even, but his casual wardrobe was sad and dated. Stepping out these days, he looked as trendy as Myspace. There was no excuse, he could afford to splash out on his wardrobe – but why bother?

He glared at his image framed in the box on his computer. Even his over-priced suit couldn't mask his uninterested appearance. Uninterested in the business, uninterested in himself and, if he was honest, uninterested in life, at least his current life. He owned a fabulous house, the latest Audi and an impressive investment portfolio. But nothing came close to filling the large hole that had developed since his wife suddenly died from cancer five years ago.

The sale of his company to the Erebus Group had made him front page news, for five minutes. *Kiwi entrepreneur attracts US venture capital.* There were alcohol-fuelled celebrations, and the local business incubator, who Will had never heard of, claimed credit in the media for creating a 'transformational, innovation ecosystem'. The business press wanted to know about the real Kiwi winner and ludicrously, as the business had operated for over twenty years, he had received a nomination for entrepreneur of the year. It was all, apart from the money in his bank account, total bollocks.

He wasn't a Kiwi winner and anyway, for every 'winner' in the business world there were a thousand near-death businessmen and women. People who turned themselves inside out every day to keep their world turning, to make money for unseen billionaires.

'What do you think, Will?' A voice from one of the boxes snapped him back to the present.

'Sorry, was that you, Rob? The connection's not great today,' he lied.

'No, it was me, Simon.'

'Right, sorry Simon. Can you repeat the question?'

'I said clients are finding the fine print in our contracts unfathomable. Can we simplify it?'

Will had already discussed this with the owners. 'The short answer is no. Because we're owned by an American company, we need contracts containing aspects of both New Zealand and US law. I'll include a note in our next communique to our resellers to let them know that's the reason for the complexity. I didn't think customers read the contracts. Click or sign and get on with it.'

'I agree,' said Simon. 'Who knows what rights we give Gates when we agree to Microsoft licences?'

Heads nodding their general agreement mixed with polite laughter.

Simon continued. 'It's the contract for street-facing extensions anyway, bugger-all customers are interested even though it's free.'

'That's a nice segue into my update,' said Will.

The faces in the boxes remained unreadable, as expected. Maintaining a poker face was an essential skill in the Benthamian world of recorded high-definition online meetings stored for ever in Iceland.

Will cleared his throat. 'Firstly, let me say the board are delighted at the progress we're making with A-Star. As you know, we are the first to trial this proactive security system and there are a lot of eyes across the Pacific taking a keen interest in our progress. They're impressed we're meeting most of the stretch goals they set.' He knew the team didn't fall for this bullshit, but he needed to say it for the recording. 'The goal we've missed is street-facing extensions. The board are eager we focus on it for the next quarter.'

'We have been,' said Simon, 'but it's not popular. I rang a few clients, they said it felt like spying, not protecting their property.'

Janine chipped in. 'We're seeing some growth, but I think that's mainly due to the increase in the street crime the media are covering.'

The boxed faces nodded their agreement.

'I understand,' said Will, 'but the board's research indicates this is an area that will grow and be a deciding factor on future customer choice. To that end, they've authorised a cash bonus of two hundred and fifty dollars for each street-facing extension and a two hundred dollar customer credit.'

The faces switched to confusion. Simon, the group's unelected leader, said. 'Free, a sales bonus and a customer credit?'

Will raised his eyebrows as acknowledgement. 'And before you ask, the Group are covering costs from reserves, so profitability won't be impacted. Your bonuses are safe.'

The faces changed again, this time to a mix of surprise and pleasure.

'Does it include existing customers?' asked Simon.

Will confirmed it did.

Simon pushed his chair back from the screen and spun around. 'Well, well. That will get the sales force excited. That's tipping blood into the water. Do they realise sales will plummet as our guys rush around their existing customers stitching them up?'

'I'm comfortable the board know exactly what they're doing,' said Will.

The rest of the meeting passed in its usual orderly fashion. They discussed the glitches in invoicing and the upcoming transfer of the call centre contract to Asia.

Will wound up the meeting. 'Okay guys, good luck and we'll catch up next month.'

Each person waved a goodbye as the mechanical female voice confirmed Will had stopped the recording. The boxes of faces didn't disappear, however. Everyone stayed online. They refilled coffees, ate and the odd face disappeared behind clouds of vape. This informal post-meeting debrief had developed by accident but was now a feature.

'What the fuck are they doing?' said Toni, the Wellington branch manager, puffing out an impressive vape cloud.

Will held up his hands. 'I know, I know. I don't get it either. They have their own agenda, which they don't share with me.'

'Customers don't want security cameras monitoring their streets,' added Simon. 'I don't want them in my street. I can't see how it's going to be a game changer.'

'I don't know,' said Janine. 'As I said, we're seeing an uptick. A couple of nights ago, some arseholes near me let off a string of fireworks at five past fucking two in the morning. I lay in bed wishing they'd been caught on camera so we could string them up by their balls.'

'It could've been girls,' said Simon with a smirk.

'String them up by their—'

'Okay,' interrupted Will. 'Only the future will tell, and anyway it's the board's decision. Let's make hay while the sun shines; we can use the increase in crime as a selling point. Our bonuses won't be impacted and we're on track for a good year.'

Without anything else material to discuss, the informal catch-up didn't last long. He suspected his managers shared a similar plan to his – make as much money as possible and get out as soon as possible. Also, like him they sensed something was off, but it was never a topic of conversation. Ignorance was bliss, albeit a touch uncomfortable.

Besides, New Zealand's economy was struggling under the Covid threat that kept circulating in varied strains. Employment options were few and his team were on strong salaries, better than they could earn anywhere else in New Zealand. That was a trap in itself. They were victims of success, and their lifestyles had no doubt swelled to accommodate their earning power. Private schools, expensive houses with crippling mortgages and luxury holidays around New Zealand had raised the bar to a height few honest people could clear.

With the meeting finished, he ate the second sausage roll; it tasted as great cold. When he finished, he balled up the bag and tossed it across the room straight into the rubbish bin. 'Three points,' he said holding his arms up in triumph. But he quickly dropped them. With nobody to share your victory, it didn't count. It was like getting a hole-in-one playing by yourself, it may as well not have happened.

With the sticky note back in place, Will put his feet up on his desk. He liked to have his webcam blindfolded, he could be himself. How can you be sure the unblinking eye is off? It was bad enough they had their post-meeting debrief online; it wouldn't be a shock if they recorded that too. But you couldn't operate as though you were constantly being watched, when would you relax? The danger mass surveillance presented was a question only the odd civic group considered. For most people, technology advances were as inevitable as death, taxes and climate change.

'The fine print, who reads the fine print?' he said, picking up an Erebus Optics contract. Lawyers, a group he had no love for, designed contracts to be impenetrable. They used legal dribble to justify why they charged ridiculous fees even though their degree took no longer than a BA in history. He drummed his fingers on the desk, he had an hour before lunch. 'Fuck it,' he said. 'Let's read the fine print.'

Ten minutes later he balled up the fine print and, unsuccessfully this time, launched it at the rubbish bin. 'Who in god's name can understand that? Why are customers even bothering to read it? Don't they have lives?'

What he needed was to talk to someone close to the action. Just Ice Security were a local contractor and Erebus's largest Wellington-based installer. Their performance was excellent but, like all resellers, they lagged in street-facing extensions. Will wanted to know why but also to check in with their CEO, Natasha Jillings, an ex-employee whose insight he valued. Instead of using the waste-of-money phone, Will used his legs.

'Mandy, can you organise a visit for me with Just Ice Security? Tash Jillings is the person I need to see.'

'Sure.'

Will paused but Mandy had turned away to dial their number.

On the way back to his desk he retrieved the scrunched-up contract, his back complaining as he picked it up. Next week I'll start back at the gym, he told himself, but he knew he wouldn't.

He smoothed out the contract, picked up a highlighter and started reading. It was such a boring task that his mind instantly wandered. The voice in his head came straight from his final year at secondary school. Dr Smith, his chiding, humourless maths teacher, was saying, 'Oh for fuck's sake William you twat, concentrate.'

CHAPTER 5

Grace sat up in bed, ripped from a deep sleep. Lightning flashed directly overhead, illuminating her bedroom like it was morning. Sean slept on peacefully, undisturbed. The sound followed quickly, too quickly for thunder. Boom. Boom. Then a crackling like ripping Velcro. Sean's dog Roxy jumped on the bed, making for Grace's lap and safety.

The fireworks display finished quickly; it was over in less than a minute. Grace puffed out a breath she realised she had been holding. The dull red of the clock displayed 3.18. She stroked Roxy, who was quiet, but her eyes told Grace she was worried. Sean, as he usually did, slept untroubled.

That was the first time it had been so close. She had heard similar displays but they had been faint, suburbs away. She can imagine the scene. A car of young men, women too, cruising around, finding a quiet street. They park up, make sure there are no signs of life, that their presence hasn't been noticed. Then quickly, they pile out of the car, let off a string of fireworks, then back in the car. Like the movie, they are *Gone in Sixty Seconds*.

If someone complains, rings the police, what? How many patrol cars are cruising the streets at quarter past three in the morning? There is nothing to see, anyway. They're long gone, waiting on a different quiet street.

Grace rolls over, stares at Sean who snuffles softly. Roxy snuggles between them. Wide awake, she contemplates getting up, doing some writing. She thinks over her stories; clever ideas come to mind, if she could only remember them in the morning.

CHAPTER 6

'Another short black?' asked the server as she picked up Jenna Parata's empty cup.

Jenna, JP to her friends and colleagues, shook her head, tapped her phone and, when the server had gone, growled quietly. She was meant to be having an unofficial meet with two CIA agents attached to the US Embassy who had turned up in New Zealand unexpectedly late the previous year. Officially, they were attachés, their role was to observe New Zealand's domestic terrorism progress post the mosque attack. But in reality, who knew?

Jenna had joined the SIS when she was losing the will to live as a trainee accountant. Starting as a surveillance officer, where she learned the ropes, she soon moved into an operational role. Now, seven years later, she was a lead agent in the domestic terrorism team. The work, the odd hours and the secrecy suited her current lifestyle. She told friends and romantic candidates that she worked as an investigator for Inland Revenue. That killed work as a topic of conversation.

Timed to perfection, just as Jenna was about to leave, in walked two men dressed as if they had come straight from *The Matrix* set. They stopped inside the door then, like twins, took off their sunglasses simultaneously. The taller man, dressed immaculately in a black seersucker suit, white shirt and black tie, beamed at Jenna as he walked over.

'My apologies for lateness,' he said. His American accent reminded

Jenna of every New York TV detective. 'Reg had an unexpected task. I'm Tom, what'll you have?'

Jenna stood up and they shook hands. She, dressed similarly, was a few centimetres taller than Tom and enjoyed his surprise. A former netball goal defence, she knew how to use her height to her advantage. 'I'm JP. I could do another short black, thanks Tom.'

Tom relayed this to Reg, adding an Americano for himself before sitting down.

'I thought his name was Jerry?'

Tom chuckled. 'That's just an in-house nickname we've unfortunately acquired. Tom and Jerry, you know, like the cartoon.'

Jenna nodded.

He leaned back in his chair. 'Great little country you have,' he said. 'We're enjoying getting to know the *Kiwi* way of life.'

'I'll bet you are,' said Jenna, as Reg, or Jerry, joined them.

Reg introduced himself and they talked shop for a while to break the ice. Although Jenna dealt with a wide range of people, it was rare for her to meet other agents. It just didn't happen. She had backgrounded them, but detailed information was scarce because the CIA sat outside the Five Eyes network. But, from what she had found, they were an unlikely choice for observers.

'Right,' said Jenna. 'From what I've been told, you two are here to see how we're handling domestic terrorism post the mosque attack.'

A serious look replaced Tom's smile. 'As you know, America has a range of domestic terrorism issues post Trump, post the attack on the Capitol. There are the usual threats from jihadist groups, but now we're dealing with inbred rednecks with arsenals in underground bunkers. With the Christchurch Call, you've become a leading voice for curbing terrorist and violent extremist content. We're here to find out how much of that has translated into reducing the influence of the alt-right, despite your odd hiccup.'

Jenna waited for the server to distribute their coffees. 'I wouldn't call a supermarket stabbing a hiccup, but I take your point. And that's the official line, but why are you really here? Agent to agent.'

Tom smiled widely.

'We know you arrived before Christmas, but no courtesy call. Why?'

He leaned forward; his voice low. 'As you know JP, we get told four-fifths of fuck all. From what we can deduce, they want us to get a feel for the level of alt-right activity in your society. You can give us the official line, hold seminars for the suits, but what's it like? Reg and I have the confidence to talk to a range of groups others may shy away from.'

'Is that what you've been doing for the past couple of months?'

He sat back, his smile in place. 'Exactly, meeting some of the more colourful characters in your fine cities.'

'Are you going to share the intel?'

'That's not my call,' he said. 'You'll need to go over my signoff.'

Jenna sniffed at the answer.

The rest of the meet was, at best, awkward. When they finished their coffees, they stood as one, adding to the awkwardness.

'I guess this is why we don't do this often,' said Tom.

'It's a little like *World Series of Poker* meets *Married at First Sight*,' she said.

Tom and Reg chuckled.

'I like that,' said Tom. 'See you around, JP.'

Sitting down, Jenna watched them leave. Outside the café they put their sunglasses back on simultaneously, as if they were part of Tarantino's *Reservoir Dogs*, before strutting away. She rolled her eyes. *What the fuck are they all about?*

CHAPTER 7

Grace stared out the window from her sunlit home office. The children next door screeched as they played on a trampoline, their dad keeping a wary eye on them while he painted the house. Turning up the classical music to drown out the excited children, she ran through her meeting with Corin, her detective contact. It had raised alarming possibilities, but it was all assumption and speculation. If it was a strange random set of events, there was no story. If, on the other hand, it was organised, two questions flashed in red lights – who and why? What she needed to do now was simple – work out where to head next.

She put a finger in her coffee and grunted, it was cool but drinkable. It wasn't great coffee but it was cheap. Her rise to fame had opened doors, but none had led to a pot of gold.

Who and why? Her list remained short. Apart from security firms, she had written down both the police, who could get additional funding, and revolutionaries as a joke. While she couldn't rule out the police, it stretched credibility to breaking point and that was the problem. It left the improbable scenario of security firms or the alarming scenario of state involvement.

The longer she deliberated, the more she concluded security firms had to be involved, even if indirectly. An internet search turned up the New Zealand Security Association, which helpfully listed its members. After dropping firms with limited geographical coverage, such as Central Otago's Cougar Security, which she hoped the owners had named after felines and not females, there were eleven candidate companies.

Before ringing the first company on the list, ADT Security Ltd, Grace looked them up on LinkedIn. Inside two minutes she knew exactly who to call – Christopher Pluck, their business development manager. Not only did she have his name, she had his entire work history. Why people worried about their privacy when they prostituted themselves on social media was beyond her.

'You've reached ADT Security; how can I help?' The male voice was overly perky.

Grace wet her lips. You needed nimble footwork to get past receptionist gatekeepers. 'Hi, Christopher Pluck please.'

'Who can I say is calling?'

'Grace Marks, NewsNZ.'

'One moment please.' The perky voice disappeared, replaced by Fur Patrol singing *Lydia*. Grace tapped along; it was one from her youth.

The receptionist was soon back. 'I'm sorry, Mr Pluck is busy right now. Can I take a message?'

'I'm on a deadline. Ask him if he wants to read the story before we print or if he's happy we run with no comment?' It was a tactic Grace developed as a parent – give two choices, both leading to the same outcome. Do you want to walk to bed, or shall I carry you? In this case, the options led towards Pluck needing to talk to her.

The line went quiet as the receptionist worked out Grace hadn't given him a choice. 'One moment,' he said less perkily. *Lydia* was back.

Another minute passed before Grace scored.

'Chris Pluck, I'm not sure I know what this is about.'

'Hi Chris, Grace Marks, NewsNZ. I'm planning to run a story on how the rise of street crime is propelling a surge in sales of security systems.' It was an accurate statement left open to interpretation.

'And you want a comment from us?'

'At this stage I'd like your thoughts,' she said.

'I understood it was finished.'

'No, what gave you that idea?'

'Steve said—'

'He must have misunderstood,' she cut in, wanting Pluck focused on the topic. 'I'm happy to feature your company in the story. How are sales?' Grace knew salespeople loved to talk sales and Pluck was an ex-salesman.

She heard him draw in a noisy, resigned breath. 'They're strong, very strong.'

Grace stayed quiet and waited.

'In fact, the strongest I've seen.'

'Wow,' she said. 'And you're an industry veteran. What gives?'

Pluck took another noisy breath. Grace didn't know what he looked like – she hadn't found a recent image – but he sounded as if he needed to drop a few kgs.

'The pandemic kicked it off. You know, money gets tight. It pushes up the crime rates, which is what we're seeing. People get concerned.'

'Right,' she said, and waited.

'That was the start of it, but over the last couple of months, Jesus. Don't print this, I wouldn't want my boss to know, but I'm not needed. Who needs business development when we're turning away work? Demand's skyrocketing.'

Grace decided to prompt. 'Is it due to the surge in street crime?'

'Sure is, I'd bet dog sales are going through the woof,' he said with a chuckle.

Grace wasn't sure if he said woof or roof but gave a flat, single syllable laugh. 'You weren't prepared for the surge?'

'Nope. I mean we'd geared up, but a four-fold increase in demand, no way. Only Erebus are coping.'

'Erebus? Like the mountain?'

'Yeah, Erebus Optics. A horrible name for New Zealand, but it's owned by Americans.'

Grace's journalist's antennae vibrated. 'Erebus,' she said slowly, gathering her thoughts. 'And they're doing well?'

'They have to be. They used to be small, not on our radar as a competitor, but they've grown quickly through an injection of Yankee dollars. It was in the business press a while ago. Interesting business model they have, it's making us rethink.'

'How so?' she prompted.

'They're not so worried about selling kit or the installation fee, just the ongoing monitoring. Clients are getting us to do the install but Erebus to do the monitoring because they're giving a two hundred dollar account credit. We can't compete with that but, as I said, we've enough to do.'

'Making hay while the sun shines.'

'You've got it. Erebus can't sustain what they're doing. We're hoping they'll go broke inside eighteen months and we can mop up their clients.'

'Hope isn't a strategy,' said Grace, her consultant's brain barging into the conversation.

'Sorry?'

'Never mind. Thanks for talking, Chris, you've a great grasp of your industry. That's rare these days.' She needed to stroke Pluck's ego so she could call back if needed.

'Thanks, I've been around the block enough times to see the patterns. When are you planning to publish?'

'As soon as possible,' she said truthfully. 'I need a little more information, but I'll make sure you get a positive mention. I'll try and run it past you first, no promises.'

'Okay, that'd be great.'

'Ciao,' she said, ending the call with a tap on the red phone icon.

The conversation confirmed it wasn't a cartel of security firms lining their pockets, not that Grace had considered this probable, but it was good to rule it out. And Pluck had given her a strong lead – Erebus Optics, owned by Americans with a business model suited to the environment. If American dollars were backing them, Pluck was dreaming if he thought they would go under. Hope is not a strategy.

The Erebus Optics website was slick, highlighting a range of offers including the account credit mentioned by Pluck. It seemed a generous offer, but as an ex-consultant Grace appreciated their cunning. An account credit didn't mean you gave the client money, just free service for a fixed period. The company's cash stayed in its bank account. So, if you've gained enough market share, and your competitors have bled out financially, who's left to switch to when the credit runs out? Erebus Optics was creating an iceberg and the other industry players were sailing towards it, full steam ahead.

On the website's *About Us* page, details were scant. No company history or mention of the US parent company, Erebus Group. There were pictures of the branch managers and CEO Will Manilow, who looked the same as ninety per cent of all CEOs – a middle-aged white man, greying, balding and overweight. He had a distant, sad look, like an accountant whose books don't balance.

She took in a deep breath, she needed to know more about Will Manilow as well as the Five Eyes alliance. If it was industrial espionage, and the US were involved, state sponsored might mean Five Eyes sponsored. She would need to be careful; she didn't want to alert the CEO to her suspicions. He could be a key player and she needed to get closer to the action without anyone hitting the panic button.

She started by focusing on social media sites, where people plastered their lives in tedious glory. There were many sites where people detailed, embellished and downright lied about their importance and skill. Grace had abandoned social media, her long-ago deleted profiles now buried in a data farm like e-dinosaur bones.

Manilow had detailed his entire career on a single site. Starting with his Wellington College school days. He had worked at a range of jobs in retail before moving into real estate in 1985. He survived in the property world until 2001, when he launched Manilow Security Ltd, servicing the lower half of the North Island but mainly Wellington. Two years ago he sold his company to the Erebus Group, the new owners rebranding the company Erebus Optics Ltd with Manilow becoming CEO. That was it. Over forty years summarised in four underwhelming paragraphs.

There was a range of stories on the sale of Manilow Security. Most were straight from an Erebus Optics press release – cut-and-paste journalism. The press release had little Grace couldn't have worked out for herself though it contained a photo of Manilow and the new American owners, beaming at the camera. The photo's date put the scene during the pandemic's height, though you wouldn't have known. They stood together, their unmasked faces beaming.

Grace decided to try her luck and contact him. To her surprise, whoever populated the site had listed his mobile phone number in his contact details. It couldn't be his real mobile but it didn't hurt to try.

After two rings, to her even bigger surprise, the call was answered.

'Hi, Will Manilow.'

Grace, momentarily lost for words, stammered, 'Hi. Will?'

'That's me. Who's this?'

'Grace Marks from NewsNZ.'

Grace held her breath. This was often as far as conversations went.

'Grace Marks. Are you the reason I'm paying a load more tax?' he asked.

'Well, not really. I was doing—'

'A great job,' cut in Manilow, in an energetic tone. 'Getting the wealthy to pay their fair share is the way it should be in good old egalitarian Aotearoa. Anyway, I'm assuming you're not ringing for a comment about tax.'

He had given Grace the few seconds she needed to compose herself. 'I'm writing a story about the rise in street crime and how it's driving up demand for home security. I've talked to a few of the major players, they say Erebus is leading the way. I'd love to hear your views on what's happening.'

He took his time. 'Okay. Are you based in Wellington?' His voice had become quieter.

'Palmerston North but I'm often in Wellington.'

Another pause. 'Okay,' he said, his voice returning to its former level. 'Send me an email and I'll book in a time.' Grace went to speak, but he didn't leave a gap. 'I look forward to meeting you in person. Cheers.' He terminated the call.

'Fuck, I let him get away,' she groaned. 'I almost had him.'

He knew her phone number now, he could avoid answering or block her. She composed an email making it sound interesting and enthusiastic, but as she clicked send, she doubted he would reply.

She turned her attention to the Five Eyes alliance. An internet search revealed a mountain of material, as she expected. Starting at the top, she clicked on the link to the Government Communications Security Bureau, or GCSB as it was known. After reading one sentence, she knew she needed help. *New Zealand is a member of the UKUSA Agreement, a multilateral agreement for SIGINT cooperation.*

If she wanted to know how the alliance worked in practice and didn't want to spend the next month drowning in impenetrable language, she needed help from an expert. Even the names of the spy agencies had changed and multiplied. Along with recognisable names, such as the CIA and MI5, were the NSA, GCHQ and SVR.

In the search results, academics such as Al Gillespie and Rob Patman regularly featured. They were the media's go-to experts on Five Eyes or international relations. One result linked to Dr Kaia Noble; a local academic who had published an article titled 'The Five Eyes alliance: Why everyone has something to fear'. In Grace's experience, high-profile media talking heads were often hard to access because the media had pumped their egos.

Grace found Dr Noble's contact details on her university website. With short purple hair, she looked wildly different to her older, white, male colleagues and that appealed to Grace. Her details didn't include a mobile number, so she sent an email outlining who she was and her interest in Five Eyes. Grace offered to buy her coffee in return for her insights.

As she sent the email to Dr Noble, a new meeting request arrived from Will.Manilow@erebusoptics.co.nz. He had invited her to his office, Solnet House, Level 3, on The Terrace, next Thursday at 12pm.

Grace clicked accept. She hadn't expected that.

CHAPTER 8

Will Manilow stared at the smoothed-out Erebus Optics contract, piecing together his thoughts from the previous week. He had covered the document in highlighter and notations, but the New Plymouth branch opening together with the relentless pressure from the company's owners to increase sales meant it had slid down his priority list.

The door opened without warning, causing him to jump. Mandy stood there, unsmiling as usual.

'You've an appointment at Just Ice at two. You'll be late, they're in Petone.'

He blinked once – the mental picture he was rebuilding was gone. 'Thanks Mandy,' he said to her back before she shut the door. He stared at the closed door. She was only doing her job but he knew where Just Ice was, he had time. She wanted him out of the office so she could surf her favourite websites or go shopping.

Packing up his laptop, he added the fine print to the reports he had prepared for his meeting. Although he disliked the term 'old school', he was old school. He hated it when people sat in meetings staring at their screen. Face-to-face meant exactly that, it didn't mean face-to-balding crown or roots-need-doing.

On his way out he stopped at Mandy's desk. 'I'll head home after the meeting, Mandy, no point coming back. Do you need me for anything?'

Mandy put on a practised smile. 'No, I'm good. Everything's under control.'

Will smirked as he left, Mandy was okay. She was doing a job she was overqualified for and, apart from the money, didn't want. She was smart which was why he was surprised she hadn't found a better job, although the economy meant good jobs didn't come up often. She would leave today at three for afternoon tea and wouldn't come back. Not that he cared; she was on top of her work and that was all that mattered.

Minutes later he was cruising along the motorway in his Audi S5 Sportback. When he was out of the office, away from the company, driving with the music up loud, he was living the dream. In three years, like the movies, he would drive off into the sunset.

When the avalanche of Erebus Group money arrived, he had spent it sparingly, investing it to prove money wouldn't change him. But the allure of his eye-watering portfolio proved too great, and he had succumbed to money's corrupting charm. He rationalised that to compensate for the sixty-hour weeks he was putting in to keep on top of the rapidly expanding operation, he deserved a home with a multi-million-dollar view and the latest Audi. It was the first brand-new car he had ever owned.

He loved driving his new Audi and, all too quickly, he arrived at the offices of Just Ice Security; he was two minutes early.

Natasha Jillings, the General Manager, was waiting for him at reception. Dressed semi-casually in designer jeans and a t-shirt carrying the words 'Blood, sweat and respect', she had short black hair left long in the front which she swept to one side. He had known Natasha for over a decade; she had started working for him as a security guard and she was clearly still a gym junkie. He had followed her career as she worked her way to the top in a male-dominated industry through merit, determination and being tough as all hell.

'You look great, Tash,' he said. 'The industry hasn't worn *you* down yet.'

'You haven't changed much, Will, though the suit's a little sharpish for you.'

He chortled. 'Thanks Tash. I think.'

'So, how long have you got?' she asked.

'The rest of the afternoon, but I don't want to monopolise too much of your time. Can we have a look around first?'

Natasha's eyes lit up. 'Sure.'

Will knew most visitors weren't interested in the operational side. The Erebus Group executives weren't when they did their due diligence. They wanted to see the financials and wine and dine everyone to show off their money. He knew security firms and he knew what to look for, he was confident Just Ice would pass muster.

The tour took over half an hour because Will kept stopping and talking. When they arrived back at Natasha's office he said, 'You run a great operation, Tash.'

'Thanks, praise indeed coming from you.'

She closed her office door and pulled over a chair for Will, before sitting behind her desk. 'What's up, Will? I mean, it's nice having the only boss I've had who wasn't a sexist homophobe on the make for a visit, but you must be crazy busy because we're crazy busy.'

'You should've worked for the CID,' said Will. 'You're right, I'm getting pressure from my new bosses. I figured, as our largest contractor, it would be easiest to talk to you first and follow up with the obligatory memo.'

'You were never a memo guy. It's about street-facing extensions, isn't it?'

He nodded.

'I knew it, we're crushing every target except that.'

'You are,' he agreed. 'Your performance on every other metric is great.'

Natasha leaned back, her hands forming a steeple. 'I've good news, we're starting to see a steady increase. Those incentives are driving my sales force to work all the hours god can send. The increase in the volume of street crime has helped too; it's worrying people.'

'That's good,' said Will. 'Not the increase in crime, that's bad, but it's good for business. My new owners are convinced safe streets and community safety will be a key decision point in the future.'

Natasha pouted. 'What's the catch?'

'No catch. Sell, make money, be merry.'

'You're not radiating joy, Will, you're radiating concern. Why?'

He closed his eyes for a moment before looking back at Natasha, who was watching him with raptor keenness. She would've made a great detective. Leaning forwards, he rested an elbow on her desk. 'Does it make sense to you?'

Natasha looked at her steepled hands. 'No. Even if you're buying market share, it's overkill. Free, a bonus and a customer credit. Your profitability, not ours, is going to take a big hit in the short-term.'

Will harrumphed. 'You'd think so, but they're underwriting the incentives with new money. Our profitability, and bonuses, won't be impacted.'

'Now it makes even less sense.'

'I know. On my waste-of-time business degree, I stumbled over the odd snippet of value, usually from other students. One woman, she was some sort of hotshot adviser for one of the big consultancy firms that fleeces government departments for stupid amounts of money, told me about the reward system. Heard of it?'

Natasha shook her head slowly.

'It's simple but it makes sense. People focus on what gets rewarded and avoid work that's unrewarded. Think about your sales team.'

Natasha's thoughtful pout gave her a seductive look. 'Sure. They focus on what makes them money, that's their reward.'

'Exactly,' he said. 'These new measures will have them, as you said, working all hours. That's a rational response. My question is, assuming my US owners are rational too, what's in it for them? I'm sure they're not doing it to help your sales team buy new cars.'

'You said they think community safety's going to be an important sales factor.'

'What do you reckon, Tash? Would it be a sales factor for you?'

'A few months ago, I would have said no. I want to protect my whanau and property, but watching people on the street, that's not security, that's ...'

'Surveillance?'

She nodded. 'But all this minor crime, the disturbances, people want the louts caught and thrown inside even though it's not going to happen. They're keen to help the police.'

'I hadn't looked at it that way. That's a change. I mean, we offer services to protect people and their property, we're not in the policing business. At least we weren't.'

'Your owners' logic makes more sense if people *want* to keep an eye on the streets. But are our streets dangerous?' she asked.

'You said yourself, these crimes are on the rise.'

Natasha's forehead creased.

'Sorry, Tash, I'm not trying to put you on the spot. The logic's easier to test by saying it out loud. It gets all twisted in my head, bouncing around randomly. I'm with you, I don't think we need to monitor our streets, but the US thinks we do, or will.'

'Surely it's about the money,' said Natasha. 'They must think it's going to help them corner the market or something.'

'And how much is the New Zealand market worth?'

'It's not that, it's like a trial. If what they do works in Aotearoa, they can export the model and nail other countries, bigger countries.'

Will rubbed his two-day stubble. 'That makes sense.' He checked the time on his large Hublot watch.

'Nice watch,' she said, a single eyebrow raised.

He reddened. 'They gave it to me as part of the deal. Anyway, I shouldn't hold you up any longer,' he said, easing himself up. 'Don't get up, I know the way out.'

Natasha, who had made to stand, eased herself back down. 'You're always welcome, Will. And I know the team will deliver, with those incentives they'd be mad not to.'

Back on the motorway, Will drove without music to give his mind space to chew over his thoughts. Crazy incentives, market share, the fine print, pressure, street-facing extensions and the burger he had for lunch scrambled together in his mind. He felt like Alice, tumbling down a rabbit hole, trying to grab the pieces and assemble them before he hit the bottom.

Mount Victoria's narrow winding roads forced him to concentrate on his driving. The Audi danced up the hill effortlessly to his house on Lookout Road that cost more than ten houses should. He bought it during the recent housing crash, the real estate shark telling him he was getting it 'dirt cheap'. It was still a ridiculous amount of money to pay for something which couldn't leave the earth's atmosphere.

The garage door slid silently upwards allowing Will to ease his Audi inside. The house lights flicked on automatically, which always made him feel uneasy, as though he too was under surveillance. The house had a security system which he never used after setting it off twice when he had drunk too much to remember the code.

Inside he put his laptop and folders on the table, took a beer from the fridge and went over to the panoramic windows. The view was spectacular. He was about to open the beer but checked the time, it had only just gone four. If he started drinking now, the evening would be a write-off. He put the beer back in the fridge and headed to his bedroom to change. A leisurely walk downhill to town would give him what he needed most, thinking time.

As he picked through his meagre wardrobe, he thought more about what Natasha had said. New Zealand was an ideal place to run a trial, but not in the way she thought. Buying market share and aiming cameras at streets was hardly a transformational, innovative, bullshit anything. New Zealand was a trial, that made sense. But a trial for what?

CHAPTER 9

Jenna Parata yawned. It was just after 10pm, but her day had started at five when her phone's alarm had blasted her out of bed for a run. She didn't need to be out now, she wasn't on duty, but she was curious. Normally minor street disturbances wouldn't get a second glance from the SIS's domestic terrorism unit, it was well outside their operational area. But the police request for information had landed on her desk. She'd answered with what they knew – nothing – and that fact piqued her interest.

Having tuned into the police radio, she was following the reports of a group of youths roaming around Johnsonville causing problems. Each time she drove to where the police reported they were, they had already gone, reassembling blocks away. The police and Jenna were playing a game of whack-a-mole. The last reported sighting was on the aptly named Cortina Avenue. Jenna parked at the bottom of the street to wait.

She heard them before she saw them. A group of youths, around ten strong, emerged from the gloom heading her way. Jenna clicked her neck. 'Finally,' she said, getting out of the car.

She had stayed dressed in what passed for her SIS uniform: black shoes, pants, jacket and a white shirt. Comfortably over six foot and solidly built, she knew how to look imposing. She strolled towards them as they walked towards her, making a racket. One had a music device pumping out a doof doof noise, the rest were singing, yelling and generally yahooing. As they neared her, they quietened as their attention turned to her. The pack split in two allowing Jenna to pass through the middle.

She listened carefully. 'Whoa mumma.' 'Milf.' 'Tidy.' 'Gagging for it.' The odd catcall was lewder, but it was tame and, importantly, no one touched her or used racist language. If she called the police, they wouldn't arrest them. It was unpleasant, but it wasn't serious.

As soon as they were past, Jenna turned and followed them. Before they noticed she was behind them, she ran her trained eye over them. Ten teenage boys, mixed race, school age, well dressed, well groomed, and they weren't spaced-out or drunk. In short, they looked like a high school cricket team, their strength of numbers giving them their confident swagger.

The first to notice her called to the others.

'Hey, the milf is following us.'

The group stopped, turned off the incessant doof doof noise and formed a semi-circle. Jenna gave them a steely once over and their cockiness quickly ebbed away, leaving a group of nervous schoolboys.

One stepped forward and sniffed. 'I smell pork.'

Emboldened, the group grunted and snorted. Jenna stayed quiet, staring hard until the noises died away, the boys fidgeting.

The same teen spoke. 'What do you want, scary lady? We've talked to the police, twice. We aren't doing anything; we're just having fun. Is it illegal to have fun?'

Jenna shook her head slowly. 'I was expecting a mob of hard arses. You're not street kids, look at you. You're a bunch of posh, well-educated school kids.' The group shuffled uneasily. Jenna pressed. 'If I followed *you* home' – she pointed at the most nervous-looking boy – 'I'll bet I find a scene of middle-class suburban bliss. Your parents will be disappointed little Johnny has fallen into bad company. Except you haven't. This is hardly bad company.'

The nervous boy stared wide-eyed. The group, unsure what to do, looked to their informal spokesperson.

'Are you going to arrest us?' he said trying to sneer.

'I am,' she said, taking the handcuffs off her belt and enjoying the genuine fear she saw in their eyes. 'Tell me what you boys are doing out past your bedtime and I might let you go.'

'We don't have to talk to you,' he said, before turning away. 'Come on, let's get away from this porker.'

As the boys walked quickly away, Jenna followed, keeping pace. The first boy to run set off the group. Stopping, she watched as they pounded away, heading towards the train station.

She sang out, '*Oma rāpeti, oma rāpeti, oma, oma, oma.*' Then she yelled, 'You better be long gone when I get to the station.' That should keep them on their toes.

Back in her car, she yawned. She needed to get to bed if she was to make her early-morning run tomorrow. Jenna wasn't sure what was going on, but she was sure it was as far from terrorism as it was possible to get. As she drove away, she asked herself, 'Why are these milksops roaming the suburbs trying to intimidate the locals? It's got to be some stupid internet meme.'

CHAPTER 10

While his house screamed millionaire, Will's clothes shouted middle-aged tragic. Comfortable shoes that couldn't be relied on to keep his socks dry, tired jeans with non-designer rips, a grey marle gym t-shirt and black puffer jacket. To his eye he looked presentable, and he had no desire to adorn himself with Gucci or Ralph Lauren or to carry a Louis Vuitton man bag costing more than his previous car.

A final check in the mirror confirmed he was exactly what he saw – an ageing, middle-class white man who needed to exercise more and drink less. The chance that any female would give him a second glance was slim, but he had come to terms with that. He wasn't heading into town to pull, a desperate goal at the best of times. He was heading to the waterfront for a drink and thinking space. Putting the folder with the fine print under his arm, he started down Mount Victoria. It was a pleasant evening and walking downhill took little exertion. Walking uphill later would be tougher.

Three-quarters of the way downhill, a boy racer's car, cut down illegally by the look of it, cruised towards him, its windows down. In the passenger seat, a ghostly tattooed figure with a shaven head yelled 'Get off the street, you old cunt'. Will stopped, watching the car disappear. He wasn't scared or angry, he was confused. Those people were a product of New Zealand society, it wasn't an image most people wanted to admit existed. How had New Zealand, a so-called bastion of egalitarianism, let itself get into this state?

Forty minutes after he had set out, a noticeably perspiring Will was sitting in the sun, sipping a beer at a waterfront bar. From where he was sitting, it amused him that he could see his house with its godlike view. He took out the fine print, eyeing it with suspicion. He suspected that this contract held, if not the answer, a clue. Every step the Erebus Group had taken since approaching him to buy his business was deliberate, but the picture their actions formed didn't appear rational.

He read the contract from start to finish, reacquainting himself with the task. He crossed out the standard clauses: force majeure (whatever that was), disputes resolution, termination, intellectual property and so on. All the irrelevant vanilla clauses. What remained were the clauses covering information privacy and access. These sections were long and littered with legal speak.

'Will.' A female voice broke his concentration.

'Toni, how are you?' he said, getting up to shake his Wellington branch manager's hand.

'Great,' she said. Holding up her glass, she asked, 'Can I join you for five? I'm meeting a friend and he's . . . running late. As usual.'

'Sure, grab a seat.'

The woman eased herself onto the bar stool, being careful to make sure her tight dress didn't ride up. At work she seldom dressed fashionably, or wore makeup, but tonight she looked ready for the catwalk. Will, who was a betting man, thought she must be on a date. Most people didn't try that hard for friends.

'How come you're here, Will?' she asked. 'That view of yours must be fantastic on days like this.'

He reddened. 'It is, it sure is. I only bought the place as an investment, though. It's a bit over the top for me if I'm honest. Besides, there's no one to serve the drinks.'

Toni squeezed his arm. 'You're so modest. You're living the dream.'

He half shrugged. 'Some days. Anyway, how about you? Getting back into the swing of things?'

'No choice, we're flat out,' she said.

They exchanged small talk before Toni recognised the contract in front of Will. 'You trying to work out what it says?'

'I know it's boring, but after our meeting I figured I should know what's in our own contracts.'

'And?'

He laughed. 'No further ahead. Listen to this: "subclause thirteen point four point one (b). Cameras installed under the street-facing extension package are subject to the same conditions as other cameras installed on the customer's property with the exception that Erebus Optics Ltd retains the right to use the images for computational and or statistical analytics".'

'What are computational and or statistical analytics?'

'Exactly,' said Will. 'I may be a dinosaur, but I preferred the simplicity of the old security systems. They recorded data on physical storage. There were no hassles about cloud storage or privacy and zero chance of computational analytics.'

Toni smiled. 'Yep, you're a dinosaur.'

They both laughed.

'I tried to count the number of security cameras on my way down here,' he said.

'You walked?'

'It was downhill.'

'How many did you spot?' asked Toni.

'I gave up at shitloads.'

'High-def cameras are everywhere now. If I bent over in this skirt' – she raised her eyebrows – 'someone somewhere would get a cheap thrill.'

Will chuckled.

'Oh, there's my friend,' said Toni, struggling to stand and keep her dress seemly.

'He's saved you from more shop talk,' said Will smiling.

Toni put her hand on his arm. 'You're great to talk to. Have a nice evening and good luck with the legal speak.'

Will studied her as she walked urgently towards her so-called friend. By the time he recognised it was her he was looking for, she had slowed into a not-bothered pace. After obvious awkwardness, they hugged. Will smirked. It looked like a first date; they probably met online.

He wished her luck as he finished his beer.

A server, having seen this, came over. 'Same again, sir? Are you here for dinner?'

Will signalled a yes to both questions.

'Are you expecting the lady back?'

'No,' he said with an abbreviated laugh. 'It'll be just me.'

'Ah. I'll bring over a menu and water,' he said before hurrying away.

Focusing back on the task, he took out a piece of paper and drew a diagram of what he knew, or at least what he thought he knew. When he had finished, he had identified four areas of interest. The focus on street-facing extensions, the protection of bonuses, the future competitive advantage, and street crime rising leading to increasing demand.

'Either the Yanks have picked it brilliantly,' he said to himself, 'meaning they're a bunch of strategic geniuses − or the game's rigged.'

If this was simply a campaign to corner the market, in three years he could put it behind him. But why the interest in cameras monitoring streets? They had that fixation before the rise in street crime. Why promote those in particular? Cameras monitoring the street weren't primarily for security, they were for surveillance. Customers pay for security, not surveillance.

'There must be a rational explanation,' he whispered to himself.

Three hours, too many drinks and one excellent burger and fries later, Will lay sprawled in his secluded barbeque area on the bottom floor of his house. Sweating and staring at the stars, no matter which way he looked the view was spectacular.

When a chill replaced the warmth from his exertion, he dragged himself inside. Setting up his laptop and folders on the coffee table, he took out the fine print and laughed. His semi-eureka moment had come when his burger arrived. After his first bite he had realised he was looking at the problem from the wrong perspective. His focus had been on individual sales, on individual street-facing cameras. He had imagined himself standing outside a house, looking at a security camera mounted on the apex of the roof and wondering what the big deal was.

Then it had hit him. Erebus weren't interested in what was happening on a particular street, they were interested in what was happening on *every* street.

He visualised looking down on the streets from a drone. Each street-facing camera covered a tiny slice of the neighbourhood, but as sales grew so did coverage. Over time, the sections of coverage would ooze into one massive blob. Were his US owners really interested in what amounted to widespread surveillance? Why? Clients weren't going to pay extra to do the police's job.

One thing was for sure, they weren't acting out of concern for the New Zealand public. It would be money, power or both. They were the usual suspects, the underlying motives when you removed all the glib marketing, business-speak and bullshit.

Taking out the diagram he had constructed at the bar, he started adding assumptions, theories and random thoughts. Soon the page was littered with words, phrases and a spider's web of lines and arrows. His energy waning, he went out onto the balcony and stared at the Wellington nightscape. A piece was missing.

As he stared out at the myriad lights from his lofty position, he said, 'Street crime. It's not *the* missing piece, but it's close.' He didn't feel the satisfaction of pressing the last piece of a jigsaw into place; it was closer to attaching two blocks together with a hard-to-find linking piece. He went back inside and wrote *COINCIDENCE?* in large block capitals.

Thumping heavily onto the couch, he picked up the TV remote. He had every streaming service available, but of late he had been seeing them for what they were, expensive distractions. A way to have your fur stroked the right way so you focused on society's three rules: make money, breed and consume. Philosophers must have written screeds on that aspect of capitalism, but Groucho had had a better chance than Karl of getting airtime in the business degree curriculum.

He had only his gut feeling and his suspicion, but he felt he was closing in on the scene of a crime. If he carried on searching, the path he was following would no doubt end in conflict with Erebus. They wouldn't appreciate him questioning their motives and operation. It would be a firing offence, and that, thought Will, made it even more attractive.

CHAPTER 11

Grace, for once, was early for her meeting with Five Eyes academic Dr Kaia Nobel. A member of the university gym, Grace arranged to meet her at a café on the university campus giving her little opportunity to be late. Still in her gym gear, her hair neatly pulled into a short ponytail, she sipped her coffee while she checked her messages.

Situated inside an old colonial house, the café had an old-world charm that reminded her of her days as a student. There had been books then not devices, debates not social media, getting chatted up not dick pics, outrage not obedience, and education not degrees. And where were the students? On her way to the café Grace walked through the concourse, the beating heart of the university, crowded and alive in her day, Chernobyl-esque now. She saw more security cameras than students.

It was mid-afternoon and the café was quiet. Right on two o'clock a woman entered. Grace recognised her though she looked nothing like her university photo. Short black hair not purple, a little more robust and in a black dress, green blouse and heels, she was attractive but looked uncertain and awkward. Dr Noble had no problem recognising Grace and she smiled warmly. Joining the short queue, she mimed if Grace wanted a coffee. Grace shook her head, pointing to her cup.

'Hi, I'm Dr Noble but please call me Kaia,' she said, when she arrived at Grace's table.

They shook hands awkwardly as Dr Noble put down her folder.

'Call me Ace.'

They chatted to break the ice, though Grace let her do most of the talking. Grace was curious about how the university sector was getting ready to meet the government's long-awaited change in direction to a collaborative model. Kaia delightedly told her that university management were crying into their spreadsheets while staff were celebrating like the war was over. Grace took a couple of notes sensing a story.

'Right,' said Grace, 'tell me about Five Eyes.'

Dr Noble lost her awkwardness as she became serious. 'Before I start, tell me what part of FELEG you're interested in. I mean, it's large and complex and you can get the basics off the internet.'

'For a start,' said Grace, 'what's FELEG?'

'That's their official name, the Five Eyes Law Enforcement Group, but I guess only academics use it.'

'Right.' Grace sipped her coffee as she ordered her thoughts. 'I know the basics about Five Eyes, swapping intelligence and spy stuff, but I'm interested in the role they have gathering data. What *can* they gather, what *do* they gather, but also what *could* they gather?'

Dr Noble nodded seriously. 'You'd assume that'd be specified in detail, but the intelligence gathering and sharing arrangements are shrouded in secrecy. There's a mass of either impenetrable or unavailable agreements setting out what they can, can't and shouldn't do. I doubt anyone in Aotearoa, including the GCSB, knows the full extent of the cosy alliance we've joined.'

'Really? I did some research after I had the pleasure of the GCSB's attention. They're not allowed to gather information, in other words spy, on New Zealanders without a type 1 warrant. That's right, isn't it?'

The academic tilted her head. 'Well . . . yes, but the alliance is disingenuously set up. Any of our Five Eyes partners can spy on New Zealanders and then share the data with us.' She picked up a document from her pile. 'It's hard to decipher but listen to this. "The alliance was set up to share continuously, currently and without request unanalysed intelligence in addition to end-product intelligence".'

Grace's face screwed up. 'That makes it bollocks. The Australians could be spying on me and handing over the information. That's lower than underarm bowling.'

'But everyone gets to claim that we don't spy on our own citizens.'

Grace scribbled down a note, underlining it twice.

'While you work out where you want to head next,' said Dr Noble. 'My research is in an area that you'll find interesting. I think it might help you get where you're heading.'

Grace looked up.

'I'm researching the "chilling effect",' the academic continued in response to Grace's confused look. 'It's related to the "If you've got nothing to hide you've got nothing to fear" argument.'

Grace's face changed to a combination of interested and confused.

She explained. 'Governments, conservatives, the state and even social media companies have used that argument to defend the idea we shouldn't fear greater surveillance or access to our personal data. If you're living an honest, clean, god-fearing life, you shouldn't care about being spied on or monitored.'

'God-fearing.' Grace made a noise between a grunt and a laugh. 'Interesting angle though. I've heard that argument, and in passing it seems fine.'

'That's the problem,' she said. 'It does. But it opens a door to a place society shouldn't want to go to. The article I'm writing focuses on the historical impact of surveillance on society. Do you act the same if you know you're being watched, that's the question I'm asking.'

'Absolutely not,' said Grace without hesitation.

'What about if it's a camera, but you don't know if it's on?'

Grace remembered when the SIS had made her wait for hours in an interview room the size of a broom cupboard. There was a camera on the wall that stared unblinkingly. 'No, you have to assume they're watching, or it's being recorded. It's Bentham's panopticon logic.'

Her companion beamed when Grace mentioned the eighteenth-century philosopher's name. 'You do and it is. And if you're watched constantly . . .'

Grace's eyes narrowed. 'You never act normally.'

'And if you never act normally, you're not you. So, who are you? That's the "chilling effect". People stop talking or acting in ways that might draw attention. Consider what life's like for activists in China, North Korea, Russia, Belarus or Hong Kong. History tells us you either become an unquestioning complier or, like Orwell's character in *1984*, you're forced to wear a mask of compliance.'

Grace sat back, eyeing her cooling coffee. 'And with the technology they're developing, cracks in regime walls might never appear. Shit, that's a bleak-sounding future. I can use it in my story though, that's for sure.' Grace looked at her notes. 'Back to Five Eyes, do you know what information they're currently collecting?'

'Officially no, they play their cards *inside* their chest. Unofficially, they're like a black hole sucking in as much data as they can get their hands on. Internet searches, browsing history, downloads, emails, SMS pings, mobile data, social media, credit card data, dating site information, surveillance cameras—'

'Surveillance cameras?' cut in Grace.

Dr Noble nodded. 'With facial recognition technology, a computer can churn through feeds, see who met who when and where. Companies are developing software that integrates facial recognition technology with AI. Their goal is to surveil entire populations.'

'Can they do it in real time?' asked Grace.

'Google "NEC surveillance",' said the academic.

Grace used her phone to perform the search. 'Jesus, it's a sales pitch for surveillance. Listen to this: "NEC's urban surveillance provides a platform for urban safety to collect and analyse information from multiple sources, such as videos, panic buttons, emergency calls, and social networks".'

'Casino software has tracked gamblers for years,' said Dr Noble. 'It's only a question of money, and spy agencies have seemingly unlimited cash. There's a gigantic data centre in Utah able to hold oceans of data and guess what's written in stone at the front gate? "If you have nothing to hide, you have nothing to fear".'

Grace groaned. 'Can the US be more fucked up? Excuse my language, but really. Taking a step back, you said Australians could be monitoring me on behalf of the SIS.'

'You said Australians, it could be any of the alliance partners.'

'I've been operating under the assumption my privacy was protected.'

'We all do,' said Dr Noble. 'When I started researching and writing about Five Eyes, I figured I'd be added to their list of subversives.'

'If you're a subversive, how would they classify me?' said Grace, checking the time on her phone. 'Oops, running late for my next appointment. Thanks, Kaia, you've been super helpful, and super worrying. Would it be okay if we meet again when I get further into the story?'

'Sure. You're interested in surveillance from a general interest perspective, I'm interested from an academic perspective. We could team up. You can have the spotlight and I get the university off my back for a while.'

Grace offered her hand, this time the handshake wasn't awkward.

Dr Noble beamed. 'I'll set up a confidential place where we can communicate and share information. We are talking about the SIS.'

'What we're doing isn't illegal, but I get your point. Those agencies have long, sticky tentacles.'

'They sure do. I have a colleague who's good with technology, we'll be secure.'

'Do you?' said Grace, her eyes narrowing. She couldn't place where she had seen the academic before, it was like trying to recall aspects of a dream.

'I do,' said the academic as she ordered her papers, her awkwardness back. 'I'll be in touch.'

Grace watched her leave. Her brain would keep chewing on the problem.

CHAPTER 12

'What's new, Mandy?' asked Will, slightly slurring his words. Would she notice?

Mandy gave him a look that suggested she did.

He had just returned from his regular lunch at the Bethel Woods Café across the road from his office. Even though it was only a short uphill walk, he had struggled, the alcohol making his legs heavy. When he arrived back, he found Mandy in her usual position behind her desk, staring at her screen and looking bored.

'Nothing urgent,' she said.

'Good,' he said, licking his lips. 'I've decided we need a proper team get-together. I want you to organise a sales strategy retreat for June. Erebus loves strategy events, they won't object.'

Mandy sat up. 'That sounds good. Where?'

'I'm leaving everything up to you. Not a main city though. Rotorua, Taupo, Queenstown, Wanaka. You know, some place interesting.'

'Okay, how long for?'

'How about we arrive on Wednesday morning, leave Friday evening. Three days talking shop, two nights getting to know each other. We'll need to beam in the US for some parts, so bear in mind Boston time when you're putting together the agenda.'

'Leave it to me,' said Mandy with a genuine smile.

He went into his office happy to have given her a task that excited her. After checking his emails, he logged on to the Erebus Group intranet.

Over lunch he reviewed his mind map, stepping through his thinking. In the light of day, sober, his logic looked both rational and like a conspiracy theory.

The pages of the Erebus Group intranet detailed the operational aspects of organisational life: company policies, strategy, a page for each operational division, HR, staff news and corporate files. He browsed through the group's operations; they certainly had a lot of fingers in a lot of pies. In the Asia-Pacific area, the success New Zealand was having securing market share received a short mention.

In the corporate area, where the security systems forced him to retype his username and password several times, he went into the New Zealand section. There were no surprises because he or Mandy had written the updates, sales reports, market analyses and budgets: the bland corporate compliance documents mandatory to create but seldom read.

Navigating his way back to the main directory, he clicked on other folders. Each click earned him a stark 'ACCESS DENIED' message. When he clicked the folder labelled 'Corporate', instead of the stark message, a list of subfolders appeared. His body jerked awake. He spent the next hour clicking in and out of a myriad of folders and files. In the 'HR' section he found a spreadsheet containing all employees worldwide, their salaries translated into US dollars. He had thought his salary was attractive, but he now discovered he was at the minion end of the continuum. Bastards.

Going into a folder labelled 'Fowler', Erebus' Vice President of International Operations and his ultimate boss, he saw a folder labelled 'B-Star'. A-Star was the innovative software system behind the success in New Zealand, but he had never heard of B-Star. The folder contained one file, 'B-Star pilot strategy'. He tried to open the file, but a box appeared demanding a password.

'Bugger,' he said quietly, staring at the password box.

Erebus password-protected all their sensitive documents. To make life easier, they had developed a cipher known to CEOs and directors. In practice this meant executive and personal assistants also knew the cipher to help their forgetful bosses.

Will pressed a button on his desk phone. 'What's the password-thingy Mandy?'

A perkier Mandy replied, 'The cipher is the last eight characters of the file reversed, then the two digits—'

'How about you pop through,' he interrupted.

A friendlier, though not friendly, Mandy came in and stood behind him, notepad in hand. 'Which file is it?'

Will pointed to the screen. 'It's this one, the B-Star pilot.'

'What's B-Star?'

'I don't know,' he said.

'What day and month was it created?'

Mandy radiated impatience as he looked for the information.

'Got it. Twenty-second of November.'

Mandy looked at the screen, wrote on her notepad and looked at Will's keyboard before announcing, 'It's y, get, arts, zero, one, at sign, at sign.'

Will turned and looked at her.

'Budge over,' she said with a touch of genuine warmth.

Will watched her type in 'ygetarts01@@' and click submit. The document burst into life, its heading reading 'B-Star pilot – UPS operational strategy'. The document's authors were the Erebus Group and SCS, whoever they were. A watermark emblazoned in red across the front page read: 'Top secret – not for circulation'.

The two stared at the screen for a long moment until he said, 'Thanks Mandy.'

She frowned as she left.

Twenty-five minutes later, Will sat back in his chair and ran his hands through his hair. This was the missing link. He rubbed his eyes with his fists like a child trying to wake from a dream. Now he had the evidence of what Erebus intended, he had to act. But what should he do, and how? Erebus was a huge multinational creature. He had no doubt, given the stakes, that they would send lawyers in their droves to wrap him in legal clingfilm, safeguarding their investment. Then there was this SCS organisation, he would need to find out who they were.

He checked the time, it was 4.15pm, Mandy would have left. She had long ago stopped saying a cheery goodnight. It was pointless staying in the office, he wouldn't get any work done now. Besides, for once he was on top of his work.

He transferred the document via a flash drive to his personal laptop. They had given him a powerful laptop for work, but he didn't like the idea of them snooping into his personal affairs. After locking up, he headed towards Wellington's waterfront, his laptop bag over his shoulder. His car could stay in the building overnight. He needed a bar and, after his discovery, some *no*-thinking time.

CHAPTER 13

As Will Manilow ambled towards Wellington's waterfront deep in thought, fourteen thousand kilometres away a computer operator in a windowless room in Beltsville, Maryland, sniffed at the unauthorised file copy alert blinking on her screen. She checked the logs; it didn't make sense. An unauthorised user had copied a classified file but there had been no alert signalling that the unauthorised user had gained access. That wasn't meant to be possible.

Her fingers danced across the keyboard as she investigated, discarding the possibilities that didn't fit until she arrived at the answer. The last person to change the password on the folder 'Corporate' had deleted the old password but not applied a new password. It was simple human error but a significant procedural failure. It had taken the second line of defence to detect that the files had been accessible to everyone in the Erebus Group for the past three days.

After she secured the folder with a temporary password, she typed in the details of the breach on a security incidence web form including the name of the file copied. She clicked submit and the system sent an alert to everyone who needed to know.

Six hundred and eighty kilometres from Beltsville, Maryland, Bill Paxon, head of security for the Erebus Group, sat in his thirty-second-floor office that looked out over Boston. After re-reading the alert, he rang his boss, Webb Fowler.

Fowler answered immediately. 'I've seen it. Jesus H Christ, what should we do? How did Manilow get access?'

'His clearance isn't high enough,' said Paxon, 'and there's no way he could have hacked in. There must have been a security failure.'

'Shit. Can we keep a lid on him?'

After a pause, Paxon slowly said, 'He's been contacted by a journalist. He's meeting her next week.'

'What? Why wasn't I told?'

In a matter-of-fact tone, Paxon said, 'It wasn't deemed necessary. We get hundreds of intel notifications every day. If we sent every one through, you'd be swamped.'

Paxon could tell Fowler wanted to argue but Fowler knew that he was right.

'Okay, but if that document gets out, the shit will hit the fan.'

'I'm sending in our IT specialist,' said Paxon.

'Can't the tech guys control it from here?'

'He copied the file to a flash drive, it's already out. I'm sending our IT specialist,' said Paxon before terminating the call.

CHAPTER 14

In frozen rural Nebraska, two and half thousand kilometres from Boston and a world away from New Zealand's summer, Marla Simmons, a thirty-nine-year-old former army special ops and information technology specialist, was in her barn doing what she loved, creating art out of discarded objects. Her dream was to be a full-time artist, but the world had little time, and less money, for art and artists. The irony saddened her. Art had captured the spirit of humanity through the ages and regularly sold for millions of dollars, pounds, yen, pesos, euros or, now, bitcoins. Yet equally through the ages the world viewed most artists as free-loading dilettantes and wastrels. Today's cult of celebrity allowed a few to flourish, like Banksy, but the majority spent their most creative years sentenced to toiling within depressing organisations, in her case it was the US military.

As she worked with an orbital sander on her latest piece, her back to the door, she saw in the frosted window the blurry image of a male figure slip into the barn. He stopped and looked around before picking up a hammer and stepping towards her. As he raised the hammer Marla turned off the sander and called out, 'No need to bang it, Lucas, I know you're there.'

When the sander shuddered to a halt, Marla turned to see her friend Lucas, hammer raised over an old oil drum. He must have come straight from teaching; he was wearing his usual sloppy jeans, his favourite old shoes, a terrible blue pullover with a strange pattern, and black-rimmed glasses. His fashion sense was dreadful, but his short curly hair, olive skin and intelligent, friendly face managed to save what otherwise would have been an undatable prospect.

'How did you know?' he asked.

Marla took off her mask and safety glasses and pointed to the window, where Lucas saw a blurry reflection of himself.

'Plus, you let in an icy draft. I felt it on the back of my neck.'

'You are the one,' Lucas said as he put down the hammer. 'I would have snuck up and hugged you but I figured I'd get my face smoothed.'

Marla dusted herself off as she walked towards him. 'Very wise.'

They embraced, Lucas's hands slipped inside her overalls and moved downwards.

'You're not wearing underwear,' he said, staring into her eyes.

Marla stared back and whispered, 'I know.'

'If I'd known . . .'

'I would've sanded your face.'

They both chuckled.

Lucas inspected the piece Marla had been working on. 'It's progressing,' he said, circling it. 'What is it?'

'It isn't anything yet.'

Lucas looked dubious. 'Right. What will it be when it's finished?'

'Whatever people see.'

'Right. Are you going to give this one away?'

'Yep.' Marla advertised her finished pieces online, inviting people to explain why they liked the piece and how they would put it on display. She gave them away to the story that most appealed.

Lucas shook his head. 'You could charge a few thousand, your *No Rules* label is collectable.'

'And you could charge corporates thousands to improve their civic image instead of teaching civics to teenagers.'

'Touché.'

'Besides,' said Marla, 'I like knowing the people who have them want them. They can't sell them, that's part of the deal. They can only give them back.' She sipped her coffee and grimaced, it was stone cold. She started coughing.

'When you want to take a break, I can buy you lunch,' he suggested.

'Now's good. I need a shower first.'

'Can I watch?'

'Pervert,' she said, turning off the industrial heater that kept the Nebraskan winter at bay. 'But maybe.'

Lucas's eyes lit up.

Half an hour later they were cruising towards the outskirts of Omaha on one of the gun-barrel-straight roads which criss-crossed the county. Marla, now in jeans, boots and three layers on top to keep warm, spent her days keeping fit, reading, keeping her IT skills polished and searching for materials to use in her art. Money wasn't a problem thanks to her quasi-government contracts. They sent her when IT skills were needed in dangerous environments, and she was paid handsomely.

They drove in silence, both enjoying the feeling of freedom cruising along a highway brings. The snow ploughs had piled snow into low walls, making the journey resemble travelling through a white arctic tunnel.

Marla smiled at Lucas, who grinned back. She loved Lucas, but she wasn't in love with him. She had never loved anyone, not truly. She'd had relationships with men and women in her past, and she acted as society expected, but she was always acting. Lucas was intelligent, fun and, importantly, if an assignment soured, she could rely on him to sort out whatever needed sorting. He was the most reliable, honest man she had ever met.

As he was paying, Lucas was choosing the lunch venue. That meant Ollie and Hobbes Craft Kitchen in Papillion. Lucas was a creature of habit.

The restaurant was warm and, after they had settled themselves in a quiet corner booth and ordered, Lucas said, 'You're the only person I know who changes their coffee order. Today a long black, yesterday a cappuccino, last week a Frappuccino, a calorific disgrace of a coffee.'

Marla shrugged. 'I'm fighting the McDonaldisation of the world.'

Lucas tilted his head.

'Why do people go to McDonalds?' she asked.

'Because they like the food, I guess.'

'Maybe, but it's hardly *haute cuisine*. There's another reason.'

Lucas took off his glasses to clean them, a habit Marla recognised meant he was thinking.

'It's cheap.'

'Sure is. That's part of it, but there's another reason.'

Lucas carefully polished his glasses as their coffees arrived.

'Nope,' he said. 'What am I missing?'

'It's their ability to carbon copy food.'

Lucas gave Marla a blank look.

'No matter which McDonalds you go into worldwide, it produces the same food. Not similar food, a carbon copy. You go to McDonald's in San Salvador you get the same food. I know, I've been.'

Lucas nodded along, following Marla's logic.

'Nobody's disappointed,' explained Marla, 'but equally, nobody experiences delight. The thrill of trying some new food and finding that it's delicious. McDonalds serves food to a population mentally imprisoned. That's McDonaldisation, the slide towards the vanilla society.'

Lucas grinned. 'I like that. I can so use that in class, the kids will love it. But isn't having the same coffee a habit rather than McDonaldisation?'

'What's habit?' she asked. 'I'd argue that always getting the same coffee is the neutralisation of delight and disappointment. That's McDonalds' gift to society.'

Lucas scrutinised his flat white, his usual coffee. 'I'm not sure about that part.'

Their food arrived and, after the server had left, Marla said, 'Think about art. Why don't artists keep producing their most successful piece? Why didn't Van Gogh keep painting sunflowers or Springsteen keep playing songs from *Born in the USA*?'

'Because that's not art, it's a production line.'

She leaned closer. 'The real question is, would the artists be disappointed?'

Lucas stopped, his burger halfway to his mouth. 'They'd be constantly disappointed. You might as well ask Edison why he didn't keep inventing the light bulb – if he invented the light bulb.' He went to take a bite but added, 'And how would they know it's their best work?'

Marla chuckled. 'You mean McDonalds could have produced the Immense Mac? Stopping at the Big Mac has denied generations of a taste sensation?'

He laughed too. 'And avoided hastening climate change because each one contained a whole cow.'

After they stopped laughing, they ate in silence. Marla coughed quietly. Lucas looked concerned.

'It's nothing,' she said. 'Too many hours in that cold barn.'

His plate emptying fast, he put his cutlery down and asked, 'How did you survive in the army for so long? Not using your brain must have driven you crazy.'

'The army helped me escape and I did use my brain, I got into tech. The army has seriously smart IT geeks, I was one of them.' Marla leaned closer to Lucas, who also leaned in. 'I was brought in to look at the IT haul when they took down bin Laden.'

'Get away,' said Lucas.

Marla arched an eyebrow. 'I was a contractor at the time, not that

I could've gone in anyway. I was special ops, that was a Navy Seals mission.'

Her phone buzzed.

'You can get it,' said Lucas.

'It can wait,' she said between coughs.

'That doesn't sound good. You should get it checked.' He leaned in close. 'You could have Covid. It hasn't gone away as folks around here like to think.'

Marla crossed her arms. 'Apart from you, I keep away from people. Besides, I'm fully vaxxed.'

'When was your last shot?'

She considered this. 'A while ago but it's just a tickle.'

He gave her an if-you-say-so look.

Only Lucas and her employer knew her phone number. As it wasn't Lucas, it would be the assignment she was on standby for. Although this was what she did, and the money was fantastic, she had decided to get out of the game. This assignment in New Zealand was going to be her swan song.

CHAPTER 15

Like most investigative journalists, Grace had several stories she was working on at any given time. She was meeting Manilow on Friday, which gave her time in the week to keep plugging away on the story closest to publication, the hidden scourge of domestic violence.

Highlighting New Zealand's domestic violence problem in the media was tricky. Grace had started researching the area two years ago, yet each draft she produced struggled to win editorial support. It seemed to her that New Zealand, the media included, wanted to pretend domestic violence was historical, cured like polio.

She was tracking the lived experience of Elle, a domestic violence victim, as she battled her way through the courts to reclaim her life from a manipulative, stalking ex. In return for Elle's help, Grace twisted NewsNZ's arm to help with her legal costs. A key part of Grace's story was how access to justice was correlated to your bank balance. Without financial help, Elle couldn't afford the legal costs and there would be no story.

Elle lived in a typical Palmerston North suburb. It wasn't the wealthiest, it wasn't the poorest. Her house was a tidy 1980s bungalow with a neat flower garden hidden from the street by a head-high, black fence. For a fleeting time, Elle's house had been worth a small fortune but, even though the self-interested real estate talking heads had declared house prices would increase for ever, the needle of economic reality had burst the housing bubble. Grace hoped Dante reserved a place in his hellish circles for real estate commentators.

It was just before five when she parked behind Elle's sensible grey Nissan Note. A wary-looking Elle was watching at the front door. When Elle recognised her, she didn't look as pleased to see her as Grace had expected: she burst into tears. Grace gave her a hug and Elle pulled herself together. Inside, after making sure her children were busy and happy, Elle made Grace a cup of herbal tea.

Standing in the kitchen, unsure about pomegranate and raspberry tea, Grace asked, 'Tell me, what's up?'

Her friend sniffed. 'It's my own fault, I shouldn't have listened to my ex. But I didn't want to spend money if I didn't have to, mine and your company's.'

Grace stayed quiet while Elle took her disjointedly through what had happened. Elle had applied for a protection order that her ex contested, meaning the case went to the Family Court. Her ex offered to save everyone time and money by agreeing to sign an undertaking in which he agreed not to act in a way that would constitute a breach of a protection order. Grace knew this wasn't uncommon, but success depended on the character of the individual making the undertaking. As it was a personal, not a legal commitment, there was no recourse if it didn't work.

'You decided to try it?' asked Grace.

'I did,' said Elle, fighting back tears.

'I guess I don't need to ask what happened.'

Elle's demeanour changed in a flash to anger. Checking her children weren't listening she said, 'What a fucking waste of time.'

'How long before he showed up?'

'As soon as I'd signed, he was back leering and laughing.'

'What did you do?'

'What could I do?'

'Oh Elle, I'm so sorry.'

'It's my own fault, I should have spent the money instead of believing another lie.'

'You still can,' said Grace. 'You'll need to gather more evidence, that's all.'

Elle's face pinched.

'I can help,' said Grace. 'My story tracks your journey, and this adds another dimension.'

Elle sighed. 'Maybe. The whole schemozzle is sucking me dry. I'm busy enough with work and the children.'

Grace was about to speak, but Elle held up her hand. 'I can hear his van.'

'What does he do?'

'Blocks me in by parking across the driveway. Waves to the kids if they see him, mouths obscenities and gives me the bird.'

'How old is he, twelve?' said Grace. 'Come on, let's give him a reason to fume.'

Elle's eyes grew large. 'Is that wise?'

'I can't see what harm it'll do.' Grace took out her phone. 'This'll record the evidence.'

Grace went out the front door first, followed by Elle. As Elle described, a white van with a leering driver was parked across her driveway. Grace recognised the driver, though he was scowling with such intensity he looked cross-eyed. She assumed he hadn't expected to see his ex-wife walking towards him holding hands with another woman. She captured the scene, completed by his middle-finger gesture before he sped away leaving rubber and smoke behind.

Grace gave Elle a go-figure look, and Elle burst into uncontrollable laughter. Grace joined in and they hugged while they laughed. Their laughter drew the attention of a passer-by in sunglasses who watched them as he got back into his car.

Back inside, Elle's children remained unaware of the altercation. Grace and Elle developed a plan of attack to collect the evidence. When Grace had time, she would help Elle by parking close by and recording his antics. Elle was going to leave her phone in the window recording before and after work.

Driving home, Grace was deep in thought. She had the depressing feeling that, no matter how interesting the story, it would be a tough sell. If domestic violence impacted more on men than women it would be front-page news; like anything to do with rugby. That annoyed the journalist in Grace and pissed off the citizen in her. While the wealthy wanted the party to rage on, take the Band-Aid off any societal problem and there, staring you in the face, was a crying, empty piggy bank.

CHAPTER 16

Marla lifted her mask and washed down a cough suppressant with the rest of her neat whisky. The burn gave her instant pleasure and relief. She pushed the flight attendant button.

A masked middle-aged female flight attendant arrived quickly. 'How can I help?'

Marla liked that Air New Zealand employed a variety of people. It made a change from flying with cookie-cutter-attractive, lithe females. That logic belonged to a time when appealing to men's fantasies was good for business.

'Another whisky please?'

The flight attendant paused, about to explain why a third whisky wasn't possible. Marla raised her sunglasses and calmly repeated her request.

The flight attendant hesitated for a moment. 'Certainly.'

Marla replaced her sunglasses. In her experience, most people took the path of least resistance when confronted with a potential scene. It was a tactic Marla had perfected over the years to help her survive in the male-dominated US army. She had power dressed entirely in black with a blonde buzz cut for this express purpose.

They were two hours out from New Zealand's largest city, Auckland. From there she was flying straight to Wellington where they had booked her into a quarantine facility, a mandatory step in New Zealand in response to the new variants of Covid. If the plan went smoothly, she would complete the assignment and be heading home within three days. The tech team would erase the records of her visit. It would be as though she had never left home.

The flight attendant returned with the whisky, putting it down wordlessly. Marla nodded her thanks and waited for the flight attendant to leave before she allowed herself a quiet cough into her mask. She'd had the cough for days now. She couldn't shake it. Having Covid overseas could throw plans into chaos so she had insisted on a test before she left. As she expected, it had come back negative.

The money she earned made her work worth the risk, but each assignment could be her last. She hadn't mentioned her retirement plans because her employers wouldn't be pleased, and she didn't trust them. The question uppermost in her mind was, would they let her retire? The assignments she had carried out, the places she had visited and what she knew would make them nervous.

Those thoughts needed to wait until after the assignment. Pouring her whisky, she took out her laptop and spent the next hour familiarising herself with the assignment.

An issue with the plane delayed her flight from Auckland to Wellington, forcing her to spend a night in an Auckland hotel quarantine facility. The replacement flight didn't leave until 3pm the following day, which put her two days behind schedule. On the plus side, she was feeling better, though jet lagged.

The next morning, two nurses dressed head to foot in protective equipment had taken a Covid swab. Marla explained she tested negative three days ago before leaving the US, but they were adamant, the US was back on the Covid red list. Once again, she endured having a bottle brush shoved into her brain.

Logging into her laptop, she opened an encrypted communications app, leaving it open while she checked her equipment: a bootable password reset drive, a range of flash drives with programmes such as Intruder, Traceroute NG and her favourite, Hashcat. Difficult-to-get items including an X-26 taser; a small bottle of the anaesthetic propofol and sedatives were in the hotel fridge when she arrived at Wellington's Grand Mercure hotel. These were easier for locals to source than having her risk smuggling them into the country. She had brought with her a range of outfits; the one she intended to use included a blonde wig that gave her an updated Farrah Fawcett look.

A silky but disturbing voice came from her laptop. 'Simmons?'

Marla shivered, it sounded like an evil Hal from *2001: A Space Odyssey*. She accepted the connection, the image on the screen was no more reassuring, a generic, sexless human icon. 'One minute,' she said, launching a process to check the integrity of the connection. 'Secure,' she said, after it returned a green tick.

'Turn on your camera,' said the voice. 'We need to ensure you aren't compromised.'

Marla made a face at the icon before turning on the camera. 'How do you know they're not hiding under the bed?'

'Thank you, Simmons. Any questions about the plan?' asked the voice, ignoring her comment.

'No questions, an observation.'

'Go ahead.'

'The plan revolves around me picking up the target over lunch. What if he's not interested? He could be in the closet.'

'He isn't, and there's no evidence of a serious relationship since his wife died. Credit card transactions show activity with known female prostitutes.'

Marla rolled her eyes. 'Great.'

'Not recently,' the voice added. 'This approach has worked before. It will allow you to access his house where you can incapacitate him and sanitise the document.'

'I know the plan. It has worked but it's failed too.'

'Acknowledged. Any other questions?'

'Why are there two mobsters pretending to be CIA agents on the ground?' When she received the assignment, she had checked which operatives were active in New Zealand. Tom and Jerry, technically in the same line of work as her, had a reputation for violence.

'They're in a different sphere of the operation.'

Marla pursed her lips. 'Right. Last question, can we guarantee the drugs dispensed are accurate? I don't want him to end up like Michael Jackson.'

'The drugs were clinically dispensed.'

'Then I'm good to go,' she said. 'By the way, I was forced to endure another Covid test this morning.'

'It's New Zealand's policy. It should be your last, you'll be on a plane tomorrow evening. Good luck, Simmons.'

The connection terminated.

It was time to go to work. The quicker she completed the assignment, the quicker she could get back Stateside and work on her retirement plan. She was thankful no part of the plan involved interaction with Tom and Jerry.

Marla packed her equipment into a large leather satchel that doubled as a backpack. At 11am exactly, she answered a light knock on her door. A man in a security guard's uniform motioned for her to follow. Dressed in a short skirt, matching jacket and a tight top, she flung her large leather satchel over her shoulder and fell in behind. Most men found her attractive, and to make sure Manilow noticed her, she had selected clothes that accentuated her figure.

She couldn't suppress a cough as they walked down the narrow, emergency staircase, drawing a stern look from the guard. After drinking from her water bottle, she whispered, 'What about the security cameras?'

'Technical issues,' was his curt reply.

After they'd weaved their way around a maze of semi-dark corridors, the sunlight dazzled Marla when they exited the hotel. The guard unlocked a gate in the steel mesh perimeter fence and pointed to a grey Suzuki Swift parked on the street. The driver was wearing the same uniform.

'A guard will be here at one in the morning; they'll escort you back to your room.'

Marla confirmed with an eyebrow raise before heading to the car. The gate rattled shut behind her. Stretching as she walked, she was grateful to be out of the tiny hotel room. It wasn't New Zealand's fault. In her experience hotel rooms were always tiny, unless you were rich.

Taking a back seat, she let out a cough she couldn't suppress. The driver scowled as he stared at her in the rear-view mirror. Drying her eyes, she tried to take in a deep breath. She picked up the tablet on the seat next to her. It would have the latest information, the route she would take, indicative timings, security camera locations and the latest photos of the target and his house.

The driver weaved through Wellington's streets, stopping at the infiltration point, a tree-lined part of Bowen Street, where he explained there were no security cameras. Marla knew this. She had spent the last hour reconnoitring the area thoroughly. Getting her bearings, she put on a wide-brimmed hat as she made for The Terrace.

At 11.45am, a server seated Marla at a table in Bethel Woods Café. Ordering a glass of wine – one never hurt – she used the tablet to review photos of her target. Several photos were of Manilow inside Bethel Woods. The 1960s theme made a distinctive backdrop, as did the recognisable server sporting a cute blonde crew cut who had just taken her order.

After she had reviewed the information, she sipped her wine. Manilow wasn't like her usual targets, he looked like a legitimate businessman. She had a policy of not researching her target's background or why those in charge deemed they needed to have their information fucked over. It only complicated assignments. It was a policy that had served her well. Turning off the tablet, she forced away the doubt.

At 12.10pm Marla watched Manilow exit Solnet House. She closed her eyes and smiled. In her experience when operations didn't run to plan, they tended to go from bad to worse. The intel said Manilow lunched here every day, alone. But as she watched him cross the road, he wasn't alone. Walking in conversation next to him was an attractive middle-aged woman. Manilow had a lunch date.

CHAPTER 17

Grace had an hour to kill before her midday meeting with Will Manilow. She decided to pop in to see if Corin, her police contact, was free for coffee. The last time she had been near the Wellington Police Station was when she had organised a press conference outside the front entrance during the great tax rort saga. She felt an odd feeling as she approached, it was as if she was returning to the scene of a crime.

A familiar face greeted Grace with a warm 'Kia ora, Ms Marks.' Behind the front desk was the police sergeant who had kept a wary eye on the press conference.

Grace walked over. 'I should know your name, but we were never introduced.'

'Call me Bobby.'

She squinted.

The sergeant chuckled. 'Can't sneak one past you, eh. It's Taine.'

Grace gave him a sideways look.

'Honestly,' he said, offering his hand.

'Okay, Taine, it is nice to meet you in altered circumstances. Call me Ace.'

'And what brings you in, Ace? No trouble, I hope?'

Grace smiled. 'No, I was in the neighbourhood. Is CT around?'

Taine checked his screen. 'He's in Porirua.'

'Bugger,' said Grace. Never one to let a chance go by, she asked, 'Out of curiosity, what's your take on the rise in street crime?'

'Are we off the record?'

'We are.'

'It doesn't add up.'

Grace stayed quiet.

'I know times are tough,' he continued, 'but the increase is off the charts. We're getting so many complaints but there's little we can do. Half the time they don't know who did it and, even when they do, it's minor. And because of all the attention in the media, it's escalating. Kids and copy-cats are getting involved to be part of the action, sharing daft videos on social media.'

'What does your gut tell you?' she asked.

Taine rubbed his chin. 'Something's off but exactly what . . .' He shrugged.

Back outside the police station, Grace decided to kill time by wandering around Wellington's CBD. Since she began researching surveillance, she had started to notice the plethora of security cameras. They were literally everywhere. Dalek eyes on stalks. Three-sixty-degree cameras hanging malevolently. Small unblinking limpets screwed onto buildings, atop all manner of poles, infesting public transport, behind counters, spider-like in dark corners and under eaves everywhere. Previously they had blended into the background, as they were designed to do; now to Grace they stood out like male canine genitals.

Taine hadn't added significantly to the picture, but he must have been on the force for decades and he had said that what was happening was new to him. Although the world was rapidly changing, the old saying 'There's nothing new under the sun' rang true. If people were behaving strangely, something was the root cause, and money was the biggest driver of behaviour.

With a long black from a coffee cart, Grace headed towards The Terrace and Erebus Optics' head office. She didn't have a plan for the meeting, it would depend on Manilow's level of receptiveness. If he was chatty, she would let the interview go wherever it went. If he was reticent, she had a list of open questions to nudge him along.

Erebus Optics' head office was on the third floor of Solnet House, a building she discovered was part of property tycoon Bob Jones' empire. She grinned. If Jones knew she was walking into a building he owned, he would have set his dogs on her. Jones was a former poster boy for the wealthy whose gloss she had helped dull.

Entering Erebus Optics' head office, she received a warm welcome from a bored-looking receptionist. Grace chatted for a few minutes, it never hurt to be nice, before she knocked on Manilow's door. In response to a muffled 'Come in', she entered. A man dressed in a suit, but no tie, stared at his laptop as he motioned for her to take a seat.

Manilow and the company's head office weren't what she expected. The company was successful, it had US owners and offices on The Terrace. She had expected full-blown corporate excess. A team of young, attractive, immaculately dressed staff. Expensive but tasteless corporate leadership art adorning the walls, an indoor waterfall with cherubs reclining and, amongst the opulence, Will Manilow, looking like a poor man's Tom Cruise. What was the point of having corporate money and not blinging up your surroundings like a would-be-if-could-be American rapper? As she had learned to do throughout her working life, Grace kept her thoughts to herself.

After a final click, he stood. 'You must be Grace Marks, please call me Will. I've heard a lot about you.' Handing her a business card, he said, as though he had read her mind, 'Welcome to our humble head office.'

Grace shook his hand, popping his business card in her jacket pocket. 'Hi Will, call me Ace. I did expect . . . I don't know, something grander.'

'We've outsourced most of the corporate functions, it's what the new owners wanted. I miss the people, but I've never liked that corporate image bullshit. It's pure ego and a waste of money.'

'I agree,' she said, 'but it's not usual. Especially as the owners are American, aren't they?'

He nodded. 'The pandemic keeps them away, but when anyone visits, I hire conference rooms at the InterContinental to appease their desire for opulence. What you see is all we need to keep the Erebus Optics world turning and give the owners what they wanted, an upmarket head office address.'

Grace semi-shrugged a fair enough.

He looked at the time and put on his jacket. 'We can chat at the café across the road, I'll buy you lunch.'

'Great.' She hadn't eaten breakfast in penance for bunking on her morning gym session.

Bethel Woods Café was more bar rather than café. The owners had styled it on the heyday of vinyl records, with vintage posters adorning the walls. A drum kit hung oddly from the ceiling like a kind of retro chandelier. Though they had chosen hideous colours and the worst fashion aspects of the era, Grace enjoyed the atmosphere. Manilow chose a table away from the bar where it was quieter.

After they had ordered and chatted about the décor to break the ice, he asked, 'Where do you want to start?'

Grace took out a notepad. 'How about starting with why you didn't want to talk in your office. I got the feeling it wasn't just hunger. Is it your receptionist?'

'Mandy? Goodness no, she's fine. A bit bored but solid.' He paused and stared at Grace. 'Look, before we get into this, what's the deal?'

'Deal?'

'You're a journalist looking for a story. I don't fancy starring, but there is a story . . . a big one.'

'A big one,' said Grace, nodding. 'Okay, let's make this chat off the record. If you, if we, want to have a talk on the record, we can discuss that later.'

'Sounds good,' he said. 'I'm pretty sure I can trust you. I did some digging, you seem honourable.'

'You make me sound Victorian.'

Their lunch arrived. A cheeseburger, fries and a pint of beer for Will, a Caesar salad and water for Grace. They each scrutinised the other's lunch before he broke into a laugh.

'This makes a bit of a statement about our respective lives.' He raised his glass. 'Good health.'

'Don't get me wrong,' said Grace, not bothering to raise her water, 'I could demolish two burgers, but female guilt would force me to bike a stupid number of kilometres as penance.'

'I shelved the male version of that a couple of decades ago.' He took a large bite of his burger and winked at her.

'Sorry to break this to you Will, there is no male version. So why not chat at your office?' She picked at her salad. The sight of Manilow's cheeseburger had made her ravenous, and jealous.

'Because I have no idea whether the office is bugged.'

'By who?'

'By my employers.'

'Can't you tell?' she asked. 'You're in security.'

'There's a difference between security and spying,' said Manilow. 'If they put a security camera on the wall, I'd recognise it. But if they've bugged my office, if the phone system is recording my conversations or they're listening in to my mobile, how could I tell? As you can see, I'm no James Bond.'

'Okay, but why spy on you?'

He put down his burger. 'Why not? If they can. I find it hard to trust them, especially now. They're primarily in home security but they have their fingers in several associated industries. If we were in my office, and I don't know whether they're listening or not . . .' He finished the sentence with an eyebrow raise.

'You have to act as though they are,' said Grace. 'Jeremy Bentham keeps invading my conversations.'

'His philosophy has never been more . . .' He struggled to find the right word.

'Apposite?'

'Nice.'

'I hear business is booming. What do you put it down to?' It was one of her prepared questions.

'The pandemic of course. Unemployment, inequality, poverty all increase crime and suddenly everyone wants protection. Cue rapid increase in sales.' He leaned closer. 'Except you know that's not right, you wouldn't be here if it was. You're not a business reporter, you like looking under the carpet where society sweeps its secrets.'

'Maybe,' said Grace. 'But isn't your company raking it in?'

He shook his head. 'Our market share is soaring at the expense of profit, at least short-term profit. Our business model is about long-term services, not short-term installations. But you knew that too, otherwise you would have looked confused or surprised.'

She chuckled. 'I'm making a note not to play cards with you for money. You're right, I talked to a competitor to find out what's going on, he put me onto your company. You're focused on the ongoing monitoring, losing money in the process.'

'In the short-term,' he agreed. 'But when the surge in installations dies down, as it must, what are the other guys going to do?'

This confirmed what Grace had gleaned from Pluck. She was about to introduce the increase in street crime, but Manilow beat her to it.

'My guess is that you're interested in the rise in crime. You're not buying the coincidence. A firm with US owners is increasing market share. Street crime is up. People are worried.'

The interview wasn't going as Grace had expected. Far from ignorant of the wider context and reluctant to talk, the businessman seemed steps ahead of her and eager to talk. 'I need a bit of background first,' she said. 'When did Erebus buy your company?'

'Just over two years ago. I started it in 2001 when I grew bored running around weekends selling houses. It was a solid business with twenty-seven employees and contracts with a range of resellers and installers. Then along came Erebus Group with their money and now I'm filthy rich and quite the catch.' He winked at Grace.

She squinted as he laughed.

'I guess I shouldn't act the clown these days, it's . . . un-PC,' he said.

'I can handle myself,' she said. 'I started work in the eighties, being groped was in my job description.'

He laughed. 'That sounds sadly accurate.'

'It's nice to meet a Kiwi who's made it, though,' said Grace. 'I was beginning to doubt they existed.'

'Have I made it? I guess I have. Anyway, Erebus injected a lot of cash into the business. We now supply security solutions nationwide and have opened offices in Auckland, Tauranga, Nelson, Christchurch and Dunedin. New Plymouth is opening soon. The real catch was I had to stay on as CEO for five years – the penalties in the contract are ruinous.'

'How long until your contract's up?'

He looked at the ceiling, a chip halfway to his mouth. 'Another two years, ten months and a few weeks. I can't wait to finish. It's not my business now, it's theirs. Sure, I've a huge house and a fancy car, but the amount I'm drinking and my diet' – he gestured simultaneously at his lunch and stomach – 'I'll be lucky to see retirement age.'

'You can change that.'

'True enough. And I should.'

'What'll you do?' asked Grace.

'Sell my far-too-big house and head to the country for a quiet life. Maybe I'll take up writing.'

'Have you got something to say?' asked Grace.

He grinned. 'That's an insightful question. You're good, Ace. And yes, with what's happening, I've definitely something to say.'

'Good luck then. In my experience, agents and publishers only read spreadsheets these days. What's different about your monitoring services?'

'Right, back to business it is,' said Manilow, smirking. She watched him contemplate his empty glass, looking around for a server though none were looking his way. 'Monitoring for most companies is reactive. If an alarm is tripped, or a client calls, they dispatch a car. We used to be the same. Now we leave the monitoring to our new technology, A-Star. If it detects an event of concern, it notifies the call centre, and they check the footage and live feeds to see if an intervention is required.'

'Wow,' she said. 'The system, A-Star, can do that?'

'Yep. The technology's new and it's a game changer, excuse the bullshit term. I don't have much time for the Americans, but they've developed a bloody clever system. A-Star integrates facial recognition technology with machine learning. Over time, the system learns who, and what, is normal.'

Her face screwed up, partly in thought, partly in confusion.

He explained, 'If the system detects a slinking shape it's never seen before, it creates an alert. The operator checks and tells the system cats are harmless events. That's cats taken care of for everyone. Every time an event occurs outside known safe parameters it sends an alert coded for how concerning it assesses the event.'

'Concerning?'

'If the event appears dangerous, like an intruder armed with a knife, it sends a higher alert. It knows all about weapons, it was developed in the States.'

'How does it figure it out, though? I mean, a knife could be a weapon, but it could be used to make a sandwich.'

'Don't ask me,' he said. 'The software was developed by clever pointy-heads. Our marketing angle is, we'll see the danger before you do. That's why we're grabbing market share, everyone else offers the outdated reactive service.'

'Do your customers know people can look at their camera feeds? What about privacy?'

'It's in the fine print,' he said with a what-can-you-do gesture. 'The privacy legislation is outdated anyway. Currently if a computer looks at data, there's no privacy breach.'

'For real?'

'Sure. Computers store your financial data and transactions then access them to calculate how much you owe. If they didn't, how could they warn you if you'd gone into overdraft? Privacy is only an issue if a bank employee looks at your data when they shouldn't, or your data gets into the public domain.'

'I never thought about that,' said Grace. 'The difference between a computer and a person. But if computers are smart enough to act, what's the difference?'

'Exactly. Be careful though, Ace, it's a rabbit hole of an issue. If they ask, we tell customers our staff can only look if the software detects an unsafe event. Their feeds are private until A-Star raises an alert or the customer contacts us directly. That's the theory.'

'Why's it only a theory?' asked Grace.

He signalled a server and ordered a second drink. He glanced at Grace, who declined a second water. 'The world's changed,' he said.

'Until recently, security cameras recorded to a physical disk, before then it was video tape. It wasn't possible to work in real time, the data only existed offline. Now with the cloud, data streams are uploaded in real time to god knows where.'

'There must be protocols to keep it secure.'

'There are, but again in theory,' he said. 'In practice, once the data is ripping along a fibre cable, who knows who can see it? I assume you're looking at the Five Eyes alliance as part of your story?'

'For sure.'

'Tell me what they can and can't do. Speargun, Prism, Stateroom and XKeyscore: who can keep track? They have the technology to poke their nose into anything and everything. Who's to say they're not trawling through the data.'

Grace's brain was working overtime merging what Manilow was saying with what she had learned from Dr Noble. 'You make it sound Orwellian – but people don't seem that concerned.'

He sat back as the server delivered his beer. 'People aren't concerned because they're distracted, but it has Orwellian potential and it's happening through political misdirection.'

'Do you think people are buying the "if you've got nothing to hide" message?' she asked.

'Misdirection,' said Manilow nodding, before drinking deeply. 'The focus is on crime, terrorists and the pandemic, not on the negative impacts of mass surveillance, individual freedom and loss of privacy. Imagine having the power to review everyone's phone conversations, emails and computer files.'

'And where they've visited and who they've met,' added Grace.

'And who decides what's acceptable?' he said. 'Same-sex gymnastics was illegal until recently. Imagine if a future government of morons reclassify it as deviant behaviour. The system trawls through its databases looking for signs of males and females up to you know what. Boom! There's a list of people for the authorities to name, shame and lean on. That's the real problem. The system is as harmless or Orwellian as those in power.'

She gave him space to keep talking. He was building to something and she didn't want to get in his way.

'The system establishes the foundation for societal control ready for the wrong party or person to come along. And once they're in control . . .'

'They'll be difficult to shift.' She finished his sentence to keep him talking, but he changed tack.

He pointed a chip at her. 'The journalistic ranks are already skinny, how hard would it be to consign investigative journalism to history?'

'Good job I'm driving,' said Grace. 'This conversation is making me fancy a drink or two. Back to the rise in street crime, how do you think it fits in? I agree, it's no coincidence.'

'That's the question, isn't it? If it's coordinated, that's dark news.' He slowly ate another of his chips. 'I need time to work out what to do. The document made it clear . . .' His voice trailed off and he drank the last of his beer, abandoning the sentence.

Grace waited, but she was forced to prompt. 'What did the document make clear?'

He stared at her. 'I'm not ready to go there, not yet. Soon.'

Grace stayed quiet.

'If you think about it in terms of business,' he said, 'the obvious conclusion is that Erebus is after money, and that's partly true. But the money's a bonus. Looking from above, each house becomes a node in a surveillance net. When you have enough nodes, you cover a city. When you cover enough cities, you cover the country.'

'And if people know they're being monitored twenty-four-seven, they'll never act normally.' Grace closed her eyes briefly, Dr Noble's logic coming back to her.

'The "If you've got nothing to hide" argument is pure political misdirection. Think about Hong Kong. The goal of surveilling their population isn't about catching criminals, that's also a bonus. It's about compliance, keeping people in line. Keeping citizens toeing the line.'

'The chilling effect,' said Grace. 'It sounds like you're saying a US corporation is interested in surveilling New Zealand. Why?'

'That Ace, is the right question.'

CHAPTER 18

The intelligence reports said Manilow lunched alone, but today of all days the target had a lunch date. Marla didn't lose her cool. Shit happened, things went wrong, and losing your cool only ever worsened the situation. But this assignment had confirmed her decision, it was her last. It was time to retire.

She ate her lunch slowly as she watched the businessman and his lunch date talk animatedly. After they left, she used the tablet to open the encrypted communications app, using Bluetooth earbuds to ensure no one overheard her conversation. While she waited, she sipped her water, finding it increasingly difficult to suppress her cough. The generic, sexless human icon appeared, the voice creepier because the earbuds made it feel intimate.

'Manilow wasn't alone,' said Marla.

'We know.'

'I uploaded a photo.'

'She's a journalist, Grace Marks.'

The name meant nothing to Marla. 'If she has a copy of the document, it will jeopardise the assignment.'

'Did Manilow hand over information to Marks?' asked the voice.

'Negative. No physical document, no flash drive.'

'You're sure?'

'I am.'

'Then she doesn't have the document,' said the voice. 'He hasn't emailed it or made it available in the cloud.'

Marla waited.

'Execute plan C,' said the voice.

Marla frowned as she stared at the tablet. Even if the camera was on, they couldn't see her reaction, it was aimed at the ceiling. 'I reviewed plan C; it's flawed. I don't do Hail Marys.' From American football, that was the term Marla used for desperate plays with little chance of success.

'Hold for instructions,' said the voice.

Marla noted a hint of ice, or was it malice?

Marla waved away the server while she waited, jumping slightly when the voice returned. 'You'll be extracted at today's infiltration point at 3 pm local time. You'll infiltrate the target's house directly tomorrow at 2 pm local time. After you've sanitised the location, you'll be transferred to central Wellington to ensure his office is sanitised. Detailed plans will be available in a few hours.'

'Acknowledged,' she said, terminating the connection. They wouldn't be impressed by the setback, or her refusal to implement plan C, but fuck those rear-echelon motherfuckers: shit happens.

The same driver-car combination arrived promptly at three. As she lay concealed in the back, the driver dropped her in a dimly-lit corner of the underground carpark. Although she was looking casual, Marla was ready for any form of attack. None came. A security guard arrived to escort her back to her room via the fire escape stairs.

After checking the amended plan, she shut her laptop and rested her head on the tiny hotel desk. Between her constant urge to cough and her brain on Nebraska time, she hadn't slept well. After picking at her dinner, followed by a long hot shower, she combined a cough suppressant with a slug of whisky and climbed into bed. She didn't set an alarm. With the operation planned for the afternoon, she could sleep the morning away.

Marla slept badly, her dreams punctuated with foreign places, people she had seen killed and psychedelic images of yesterday's bar. Although it didn't feel like it, she had been asleep for ten hours when a loud knock roused her. A rapid surfacer, she sat up alert only to succumb to a coughing fit.

'Hang on,' she gasped, gulping water from a glass beside the bed.

Surveying the room, she checked to make sure there was no evidence of yesterday's activities: there wasn't. She typically hid all incriminating items as soon as she returned from an assignment to ensure she couldn't be taken by surprise. She opened the door to two humanoid figures, presumably nurses, kitted out in personal protective equipment.

'What's going on? What time is it?' she asked, her voice hoarse.

A male voice said, 'Kia ora, it's seven thirty Miss Simmons, sorry it's early. I'm afraid your Covid test has come back positive.'

Marla stared at the nurse. This couldn't be happening. 'There must be a mistake.'

'No mistake, you've contracted Covid-19, the dangerous new variant. Given the timing, you probably caught it before you came to Aotearoa. Other passengers and crew from your flight have also tested positive. You're transferring to the quarantine wing.'

'I thought this was quarantine,' she said, her voice returning to near normal.

'This is managed isolation. The quarantine wing is in the hotel, but it has additional security. It allows us to monitor you closely, limit the chance of spreading the infection and make sure you recover.'

Marla shook her head. This could not be happening.

'You don't have to move immediately, you'll need time to pack,' said the nurse, his sympathetic smile elongated clownlike by the curved perspex face shield. 'This room will be deep cleaned to make sure none of the virus survives. You're scheduled to move tomorrow morning. We need to make sure we take precautions to limit the chance of spreading the virus.'

After they had gone, Marla slumped on the bed. She had Covid but she couldn't afford to have Covid. This was bad. This was dangerous. Not the virus itself, although she knew it could be deadly, it was because they would want to trace her movements and that wouldn't end well.

Logging into her laptop, she opened the encrypted communications app, turned on her camera and sat in front of it, cross-legged on her bed. It took longer this time before a similar but different voice asked, 'What's happened?'

'I've tested positive for Covid. They're transferring me to the quarantine wing in the hotel tomorrow.'

'That's unfortunate.' The voice said indifferently. 'Hold for instructions.'

Marla refilled her water glass in the bathroom. Looking at herself in a large mirror, she let her senses check her body. She felt okay. Her chest was sore from coughing, but that aside she felt she could run a marathon.

'Simmons?' The voice brought her back to the present. She sat back in front of the camera. 'Your assignment can still be completed this afternoon before you're moved. We have no ability to extract you from quarantine. You're to be extracted immediately after your quarantine period.'

'I am not spending a fortnight in a shoebox.' Marla's outburst brought on a coughing fit.

Ignoring Marla's coughing, the voice said, 'Understood, we'll work on an alternative extraction plan.'

Marla heard the connection terminate. When she stopped coughing, she lay on the bed staring at the ceiling. 'The doctor said I probably caught Covid before I arrived. But I'd tested negative before I left, or had I? This is bad.'

CHAPTER 19

Grace dropped a piece of penne pasta for Roxy, her partner Sean's grateful retriever, who expertly intercepted it before it hit the ground. Grace had made carbonara but as usual she'd made too much, so leftovers were in ample supply. Grace's children had devoured dinner in record time and disappeared to 'study'.

'What should I do?' she asked Sean. She had given him the highlights of her meeting with Dr Noble and the realistic possibility she was under government surveillance. Then she ran through her meeting with Manilow, highlighting his mention of a document.

'About being spied on?' asked Sean. 'What can you do? I can't imagine the GCSB, or whoever else is involved, would tell you. And as you said, they can deny involvement while being in it up to their necks.'

'I can ask the GCSB what information they hold about me,' she said. 'I'll be on their watch list, but with the number of escape clauses they've left themselves, the rules are like Swiss cheese.' She picked up a liberally highlighted document. 'Listen to this: "In some instances, the GCSB is able to neither confirm nor deny the existence or non-existence of information. This is done in cases where declaration of the GCSB holding such information would prejudice the interests protected by sections . . .", blah, blah, blah bullshit.'

Sean's face soured. 'We should – I'm talking citizens here – know how this works. When you started chasing this story, I assumed it would be relatively straightforward. But hell, the legislation is mind-numbing, and I'm a lawyer.'

'I'm sure they write it to be impenetrable,' she said. 'It puts people off asking awkward questions, asking *any* questions. And even when super-smart journalists,' Grace gave Sean a theatrical wink, 'manage to get it into the media, it's too dense for the public to swallow. What's left is a regurgitated mess splattered on social media.'

Sean laughed. 'Social media and pavement pizza, an apt analogy.'

She was in full stride. 'All we're left with is the chilling effect from the "If you've got nothing to hide, you've got nothing to fear" bullshit logic.'

'I don't know if that message was crafted,' he said, 'but it's simple and seductive.'

'It's been used for as long as humans have worshipped gods. It's evolved in modern times, including in 1933 when a certain Minister of Public Enlightenment and Propaganda called on the "volk" to keep an eye on things.'

He grimaced. 'Goebbels.'

'It's what the Nazis did, except they didn't have the technology we're developing. They relied on citizens informing on other citizens. Children informed on their parents, got them shot. How revolting is that?'

'As revolting as it gets.'

'Imagine the Nazis, Stalin or the Stasi with HD cameras and facial recognition technology.'

'It would have made them near impossible to topple. They would've crushed resistance like' – Sean clicked his fingers – 'that.'

'When I started this story, it felt like the state versus citizens. But people are keen to put cameras on their houses to help the state. It feels like we're on a similar slope to the Germans.'

'Not as extreme, though.'

Grace shrugged.

They sat silently until she asked, 'Are you thinking what I'm thinking?'

Sean nodded. 'Trump, Putin, Kim Jong-un, Bolsonaro. And, closer to home, what about Seymour, Luxon or, heaven forbid, someone like a Lee-Ross?'

She laughed. 'Seymour would so grow one of those little moustaches.' She put her hands on her face in an impromptu impression of Munch's *The Scream*. 'Imagine any conservative with that power, they'd fashion themselves as the new Volkner.'

'Volkner?' he asked.

'You know, *Sleeping Dogs*.'

'Was that the despot's name? Anyway, as Lenin himself asked, what is to be done?'

His question ushered in another period of silence interrupted by Roxy's plaintive moan to remind them she was still there, as were the leftovers. Sean tossed her another piece of pasta.

'What angle is your story taking?' he asked.

'I'm trying to show that monitoring people twenty-four seven is a terrible idea and that the "If you've got nothing to hide" argument is flawed to the point of absurdity.'

'What about Erebus, the document and . . . was it Manilow?'

Grace nodded. 'There's something going down. Will said it was something big, but . . .'

'But?'

'But I can't use any of it, not yet. It's all supposition, I'd sound like a conspiracy crank and there's enough of them already. The Americans are coming to spy on everyone, run for the hills, put tinfoil on your head.'

Sean chuckled.

'Don't get me wrong,' she said. 'It could be huge, but I need something concrete. I've got to believe it myself first. At the moment, even though the dots are joining, it still sounds whacky. In the meantime, I'm focusing my story on the general evils of surveillance.'

'Will people get it? And will people care?'

'What do you mean?' she said. 'They should.'

'They should, doesn't mean they will. Your tax story demonstrated that you need more than just a story. People had written about the wealthy rorting tax for decades, but you—'

'And Michael Thompson,' interrupted Grace, referring to the Inland Revenue whistle blower at the centre of the story.

Sean squinted. 'Are you ever going to tell me who he is?'

'Nope. He'll still be safe after the SIS have waterboarded you.'

'Charming. Where was I? That's right, that politician sounding off in the media. That turned it into an event. An event that sparked the public's imagination. Result, real change.'

Her brow furrowed deeply. 'Okay, but a story—'

Sean cut in. 'Will be just another story.'

'But exposing the tax rort started with a story,' she said.

'It did, but it needed that MP losing his political shit in the media to light the fire.'

'You're right,' said Grace. 'That was the spark. Otherwise, it might have sunk without trace, and I'd be pushing for work in the second oldest profession.'

Sean tilted his head. 'Consultancy?'

'No, that's the business version of prostitution. I was talking about politics. Running for one of the councils or an equally useless role in an economic development agency. There are less junkets now Little's ditched health boards, but bloody hell someone had to.'

'You'd get into the council easy enough. People have heard of you, unlike the current lot.'

Grace chuckled before groaning. 'All right, my co-conspirator, any sparks of inspiration? And remember, I'm a journalist, nothing more. I write so the public have the opportunity to be informed.'

'True,' he said. 'Whatever you do, it has to get the public sitting up, taking notice and acting.'

'The story could provide the fuel,' said Grace, 'but what's the spark?'

'Maybe you could make politicians explode again,' said Sean.

Grace's eyes widened, she uttered a short, orgasmic 'Oh' before saying, 'I've got it.'

CHAPTER 20

In a floral dress, white jacket, a wide-brimmed floppy sunhat, sunglasses and a black designer face mask, Marla surveyed herself in the bathroom mirror. She had chosen more practical clothes now that picking up Manilow wasn't part of the plan. On the downside, now she knew she had Covid, her urge to cough had quadrupled.

A light knock on the door and the same security guard escorted her to the underground car park. Even though her body wasn't operating at one hundred per cent, she switched easily into high alert mode. The Covid diagnosis was problematic, and underground car parks were a perfect venue for tidying up problems.

'Why the change?' she asked quietly.

The guard gave her a how-the-fuck-should-I-know look.

They knew she had a taser – it was in her large shoulder bag-cum-backpack – so she should be safe. Besides, they needed the document sanitised and she was the only one who could do the job. From an IT perspective, their other option, Tom and Jerry, would be like sending in Fred Flintstone and Barney Rubble.

The security guard held up a hand and the same grey Suzuki Swift pulled up. Marla relaxed when she saw the car was empty except for the driver. Even with a face mask she recognised him from the day before. She got in the back seat, lying down as instructed so the security cameras wouldn't register a passenger. Cramped on the dirty car floor brought on her cough which made the driver swear quietly.

The Suzuki Swift weaved efficiently through Wellington's streets and up Mount Victoria, stopping on the corner of Lookout and Thane Roads, a two-minute walk from Manilow's house. Stepping onto the footpath, the driver buzzed down the passenger window and handed her a piece of paper which she took wordlessly.

The transfer to The Terrace was set for 3pm, which gave her forty-five minutes to eliminate all copies of the document. Strangely, they wanted her to day-zero his laptop — it was code for resetting it to its factory settings. They must want to send Manilow a message because it wasn't necessary, not once she had sanitised the document.

Marla was impressed by the spectacular view from Manilow's house. From the street, it didn't look large, it was only when she was inside, having entered the door code given to her by the driver, that she realised how massive it was. There were multiple levels, but it was obvious Manilow only used a fraction of the house. Satisfied there were no devices of interest in his bedroom, the one lounge he used or the kitchen, Marla settled herself at his desk with a glass of water. At least she could cough without fear of spreading Covid or attracting glares from strangers.

His laptop was password-protected and Marla used her bootable password reset drive to beat the security. She found the document and checked the computer logs to track what actions Manilow had taken. He had copied it on to his laptop from a flash drive, which conveniently remained plugged into one of the laptop's USB ports. The logs recorded that the document had been opened several times and printed once, the previous night around midnight. This physical copy was on his desk, neatly stapled with two words written in large red pen on the front page: 'For Ace'.

Marla permanently deleted it off the laptop and flash drive then checked his backup arrangements. Manilow was clearly proficient with IT; there was an automated daily process to back up changed files to a cloud drive. After deleting the document from the cloud backup, she sent an encrypted message to an IT service they used to find and delete any replicated or cached copies across the cloud storage data farm.

Lastly, she initiated the day-zero reset, which she estimated would take twenty minutes. While she waited, she flicked through the document. Manilow's company was involved with the SCS piloting a new technology system and they were using New Zealand as a guinea pig. No wonder they wanted it sanitised. Politically, anything that involved the Special Collection Service, a clandestine part of the US spy network, was a ticking bomb.

When the day-zero reset had finished she logged a report of her actions, leaving out her discovery of a printed copy. Now that she had wiped the laptop, she was the only person who knew a printed copy existed. She coughed again, her infection feeling as if it was getting worse. Focusing on the present, she put the printed copy in her bag. It didn't hurt to have leverage.

She stared out across Wellington, her mind running through possible scenarios. She was on her second glass of water when her phone vibrated in her pocket, it was time to leave. Washing the glass and putting it back in the cupboard, she double checked to ensure she left no physical evidence of her visit. She arrived at the rendezvous point the same time as the grey Suzuki Swift. Fifteen minutes later she was back, heading for the Bethel Woods Café.

Taking a window seat, Marla ordered a burger with chips and a whisky sour. If this was her last meal before they locked her away in quarantine, or worse, she was going to enjoy it.

It was 3.30pm on a Friday and the bar was almost full. From her table she had a clear view of Solnet House. According to intel, the receptionist left promptly at 4pm and Manilow was due at a business function across town at 4.30pm. Marla had an office key, if Manilow left around quarter past four, she would have ample time to check his work laptop, backups and any portable drives.

At 4.03pm, Marla recognised the receptionist as she walked within a metre of her and the café's front window. She wasn't unattractive but, dressed in black with her long hair in a severe ponytail, she gave the impression she was off to a funeral. The time, 4.03pm, confirmed that Manilow was still in the office; she had left at four on the dot. If Manilow hadn't been there, she would have likely bunked off early.

Marla toyed with ordering a second drink because the alcohol seemed to be suppressing her cough, but she needed to remain alert. Putting her mask back on to limit both the chance of spreading Covid and her exposure to the security cameras, she signalled the server over.

'Another whisky sour?' asked the bright-eyed server.

'I need to go soon,' said Marla. Taking out two one-hundred-dollar notes, she said, 'One to cover the bill, the other is for you for sorting it out for me.'

The server looked at the money with large eyes, pocketing one of the notes as subtly as she could. 'Thank you,' she stammered.

At 4.12pm, Marla received the go signal. The tech team had secured access to the building's security systems and were monitoring the office. Manilow must have left by car as she hadn't seen him leave the building.

Strolling towards Solnet House, the alcohol seemingly sharpening rather than dulling her senses, she ran through a mental checklist. Security cameras covered her every movement, so each step was vital. She had an hour to complete her assignment before she needed to exit at 5.15pm. The tech team would replace her entrance to and exit from Erebus Optics' office with a loop of uneventful empty corridor footage.

After exiting the building, she would walk up the street to the Novotel, entering via the car parking garage. In a secluded part of the car park was a bag containing a security guard uniform. Exiting via the security camera-free back entrance, she would emerge as a security guard, a cap, sunglasses and face mask obscuring her identity. It was a ten-minute circuitous walk to the extraction rendezvous, a surveillance blind-spot on Everton Terrace where a car would be waiting. Back at the Grand Mercure, she would change in the fire escape, abandoning the uniform in a rubbish bin on the third floor. Then it was either quarantine or extraction.

Marla stood briefly in front of Solnet House. When she reconnoitred the area online, she had played with the idea of abandoning the assignment, disappearing into Wellington. She didn't trust her employers, they were treacherous, but winging it was always the option of last resort. She was carrying everything she needed to disappear, but that was because she always carried them. Cash, burner phones and a change of outfit including a wig. Combined with the bank accounts her handlers didn't know about, that meant she could, if needed, blink off the radar in a heartbeat. But the logical option was to continue the assignment as planned, get back Stateside as soon as possible and retire on her own terms.

Taking the lift to the third floor, she kept her head level so that her hat obscured her face from any security cameras. The floor was empty, which was ideal. Security cameras would be recording the corridor but the tech team, who were monitoring the cameras, would alter the footage so there was no record of her visit. What she didn't want was to run into a physical witness who could describe her to the police.

She knocked confidently on the Erebus Optics Ltd door. As expected, there was no reply nor any sound of footsteps approaching. Unlocking the door, she went into the reception area and frowned. She expected it to be trendy and trashy, not plain, tidy and functional.

The only other door in the room lead to Manilow's office. Marla opened it assuredly, eager to get her part of the assignment finished. She took a step into the office and stopped. Manilow's work laptop was on his desk, perfect, but what she hadn't expected to see was Manilow himself.

He was meant to be on his way to a business function.

But he wasn't. He was lying on the floor, dead.

Taking in a calming breath, she looked carefully around the room. There was no need for alarm. Like the reception area, his office décor also spoke of function rather than style, though dusty family photos covered the top of one filing cabinet. Taking out a pair of latex gloves, she walked towards Manilow's desk.

Everything was as she expected – except for the businessman's body in a still widening pool of blood, a confused look on his face. This was not part of the assignment, at least to her knowledge.

She took a step towards the body. It took only a cursory glance to confirm he had been killed with a single shot to the temple, presumably from the SIG Sauer P228 that lay discarded next to his body. There were no signs of a struggle, so it was odd the killer had left the murder weapon behind. The chances she had walked in on a random professional hit were a billion to one, probably longer. This had the smell of Tom and Jerry all over it and, Marla surmised, only her handlers could have coordinated the hit and her incursion. The real question was, why hadn't she been informed?

With her gloves on, she turned on his laptop. What she did in the next fifty minutes would determine whether she would get home, she would have to run, or she would end up like Manilow. Glancing at the document in her bag, she imagined she could hear it ticking.

CHAPTER 21

After trying to kill herself at the gym – it was an airless twenty-seven degrees – Grace popped into the supermarket on her way home. She hadn't yet embraced the idea of online shopping, preferring to wander around at her leisure buying whatever took her fancy. She wasn't the sort of person who could create a menu for the week and then buy all the right ingredients, that was surely an urban myth.

As she prepared dinner, Grace watched the end of *The Chase*, which appeared to own the slot before the news. She had spent the day, and a lot of the weekend, in cafés and libraries polishing her story on the growth of surveillance. Calling it 'If you've got nothing to hide, you've got nothing to fear. Yeah, right!', it was shaping well. Over a virtual coffee her editor at NewsNZ had liked the concept, though he made an unpleasant face at the title.

Grace was pottering around the kitchen when the news started. The first story went from shocking to strange then, as she joined the dots, concerning. Making sure dinner wouldn't burn, she replayed the story.

'A man's body was discovered in a Wellington office building early this morning. Police say a receptionist discovered the body at eight when she arrived at work. Maiki Sherman is at the scene.'

The shot changed to the well-dressed, attractive Maiki Sherman, who was standing outside Solnet House, its signage artfully included in the shot. In the background two uniformed police officers, their weapons on display, stood guard in front of police emergency tape.

'Kia ora Simon. A body was discovered in the building behind me, Solnet House, an office block on The Terrace. Police are yet to release the full details but have confirmed a male in his fifties was found deceased at eight o'clock this morning. They're currently studying CCTV footage to gain a clearer picture of events. The Terrace is a busy part of Wellington's CBD and police have said it will take time to trawl through the footage as the death could have occurred at any time over the weekend, or even Friday evening. They will be releasing a statement tomorrow but are treating the death as a homicide.'

'Ngā mihi e hoa,' said the newsreader.

The news continued, but Grace's mind was running through permutations and combinations. The chances that it concerned Erebus Optics, and that it was Will Manilow, were low but not zero. It was pointless ringing his office, it was after six, but he had given her his business card which she remembered putting in her jacket pocket.

Finding the card exactly where she thought it was, a rare occurrence, she rang his mobile. After five rings the call went to voicemail.

'Hi, you've reached Will Manilow of Erebus Optics, formally Manilow Security. I'm not available at the present but if you leave—'

She terminated the call. 'Shit.'

It didn't prove Manilow was dead, most people don't answer work phones in the evening, but it added to her concern. She went back to making dinner, thinking it was a tragic event but not necessarily sinister. Maybe an accountant, excited about the latest figures, had had a heart attack. Grace chuckled briefly at the thought that it could be Bob Jones himself, the owner of the building. There would be a decent queue to see him off given his business dealings over the years. But then she realised that if Jones was missing, journalists would be all over the story.

Putting chicken in a frying pan, Grace cleared away this unhelpful line of thinking. It wasn't funny; someone had been murdered in Solnet House between Friday evening and Monday morning.

'Dinner's ready,' she called in her most melodic voice. She received an answer of silence. Dinner was still five minutes away, but this was a necessary tactic to stop her exploding at her slothful children, who were always five minutes late.

Grace's mind craved closure. The chances were against it being Will Manilow – that would mean that there were no implications for Grace. But if it was him, the story, at least the future story, had quadrupled in interest and possibly danger. Her previous encounter with the shadowy SIS had taught her that they were capable, happy even, to operate outside the law. But she couldn't imagine they would stoop to murder. The spectral figure of Five Eyes photobombing the picture was more likely, and with them who knew what was possible.

'Oh god.' Grace said, massaging her brain through her temples. If it was Manilow, she had met with him on Thursday, stood in his office. She would be all over the CCTV footage they were currently salivating over. And she'd just rung his mobile. Grace groaned. If it was him, she would be hearing from the police, or the spooks, about now.

'I hope it doesn't get here,' her daughter said.

'Sorry?' said Grace, her thoughts interrupted as she turned off the element.

Her daughter pointed at the television. 'Covid, the new variant,' she said. 'I saw it on my feed. A few passengers on an Auckland to Wellington flight caught it but everyone infected is in MIQ.'

Grace had heard the news item, but because Covid was constantly in the news and the government didn't use lockdowns now, she had paid it no attention. 'Did they say when the flight was?'

Her daughter took out her phone, humming as she searched. 'The flight landed in Wellington on Wednesday.'

Grace pursed her lips. She had been in Wellington on Thursday – but so had a quarter of a million people. Dinner was ready and her starving daughter leapt towards the kitchen while her son slowly unfurled fernlike from the couch. Grace had no idea how long he had been there.

It was, as usual, a nice, simple, healthy dinner. While her children made quick work of theirs, Grace ate slowly. The murder, the fact she visited the building the day before and Manilow not answering his phone were combining to change her lingering doubt into a wailing banshee.

CHAPTER 22

Jenna Parata watched the members of the police suspects team as they trooped in, coffees in hand. Once everyone was settled, the officer in charge asked, 'What do we have, Rogers?'

In a large meeting room inside the Wellington Police Station, the suspects team assigned to the homicide in Solnet House were having their first debrief. Jenna was sitting in for the SIS in case it was determined that it was an act of domestic terrorism. The scene examiners and general inquiries team were still combing the scene and interviewing possible witnesses.

Detective Rogers opened a file. 'The deceased is Will Manilow of Lookout Road—'

'Lookout Road?' interrupted the OC.

'Yep, looks like he was loaded. We're checking into his finances and business deals. He was CEO of Erebus Optics, a firm specialising in home security systems. He was killed with a single shot to the left temple.'

'Execution style?'

Rogers nodded. 'Forensics are still at the scene but so far they've found little else.'

'Time of death?'

Detective Ferguson picked up the story. 'The security camera in the corridor captured the action. The receptionist, Mandy Goodson, left right on four o'clock.'

'Did we get anything from her?'

Rogers shook his head. 'She said he was in his office, alive, when she left but she didn't say goodnight so had no idea what he was doing.'

'Then . . .' Ferguson tapped on a keyboard and the grainy image of a woman, a large hat obscuring her face, stood in front of the door to Erebus Optics. 'This woman arrived at four eighteen, the time stamp on the footage is accurate. There are no cameras inside the office but . . .' Ferguson let the action advance. 'If I slow it down, you can see she knocks, waits, then unlocks the door.'

'Where did she get her key from?' asked the OC.

'We're onto it,' said Ferguson, clicking on a file. A colour image of Manilow's body appeared, sprawled face up on the floor, his head lying in a crimson lake. 'Manilow was killed in his office. The assumption is she shot him straightaway, making it around four nineteen. We have to wait until forensics get the bullet to identify the murder weapon.'

'That's a hit, pure and simple,' said the OC. 'No discussion, no argument, no chance to have a falling out over money or sex.'

Jenna nodded her agreement.

'Motive?' asked the OC.

Rogers shrugged. 'Nothing yet. He was wealthy but there's no indication of robbery. The most likely angle is blackmail or a business deal with the wrong people. We're checking.'

The OC nodded.

Ferguson increased the speed of the footage. 'She stayed in the office for fifty minutes, leaving at five fifteen.' The screen showed the woman exiting the office, leaving by the stairs. 'We think she used the victim's computer. The IT boys are checking it over. The only prints we've found so far are the victim's and the receptionist's.'

'Do we know how the killer left the area?'

Ferguson shook his head. 'We tracked her movements from security camera footage.' The screen changed, showing footage of a woman walking up The Terrace, her face obscured by her hat and a face mask. 'All we have is she's around 170 centimetres, of slight build.' The last image showed her walking into the Novotel car park. 'That's where she disappears. No sign of her coming out and we've checked, she's not there.'

The OC harrumphed. 'We shouldn't be surprised if she's a pro. What about his house?'

'No sign anyone except Manilow had been there recently,' said Rogers. 'We've sent his personal laptop to the techs too.'

'Do we have *any* leads?'

'We've been reviewing security camera footage starting two weeks before the murder. They sent this through about an hour ago.' Rogers nodded to Ferguson who worked the keyboard until an image outside Erebus Optics' door appeared. It looked similar except the woman in the hat was now a woman dressed in business attire, her blonde hair in a neat ponytail. 'It's the day before, Thursday at midday.'

The OC and Jenna leaned closer.

'It looks like the same woman,' said the OC. 'If she's a pro, it's pretty sloppy.'

'It can't be,' said Jenna.

They all looked at her.

'That's Grace Marks, I'd recognise her anywhere. Why the fuck is she there?' Jenna's involvement with Grace had started during the events surrounding Grace's attack on how the wealthy rorted the tax system. Their paths had crossed several times, never pleasurably.

Rogers checked his notes. 'That's right, Grace Marks the journalist. The deceased's diary confirmed she had an appointment, they had lunch at Bethel Woods. She also rang his mobile phone after six last night.'

'She might be involved,' said Jenna. 'But she's not the killer.'

'I agree she's likely doing what journos do, but' – the OC stared pointedly at Jenna – 'she's at the murder scene the day before and she fits the killer's build. Are you telling me it's a coincidence?'

Jenna, standing tall, stared back. 'It's not a coincidence, but she's not the killer.'

'Fine,' he said. 'We need to bring her in though. She's involved with Manilow, and we need to find out why. She may be more involved than you think.'

CHAPTER 23

Grace pulled alongside the only car parked outside the Whenua Tapu Cemetery gates near the town of Plimmerton. She didn't need to check, she had been in Corin's large, thirsty Holden Commodore many times. She tried to convince him it wasn't good for the planet, he agreed but argued it suited a detective's image. As they got out, he offered her a coffee, which she gladly accepted. It was 8.45am and the sun had yet to warm this part of the world.

Grace made a why-the-fuck-did-you-choose-here gesture.

'This is one of the few places left not infested with security cameras,' said Corin.

'The doggers must love it,' she said smirking.

'I'm sure they do, but it's a bit early for them. And cold.'

Grace sipped her coffee; even though it was lukewarm it provided a needed jolt. 'Thanks for meeting, CT. I figured a heads up before I ventured into the lion's den couldn't hurt. I can't believe it was Will Manilow. He seemed so – nice.'

Corin shrugged. 'It's a strange one. When your name came up I figured it must be in relation to your interest in street crime. The word is it was a professional hit. Single shot to the head.'

Grace's eyes widened. 'Really? Fuck.'

'What were you doing there?' His tone suggested he was interviewing a suspect.

'What you said, following a lead,' she said, glowering. 'Will Manilow was CEO of a security company pushing the rollout of home security cameras, and they were pushing hard. We talked over lunch.' Grace related most of what she had learned and the shape of her story, leaving out her meeting with Dr Noble. Corin listened intently, asking the odd question, especially when she related parts of her lunch with Manilow.

'Were you in Wellington Friday?'

She shook her head. 'I was DIYing at home.'

A serious Corin nodded. 'That's how I thought it would've gone down. You were in his orbit, but that's all. From what you said, it sounds like whatever he was doing might be the reason he was killed. No other motives are floating around.'

Grace checked her phone. 'Sorry, CT, I haven't much time. Is there anything I need to know?'

He hesitated, licking his lips. 'Nothing that'll help. Be careful though, Ace, they've little to go on and you know we love to reassure the public with a quick arrest.'

She squinted. 'I fucking well do.'

As they had requested, Grace arrived at the Wellington Police Station at 10am. The officer on duty took one look at her and buzzed her straight through; she was expected.

An unsmiling Sergeant Taine was waiting. 'Kia ora Ace, they're expecting you.'

'Kia ora. Tell me, Taine, are they going to make me wait for a decade in the broom closet again?'

Taine smiled sympathetically. 'You're in a standard meeting room. And I've organised coffee and biscuits.' He said the last part with the subtlest of winks. 'Follow me.'

The room was as Taine described – a large meeting room with a steaming pot of coffee next to a plate of Belgian biscuits. A computer screen, or possibly a smart TV, occupied one wall and on the opposite wall was a large, mirrored window. Grace assumed it was a two-way mirror with serious faces glaring at her. She suppressed her desire to flip them the bird. Already in the room were two casually dressed males, whose manner and posture shouted 'We're detectives'.

'Okay, let's get under way,' said one of the detectives. 'This isn't a formal interview, you're here of your own volition so we're not recording it. Can we call you Grace?'

'Sure,' she said with a shrug. It might not be a formal interview but there was no such thing as an 'off the record' police interview.

'Great. I'm Detective Rogers, he's Detective Ferguson. Coffee?'

Grace nodded. While Rogers poured her coffee, she took the opportunity to take in the detectives. Rogers had been leaning forward, smiling and making eye contact. Ferguson lounged with his feet sprawled under the table looking bored. They were playing a version of good cop, bad cop. This was attentive dick, bored dick.

Rogers started off the informal interview. 'Take us through your movements since last Thursday, from when you met Manilow.'

'Okay.' Grace dragged the coffee over and took a biscuit. 'I drove to Wellington on Thursday. Left about nine, met *Will* as you know at midday and we talked over lunch.'

'What did you talk about?' asked Rogers.

'I'm doing a story on the increase in street crime. He was CEO of Erebus Optics, who are doing well partly because of the increase. I didn't think he'd want to talk to a journalist, but he had some interesting insights which he shared.'

'What insights?'

Grace gave a short history of Erebus Optics and why they were doing well. As she was explaining the chilling effect, Ferguson obviously decided he had heard enough.

'Yeah, that'll do. We don't need a lecture on your views of society.'

Grace gritted her teeth but looked at Ferguson impassively. 'Fine.' She hadn't yet got to Manilow's concerns regarding surveillance or the possible US connection. It seemed to Grace these two had a one-track focus – why did she kill Will Manilow?

'What happened after the meeting?' asked Rogers.

'Nothing.'

'How did the meeting end?'

'With a handshake.'

A flicker of annoyance crossed Rogers' face. 'You mentioned Manilow had interesting insights?'

'He did.' Ferguson had started the pissing contest. Grace was happy to play.

Rogers waited. Grace stayed silent.

'And?' said Rogers, holding his hands out as though she could physically pass the insights over.

'And what?'

Fergusson grunted while Grace watched Rogers breathe in through his nose.

'What were the interesting insights?' Rogers tried, but failed, to mask his annoyance.

She smiled sweetly. 'The stuff I was about to tell you about before the *nong* next to you opened his big mouth.'

Grace and Ferguson exchanged glares until Rogers intervened.

'Let's all step down. Tell us about Mani—' – Rogers licked his lips – 'Will's insights.'

'Sure.' Grace picked up a second biscuit, pointed it at Ferguson but looked at Rogers. 'Why is he acting like an arsehole? I don't need shaking down. I came to help.'

'Homicides make us edgy,' said Rogers. 'Cut him a little slack.'

She looked sternly at him before signalling a reluctant okay. Without looking at Ferguson, she explained what Will had told her and what his thinking led towards, but she didn't mention the document. Then she walked them through her movements after she left Wellington through until she arrived at the police station today. She left out both Corin's and Dr Noble's involvement, a journalist is allowed to protect their sources.

Rogers stated rather than asked, 'You were in Palmerston North on Friday between 1.00pm and 7.00pm.'

Grace took in the information. It must be the window of time in which Will was murdered. 'I told you. I was at home, prepping my bedroom wall for painting.'

'Was anyone with you?'

'Let me see.' She thought back through Friday's events. 'My children didn't come home until eight or nine. Sean, he's my partner, he worked late and didn't arrive until after the children. I had Roxy helping me.'

'Can Roxy verify this? What's her surname?'

Grace laughed. 'She doesn't have one, she's my partner's retriever. Her version of helping is dropping a ball and looking hopeful.'

Her laughter petered out as neither detective saw the funny side.

'No *person* can corroborate your alibi?' asked Rogers.

'Alibi? Why do I need an alibi?'

The detectives remained silent, they wanted her to do the talking. It was an interview tactic she used herself, so she stayed quiet. After another prolonged pissing contest, Ferguson said, 'We're trying to eliminate people from our inquiry.'

'What? I'm a suspect? You think I shot Will? That's ridiculous . . .' Her voice trailed away when the detectives exchanged a glance, made obvious by their different postures. She mentally kicked herself. Corin told her Will had been shot. It wasn't public knowledge.

Hovering her hands above the table in a calming gesture, she said, 'Don't leap to conclusions boys, I'm a journalist. The word on the street is it was a professional hit. I figured he'd been shot.'

'Would you care to elaborate on who gave you the word?'

'No, I wouldn't. And no, I don't have to.'

Ferguson sat forwards aggressively. 'This is a murder inquiry, Miss Marks.'

She followed suit. 'No shit Sherlock. And if you're looking at me as the professional killer, you've got rocks in your head. Have you checked the security camera footage?'

Poker-faced, Ferguson sat back and pulled over a keyboard. Fifteen seconds later Grace was looking at her own image standing outside Erebus Optics.

She made a so-what gesture. 'You know I visited him on Thursday, what's that prove?'

The detective clicked and the image morphed into the same scene with a different woman standing outside the door. 'This is from Friday.'

Grace studied the image carefully, noting the time on the screen, 4.18pm. A woman stood outside the office door hidden beneath a large hat. If she hadn't known, and they'd asked her to speculate, she would have said it was her wearing a large hat.

'This image was taken one minute before the victim was killed. I should say shot, as it's common knowledge.'

The detectives stared at her. She seemed lost for words, but she wasn't. She was processing the new information. More to herself than to the detectives, she said, 'A lone female assassin shot Will soon after four eighteen on Friday. As you're suspecting me, she's disappeared. Bugger, I'm going to have to change my story.'

Ferguson sneered smugly. 'We're listening, Grace.'

Grace grunted with annoyance. 'Not my story, my story. The story

I'm writing. My alibi, as you're calling it, doesn't need to change because it's true. And, now I think of it, I downed tools on Friday around two thirty to buy a late lunch and, while I was out, I nipped into the TAB to put twenty dollars on the Black Caps to beat the Aussies. Hang on.' She groped around in her bag before tossing the ticket onto the table.

Rogers picked it up casually. 'Two forty-nine pm Friday. You got them at three dollars fifty, nice.' Handing it back, he said. 'You don't look like the gambling type Grace.'

'What type do I look like?' she asked, flashing a patronising smile. 'The rich git type who doesn't need money? Maybe I should have flunked high school and joined the police too.'

'Sorry,' said Rogers, holding up his hands. 'That was dumb. We'll check out your story, but we never had you in the frame for this. The coincidence was too strange to ignore, so we needed to shake you a little. Forgive my partner. As you know, it's what we do.'

Ferguson gave Grace a what-can-you-do look.

Rogers asked, 'About your story, the one you're writing that is. Any chance you could hold off for a while?'

'Do you have a police slush fund you can dip into so the bank doesn't rock up and demand my first born?'

'I wish,' said Rogers.

CHAPTER 24

In an anonymous mirror-glassed office building in Wellington's CBD, in a meeting room devoid of corporate art, Jenna sat waiting at the boardroom table. There were two men in the room, one an SIS colleague. The other man, who Jenna had recently met, wasn't a colleague although they were officially on the same side. Tom's official position, and cover, was as an attaché for the US Embassy. Although the trio were similarly dressed, Tom's clothes were clearly high end: a dark green seersucker suit, white shirt, over-priced Louis Vuitton black shoes and Ray Bans that he wore despite being in a windowless room.

Their boss, a no-nonsense looking woman with a large, heavy face, bustled into the room taking the seat at the head of the table. Even though she was dressed identically, her manner communicated forcefully that she was in charge. She was older too; Jenna and her colleague were in their thirties – she was closer to sixty. To her subordinates, Jenna included, she bore a striking resemblance to the Governess from *The Chase*. They referred to her as Anne, though not to her face.

'Kia ora team,' she said, settling herself before looking at the attaché. 'Good of you to come, Tom. It seems events have gone badly wrong.' Anne looked over at Jenna. 'First bring us up to speed, JP.'

Jenna nudged her laptop out of sleep mode. 'As you're aware, in conjunction with Five Eyes and the police, we're conducting a series of trials to identify and track suspected criminals and terrorists under the code name Hubble. Despite these becoming public knowledge, causing a delay, we're making steady progress. The rise in street disturbances and the murder of the CEO of Erebus Optics, they're both police matters. There is no overlap with Hubble.'

Jenna looked at Tom as the American slowly took off his sunglasses, his face transitioning into a smile, his teeth an Osmond-esque white. He was confirming that her first impression of him was right; he fancied himself.

'I can fill in some gaps here if that's useful,' he said.

Anne said, 'It would be useful, Tom, thank you.'

'Okay,' he said. 'The US parent of Erebus Optics are behind the development of the software they're using, a product called A-Star. From the information I have, the NSA and CIA were involved in its development, but they're not involved in Erebus's day-to-day operations.'

'None of that was communicated to us,' interrupted Anne.

'Everyone assumed Erebus would keep it as a domestic product in the US, but it appears they decided to trial it in other theatres.'

Anne's eyes narrowed. 'Go on.'

'The local CEO, this Manilow, got carried away. Crazy incentives. He may have been involved in creating the trouble in the streets, we don't know.'

'Creating?' Jenna stared at Tom. 'Have you got anything concrete?'

'No and it's kind of by the by,' said the American laconically. 'He sure pissed off someone. We're still piecing it together ourselves but before we could act, we have a mess we need to keep a lid on. The agent who performed the hit—'

'Agent?'

He nodded slowly at Anne. 'An ex-agent. More likely a merc. We don't know who she is or who's payroll she's on, certainly not ours. Officially she doesn't exist and, as much as it'd be nice to throw a foreign competitor under the bus, we don't know which one to chuck. However, we understand she's left New Zealand.'

Anne took her time before responding. 'It's good she's out of the country. If the police arrest her . . . well, you know how that would play in the media. Here, the alliance works because we keep it out of the media except when the likes of Dotcom and Snowden grab their fifteen minutes of fame. Assassinations in office buildings don't help. I assume from what you've said' – she glared at him – 'Five eyes had no part in this?'

Tom shifted slightly but kept his smile in place. 'I only know what I've been told.'

Her face pinched slightly, a sign Jenna recognised, her boss was less than impressed.

Anne took a long breath in through her nose. 'Okay, thank you for your time.'

The American acknowledged each of them, put his sunglasses on and sauntered out. They sat in silence. After a minute Jenna checked the corridor. 'He's gone.'

'Well?' asked Anne.

'It doesn't feel right,' said Jenna, leaning back in her chair. 'I observed Marks' interview. She painted Manilow as concerned with what was happening, not a loose cannon.'

'I'm with JP,' said the male agent. 'It's got more a black op feel than a rogue foreign op.'

'Exactly,' said Jenna. 'It's more likely the hit was sanctioned, and they've extracted the agent to tidy loose ends.'

'But why kill Manilow?' asked Anne. 'They could have fired him, taken his access away.'

'As he said, maybe he pissed the wrong people off,' said Jenna.

They sat in silence.

Pressing her fingertips together, Anne said, 'We probably have a black op in our backyard which, if true, needs reigning in. There's an unsolved murder that will agitate the police and the media. We may have been able to keep a lid on the story if it wasn't for our last problem. Marks is involved.' She paused before adding, 'It would be handy if Marks did kill Manilow, it would kill two birds with one stone.'

'Didn't happen,' said Jenna.

'Pity. In that case we'd better be prepared for whatever she writes. She's got enough ammunition to be dangerous. JP, see what the records tell us. It would be nice to know who the killer was and how they managed to bring her in without our knowledge. They must have local assets we don't know about. I want to know who they are.'

Anne turned to Jenna's colleague. 'Find out about this possible black op. Use official and unofficial channels. I want to know what's going on. If they are prepared to use lethal force, it can't be minor. And put eyes on Marks.'

'Why?' asked the agent.

'Because she's not going to let this go. I want to know what she's doing and who's she doing it with. And make sure our colleagues know that Marks is a no-go. If they did have a hand in this, and we can't be sure they didn't, Marks may be next. We've only their word that the killer, the agent, is offshore and we do not need a dead journalist. There's no way to cover that up. Marks may be a pain in the arse alive, but she'd be worse dead. Any questions?'

'Just one thought,' said Jenna. 'The easiest way to get an agent euphemistically *out of the country*, would be in a body bag.'

CHAPTER 25

Putting the murder weapon in her bag, Marla frowned as she took a last look at Manilow's body. This was not part of the assignment she'd signed up for.

After completing her assigned tasks, she had used the rest of her time productively. She was wary because she didn't know whether she was walking into an ambush or to the scheduled rendezvous that would facilitate her rapid departure from New Zealand. She had used her time to effectively place a chip on both red and black.

No one witnessed her exit from Solnet House and, making sure her hat concealed her face, she walked purposefully up The Terrace. In the Novotel's car park, the bag containing her change of clothes was where it was meant to be, a positive sign. Exiting from a secluded back entrance, she was now dressed as a security guard complete with a peaked cap, sunglasses and a plain blue surgical face mask. The circuitous route to the Everton Terrace rendezvous point meant even the most sophisticated surveillance operation would struggle to follow her.

Everton Terrace was steep, and Marla found that trudging up it in steel-capped boots wearing a backpack wasn't easy. Rounding the corner, she tensed when she saw a car parked fifty metres up the road. In the early evening shadows, the trees and the hill cloaked a sleek black BMW in darkness.

She monitored her surrounds as she walked towards the car. The leafy Wellington suburb appeared deserted, although the noise of the nearby motorway provided a constant background hum. All signs pointed to a typical extraction – but now a light started flashing in her animal brain. She slowed, allowing more time to process the scene. It wasn't the grey Suzuki Swift they had been using but she had no reason to expect the same car. Every step of the extraction plan had run smoothly, so she kept walking slowly, ignoring the flashing light.

Three steps later, a car coming downhill with its lights on momentarily illuminated the BMW from behind. Marla now saw the silhouettes of two large men, one in the front and one in the back. Although it was a fleeting glimpse, she knew it was Tom and Jerry fresh from killing Manilow. She also knew that they had classified her, like Manilow, as a liability. The flashing light turned into a tsunami-warning klaxon.

The car coming downhill slowed as it rounded the tight turn past the BMW. As it did this, it briefly hid her from the ambush. She used the time to turn and sprint as fast as her clothes and boots allowed up a side street. As she disappeared from their view, she heard the distinctive fizz of a bullet fired from a suppressed pistol. It thudded into the hill behind her as the car's engine roared into life. She heard its tyres screech, and she ran faster.

Despite the hurriedly put together plan, Marla had done extensive homework on the area. She knew she was running up a winding no-exit street that led to a university halls of residence. A third of the way along the street, as the car rounded the corner at speed, she leapt onto the steep bank. Desperately grabbing trees and shrubs for purchase, she disappeared up into the undergrowth, losing her mask and cap in the process. The car skidded to a stop. As she smashed her way through the vegetation, she heard a door open and close before the car screeched onwards. One pursuer was on foot behind her, the other was trying to get ahead of her.

Breathless, she burst out of the bushes emerging at the back of the university buildings, startling two young university students furtively smoking a joint. Whoever was chasing her was faster and not wearing steel-capped boots. Crouching behind a beaten-up red car, she rifled through her bag. She had the choice of the Sig they used to kill Manilow, which she had taken as insurance, or the taser. Although they deserved to die, she selected the taser.

Her pursuer, recognisable now as Jerry, burst into the open and stopped, his attention momentarily drawn to the stunned joint-smoking students. At impossible-to-miss range, Marla fired the taser into his back. He tried to turn around, but his body stiffened before he toppled over, hitting the ground face first. The joint smokers watched the action wide-eyed until she yelled, 'Get the fuck out of here.' They ran.

She abandoned the taser, grabbed her bag then kicked the writhing agent in the ribs with the toe of her steel-capped boot, hard. She spat, 'Psycho fucker.' He was in no state to feel the pain her kick delivered, yet.

She went to turn him over to take his gun, but the sound of squealing tyres reminded her Tom was charging her way. As she had seen online, a narrow path ran between the buildings and back to Everton Terrace. There were multiple other paths to choose, and Jerry was in no state to point the way. She could hear the car's tyres approaching rapidly but, after a few twists and turns, she plunged back onto Everton Terrace, fifty metres above the murderous rendezvous. Running up a steep pedestrian walkway, she disappeared from view.

As the path flattened out, Marla picked a grassy spot to take off her backpack and sit down. As she caught her breath, she took the pistol and held it hidden in the grass between her legs. If any of the kill team came around the corner, they would die.

Her finger moved to the trigger as a couple rounded the corner, running towards her. One of the red-faced female joggers gave her a tired smile as she passed which Marla reciprocated, her finger moving back off the trigger. After two minutes she carried on up the path. She had lost them, at least for now.

The walkway emerged onto a large park. Although walking in the open wasn't ideal, it was only a few hundred metres to the relative safety of busy streets. They wouldn't have a drone, that would be to admit they might fuck up.

She crossed the park without incident and approached a major intersection. Now out of the area she had scoped, she had a decision to make. One street led downhill, presumably back to The Terrace, the other uphill. She took the uphill option, hopefully away from danger. As she slowly walked, the breeze started drying the sweat from her hair and shirt. Now that her adrenalin had dissipated, each step was a little harder than the last. Covid was adding its weight to the damp uniform and heavy boots.

Outside a busy university building, she rested in the corner of a bus shelter and used a burner phone to plot an escape route. On the other side of the street, she saw a bus coming slowly in the snarling traffic, its destination Wellington Central. Nipping deftly through the slow-moving traffic, she boarded. She took a mask from the driver, who didn't look pleased when she handed him a fifty dollar note. She apologised in Spanish to avoid a debate. The driver cursed in English while he counted her change.

The bus was nearly empty, which made social distancing easy. Taking a seat opposite the rear door, she surveyed the bus. There were four security cameras; in a worst-case scenario they were watching live, but as they had no idea where she was it was unlikely. As the bus crept downhill, she used her burner phone to plot a route to Newtown, the suburb she had selected for a situation such as this.

Ten minutes later, the bus eased into the main terminal. Marla waited until last, checking the background for suspicious activity; she saw none.

Leaving her boots on the floor of the bus, she went into the toilets to change. Discarding the security guard uniform in the trash, she dressed in her emergency outfit of leggings, a tight sports bra, peaked Nike cap and jandals. It wasn't a look she liked, or which suited her, but with a face mask on, she looked much younger. She repacked her items into a thin orange carry-all bag which she carried for emergencies.

There had been no sign of her pursuers, but they would be looking. They weren't the sort of people, and it wasn't the sort of organisation, that gave up. Desk-bound agents would be poring over security camera footage and live feeds, but even if they managed to spot her uniform at the bus terminal it was about to be a dead end.

Using her burner phone, she unlocked an e-scooter and enjoyed a leisurely journey around Wellington's waterfront and out of security camera coverage. Leaving the scooter, and its record of her journey, she walked until she reached the secluded Port Nicholson Yacht Club starter's box. It took her ten minutes to wave down a taxi, riding to Newtown Avenue. She sat in the back, face mask on with the window down to limit the chance of transmitting Covid to the driver. Some interactions would be impossible to avoid, but she would minimise these until she was better. The driver slumped when she gave him a fifty dollar note, but he beamed when she said, 'Keep the change, gov,' in an average British accent.

It was dusk when Marla checked into a cheap motel free of security cameras, paying cash for five nights. She had stopped at a supermarket to buy food and replace her toiletries, which would now be in an incinerator along with any evidence she had been in managed isolation. Once the techs erased her records, she would be a ghost in the city. New Zealand would have no record of her arrival or existence, though they would have an orphan positive Covid test. What would they do with that?

She took a long shower then ate her uninspiring supermarket dinner before collapsing into a deep, restless sleep. Although she was extremely fit, Covid on top of everything else meant she was beat. If they came for her tonight, she was defenceless.

The combination of an uncomfortable mattress, the noise of the streets, her cough and jet lag meant she slept poorly. She dozed until 9am when she could no longer ignore the light streaming through the threadbare curtains. Letting herself wake slowly, although it had been a disturbed sleep, she felt okay. Weak but okay. There was no rush. They didn't know where she was, because if they did, she would have learned that already.

Assuming she could stay hidden in the motel, her plan was to stay put until she had shaken off Covid. There were a few items she needed urgently: a replacement laptop, additional burner phones and lots of clothes – she would need a minimum of three different looks. Although she wanted to stay holed up, these she would have to venture out for today.

After another long shower, she dressed in her plan-B clothes from the day before with sunglasses and a fresh face mask. The weather forecaster had said it would be chilly but compared to the Nebraskan winter she had come from she found it balmy as she headed to the Newtown shopping precinct. In the Opportunities for Animals second-hand shop, she bought a myriad of clothes and a serviceable suitcase. Paying with two fifty-dollar notes, she insisted they keep the change, explaining to the Gothically shaved assistant that she *loved animals*. At a computer shop she purchased a new laptop and two second-hand phones. Lastly, she stocked up on food, underwear – which she refused to buy second-hand – hair dyes and a range of cheap eyeglasses.

Later that evening, Marla carefully scrutinised her look in the mirror in the dimly-lit bedroom, her hair dyed from platinum blonde to jet black. Content with her work, she checked the three sets of clothes she had chosen: a new-age hippy outfit, a butch, biker-chick look, and one designed to look like a middle-class struggling single teacher. The last of her energy draining away, she lay back on the hard bed, surveying the clothes with satisfaction. They needed washing, but she had plenty of time.

Once she was better, she planned to buy a cheap, anonymous used car. As she thought through her next moves, she paused on the question of how long she would need to hide. A year? For the rest of her life? And how long would that be? She let out a sigh that ended as a cough. For now, she needed to get better and survive one day at a time.

There were tasks that needed attention. She would have to contact Lucas with the bad news that she wouldn't be coming home any time soon. She would get him to pack her personal items and her art and store them at his house. Everything else was disposable. They would be monitoring his communications, but she would make sure he would be of no interest to them. They would visit him, tell him a range of lies, but she had warned him of that. She would miss Lucas, but to return home, to enter the US, was to commit suicide. At least for now.

Then there was Grace Marks, the journalist who had been working with Manilow on a story. Marla's last thought before sleep claimed her was that if she was going to disappear for ever, she needed to make sure her tracks were well and truly covered.

PART 2

CHAPTER 26

At 4.05pm on a warm Friday afternoon, Grace pulled into the Whenua Tapu Cemetery. She parked next to Corin who would have, she knew, arrived right on the dot. He was obsessed with time, if there was a chance he would be late, he would have used his sirens to shift traffic. Two other cars were parked nearby, the occupants presumably wandering the cemetery grounds. Those two cars aside, they were alone.

Grace handed Corin a coffee. 'I planned to be early, but finding a decent coffee around here is a mission.'

Putting his sunglasses on top of his head, he said, 'You're not built to be on time, Ace. I bet you were late as a baby.'

'Was I?' said Grace. 'Thanks for the coffee, Ace. You're welcome, Detective.'

Corin smirked. 'Thanks. Take your time in the future.'

She drew in her breath. 'What did I see in you again?'

'Do you want me to show you?'

She was about to reply but she laughed. 'Enough banter. Shall we get started? Let's swap what we know.'

'Sure,' he said. 'You start.'

She took him through the ins and outs of her interview with the police detectives. When she reached the point in her story when they showed her the image of the killer, she asked, 'Had you seen what they had?'

He shrugged. 'You knowing wouldn't have helped. I'm sure you acted surprised and indignant, as appropriate.'

'Hmm.' Grace stared at him. 'It sure took me by surprise and you're right, I didn't need to act.'

'I looked at the footage when your name came up as a suspect. Did I date a professional killer?'

'She's a professional?'

'Sure is,' said Corin. 'The word is she's already left the country.'

'How did she manage that?'

'She'd be well connected. This is obviously big.'

'If it's big,' said Grace, 'we must be in on it.'

Corin made a face. 'You'd think so, but it doesn't sound like the SIS know much.'

'So how do they know she's left the country?'

He paused. 'This is off the record. You can't use it, okay?'

'Okay,' she said, trying to read him.

'The story I've heard,' he said, 'is that she's a merc, but nobody knows who brought her in. It could've been our side.'

'A mercenary? And which is our side?'

'The Five Eyes side, not the New Zealand side.'

'Isn't that meant to be the same?'

Corin choked back a laugh. 'I told you, the SIS are in the dark. America believes they're on a mission to save the world. We're a speed bump if we get in their way.'

'Own the world more like it,' said Grace. 'Why are we in bed with them?'

'Because not being in bed with them is worse. We can see them trying to rape us rather than being surprised from behind.'

'Charming.' She had to physically shake the image away. She drank the last of her coffee. 'The hit must have been ordered, but why?'

'Manilow must have become a liability. Did he say anything to you?'

She pursed her lips.

'Come on,' he said. 'Free and frank.'

'Okay,' said Grace. 'He thought what was happening was dark and he mentioned a document. I gave him space, but he said he wasn't ready to go there yet.'

The detective spoke slowly. 'Whatever he had, it was fatal. His personal laptop had been reset to factory settings, so the assumption is that the woman was in his house at some stage too.'

Grace kicked her car's tyre. 'I'm going to wander around the cemetery for a bit. I need to think.'

'I'll come,' he said. 'I've got time.'

They put on their sunglasses as they walked through the cemetery gates, turning right towards long lines of headstones. They strolled in silence past the orderly graves of people like them. Grace found cemeteries reflective and peaceful, not sad and mournful.

She started ordering events as Corin walked next to her, occasionally stopping to inspect the headstone of a name he must have recognised. They ended up on a bench in the memorial garden that overlooked the lower cemetery. The sun was fading but it remained warm.

'Right, CT,' she said, turning to face him. 'Jump in if my logic has holes.' She held up a finger. 'First, there's been a rise in minor crime. At least some of it's organised and the only logical reason for it is that it increases the number of security cameras watching and recording our streets.'

'People want to feel safe,' he said.

'But it's an illusion, people are safe.'

'But they don't feel safe,' he said. 'And their perception is their reality.'

'Good point. The rise in crime is creating an alternative reality, one that ties in neatly with the increased acceptance of surveillance as a method of stopping terrorists and pandemics. New Zealanders don't want another mosque attack or lockdown.'

'But, as you said, it's an illusion. Surveillance only stops terrorists by chance, and we'd need an army of track-and-tracers.'

'Unless you monitor everyone,' she said.

'But that's impossible.'

'It used to be. An academic I interviewed said they've developed software that integrates facial recognition technology, phone data, surveillance cameras, artificial intelligence and the kitchen sink. The goal is to be able to monitor entire populations.'

'Fuck,' he said, folding his arms.

'Exactly,' she said. 'Fuck. Let's finish the logic. Will Manilow is . . . was,' she corrected herself, 'working for a US company that benefits from the surge in street crime. But he doesn't buy the coincidence and starts looking into what's happening.'

Corin continued the train of thinking. 'He finds a document and becomes a liability. The liability gets mitigated.'

'But who mitigated the liability?'

'The same people,' he said, although not with confidence.

'The same people,' she echoed. 'It's got to be, doesn't it? Otherwise, it's a random, motiveless assassination by some unconnected group.'

'What that means,' said Corin, 'is that they brought this hit woman in from overseas and extracted her again without anyone, including the SIS, knowing. That's heavy duty.'

She stood and stretched. 'We should get going.' She set off briskly towards their cars. 'I need to adjust my story.'

'I assume a light went on,' said Corin, catching up with her. 'Care to share?'

'Not exactly a light. If the US intelligence agencies are behind an operation in New Zealand worth killing over, the stakes are high. But it's the irony which hit me.'

'Irony?'

'New Zealand's about to become one of the most monitored societies on the planet because we think we're under attack from terrorists, local hoods and viruses. But in reality, we're the focus of the marketing campaign of an American company. The real question is the one Will suggested: why?'

Her phone buzzed. She checked the message as she walked before stopping suddenly. 'For fuck's sake.'

'More bad news?'

'It's a Covid alert, a Bluetooth one.'

'You're a close contact,' he said, stepping backwards and eyeing his coffee cup with suspicion.

'Piss off!'

He turned serious. 'When were you exposed?'

She frowned. 'Why don't they put the day as well as the date?' She screwed her eyes shut. 'Last Thursday,' she finally said.

'Where were you?'

'In Wellington, meeting Will Manilow.'

'If you've got nothing to hide, you've got nothing to fear. Yeah, right!' said Grace. She was sitting outside on her deck in the sun with Sean who was frowning.

After she left Corin at the cemetery, she had driven to a drive-through Covid testing station in Palmerston North. After letting Sean and her children know she had to self-isolate, it dawned on her that Covid had gifted her uninterrupted time to finish her story. If she didn't have Covid, it was an unexpected bonus. Her children would have to make their own meals, which likely meant takeaways, but what could she do?

Sixteen hours later she received a negative Covid result, but she didn't tell her children until the following day. She followed news of the outbreak closely. The health authorities were on alert and the track-and-trace team was busy running down contacts as they searched for patient zero. The vaccine distribution was impeding the virus's progress but, as lockdowns were no longer employed, the mutated strains were becoming both more transmissible and more virulent.

Sean, still frowning, repeated the title of Grace's story. 'If you've got nothing to hide, you've got nothing to fear. Yeah, right!' His face scrunched, as though he was picking up dog poo. 'It's a bit . . . clumsy.'

'Clumsy?' she tried to look insulted.

Ignoring her, he asked, 'Who are you pitching it to?'

'Times have changed,' she said, raising her eyebrows. 'Both the *Listener* and the *SST* are interested. The rise in street crime has everyone gagging for relevant stories, and my angle's a bit different. I'm leaning towards the *Listener*. They took a chance last time and it turned out well.'

'You're in demand, that's great.'

Grace allowed herself a broad grin. 'I know, not bad for a *clumsy* journo.'

He rolled his eyes. 'How's the story shaping up?'

'Solid. Most outlets have covered the hit, or the murder as they're calling it, but they haven't joined the dots and linked it to the rise in street crime or surveillance.'

'Are they positive it was a hit?'

'No doubt about it. Poor Will,' she said with a sigh. 'He was a real-life rags-to-riches success story and now he's dead. He was looking forward to escaping to the country.'

'I hate to point out the obvious, Grace, but you need to be careful.'

'I know, it's crossed my mind, but what am supposed to do? As a journalist, if I don't write what I find because there are criminals out there, what's the point of journalism?'

'I get that,' he said. 'It's a catch-twenty-two that shouldn't exist, not in a democracy. How far away are you from finishing?'

'It's all but finished. The problem I had was to make it interesting *and* understandable for the average person in the street. I didn't want to waste my time, as academics do, writing a brilliant, insightful, earth-shattering story which three people read. It's what you said, if it's just another story, it'll soon be wrapping fish and chips.'

'What's difficult to understand?'

'For starters, trying to make a conspiracy theory not sound like a conspiracy theory. And now' – she glowered at Sean – 'come up with a less clumsy title.'

'Have you included the Covid angle?'

She shook her head. 'I can't make sense of it, not yet. CT said' – Grace held up a warning finger in response to Sean's look – 'don't go there.

CT said Will was Covid negative but the police tech who checked the laptops got it.'

'What does that mean?'

'I don't know, not yet. CT has an annoying habit of giving an explanation that needs an explanation. Equally confusing is that initially the emergency management team at Wellington hospital confidently stated patient zero was in quarantine. Two days later they stated, equally confidently, that they'd soon identify patient zero. Something's off.'

They both lapsed into thought.

Sean broke the silence by suggesting. 'How about, "1984 has arrived"?'

'What?' said Grace. She shook her head, sighed then stared at him, her eyes lighting up. 'That's fucking brilliant.'

CHAPTER 28

Marla had been cooped up in the tiny motel room for six days, it was her own self-imposed Covid quarantine. It hadn't been the best six days of her life, but it hadn't been the worst either. She had anticipated kicking the virus quickly, but it had been nasty. For the first few days, with no adrenalin to keep her alert, she had scarcely been able to get out of bed. She watched TV, read books and slept.

She forced herself to venture out on the third day because she was running low on food. Waiting until late in the evening when the streets were quieter, she bought enough to last a week. It was mainly dry and tinned goods as the unreliable motel fridge was the size of a loaf of bread.

When she was awake, she kept a close eye on developments in the Solnet House murder case. When the police released a grainy photo of her standing outside Erebus' head office, she knew, as she suspected, that they had neatly framed her. The techs must have erased Tom and Jerry's visit but not hers, making her the prime suspect and looking guilty as hell. That was why she took the Sig from Manilow's office – they would only have left it if it had added to the evidence against her. And knowing Tom and Jerry were out there searching for her, it felt good to have a weapon.

When she had been in Manilow's house, and she hadn't known what they intended, she had performed her assignment as ordered except for keeping the untraceable printed copy of the document. After she discovered Manilow's body, and her trust levels plummeted, she had left a printout of a log file showing Manilow stopped using his computer at 4.04pm, well before she arrived. The techs should identify that, but it didn't hurt to point them in the right direction.

She was confident she had covered her own tracks in the short-term, though her former employer's actions had painted her into a corner. They wanted her dead, that was clear. The local police would arrest her, and the charges would stick, her former employer would make sure of that. Equally she couldn't approach the local SIS. Handing her quietly back would be their easiest option. She needed to lie low, but if they thought she would meekly accept her fate they were in for a surprise.

As her health improved, she began researching New Zealand in general and Grace Marks in particular. In Manilow's office she had downloaded Grace's SIS file from a replicated server in Australia. The material covered the dull aspects of an ordinary life, but it also provided details of her background including, importantly, her address. It also catalogued an SIS attempt to nullify her ability to write about the theft and publication of tax records.

After six days in solitary confinement, the agent's body was beating back Covid. She was feeling near full health and relieved to have ditched her persistent cough. Paying for another week's accommodation in cash, she planned to leave when the week was up.

Bored and browsing various news sites on her second-hand untraceable laptop, a story on the NewsNZ website caught her attention: *1984 has arrived!* She knew immediately that Grace Marks had written it. She skimmed through it to see if the story compromised her. The journalist had included the murder of Manilow and hinted at a link to the rise in street crime and surveillance, but only in passing. Without evidence she had been careful to avoid sounding like a conspiracy nutjob.

Having satisfied herself the story didn't change her situation, Marla read the story carefully. The journalist had written attractively and had crafted an easy-to-follow story; that was a gift. The story commenced at a lively pace:

You might have heard the phrase 'If you've got nothing to hide, you've got nothing to fear'. It's been around for as long as religion. There was no hiding from God.

Recently it has been adapted and used by regimes around the world to reassure law-abiding citizens that being watched under a microscope is tolerable if you've got nothing to hide.

But it's a long way from being tolerable. Recently the merging of three technologies – facial recognition, high-definition (HD) cameras and artificial intelligence (AI) – has taken surveillance to a new, concerning level.

Marla read the story slowly and deliberately. The story was saying that while most people aren't terrorists or engaged in criminal activity, that didn't mean their privacy doesn't matter.

Through the widespread implementation of HD cameras, facial recognition software, vehicle plate number identification, mobile phone data and AI, companies such as NEC, a leading Japanese firm, have developed the ability to biometrically identify individuals and track them in real time. Scale this to an entire population and we have arrived at Orwell's 1984 dystopic predication.

The story took the space to flesh out this situation. It risked losing readers with its technical jargon but, when Marks introduced the Stasi, the story came back to life.

A population subject to mass surveillance is an obscenity inevitably leading to misery, as it has done every time in human history. Many

regimes have tried to spy on their population; take the Ministerium
für Staatssicherheit, the secret police of East Germany, the Stasi.

Formed after World War II in the Cold War era, the Stasi's goal was
to infiltrate every institution of society and every aspect of daily life,
including intimate personal and family relationships. It accomplished
this through its official apparatus and a vast network of informants
and unofficial collaborators, who spied on and denounced
colleagues, friends, neighbours and even family members. The Stasi
eventually fell, along with the Berlin Wall.

The Stasi's real goal was to suppress the ability of citizens to
challenge the status quo, to change society. The state was freezing
society at its 1950 settings: homosexuality, gender, trade unions,
political dissent, equality, woman's rights, freedom of travel and
freedom of speech, all suppressed. Germans today can be thankful
the Stasi didn't have today's technology at their disposal.

Marla appreciated the analogy; it was exactly what the Stasi had intended.
And it was exactly what Putin was trying in Russia, Xi Jinping in China,
Kim Jong-il in North Korea and Lukashenko in Belarus. Marla could
hear the warning bell Grace Marks was ringing.

Advocates of mass surveillance point to the often-cited benefits of
catching terrorists and thwarting pandemics, but mass surveillance
creates the means for dark, undesirable effects and it is a slippery
slope.

It gives the state the ability to catch those engaging in any activity
it deems anti-social. It stops people joining anti-state activities – we
only need to look at what happened in Hong Kong. Ultimately it has
the power to stop people even thinking about change, à la North
Korea. Citizens become unthinking, uncritical, docile, economic
slaves of production, exactly as described by Orwell.

The situation described is not only of academic interest. There has been a series of concerning events in Aotearoa New Zealand. The dramatic rise in street disturbances has sparked a surge in demand for home security systems, many with cameras monitoring the streets. Will Manilow, the CEO of a security systems company, who was concerned at this unexpected rise, was murdered. The killer and their motive remain a mystery.

Lastly, but as important, the police and SIS are involved in a range of secretive trials of new technology. These events may be unrelated, but they bark like a dog.

It was the last part of the story which Marla considered the sharpest, the bit most journalists avoid. Marks had added a call to action.

I don't believe the New Zealand Government is actively pursuing a policy of mass surveillance, but they're sleepwalking towards the slippery slope. One way to wake them is to give every MP a taste of twenty-four-seven surveillance. It's not illegal to photograph our politicians in public places or wait, paparazzi-like, outside their houses. Oddly, it's only illegal to peer into their 'dwelling house' at night, it's fine during the day.

I think that before Parliament buys into mass surveillance, they need to take it for a test drive.

Marla lay back on the hard bed smiling. Grace Marks was trouble for everyone.

CHAPTER 29

Brandon Cantwell, the New ACT Party list MP, silently closed the front door of his lover's Wellington house, anxious not to wake his neighbours. Cardigan Way was quiet, as it should be at 5am. He was taking no chances. Since Marks' story had incited people to stalk MPs, the party whip had warned everyone to be careful. Cantwell had gone to great lengths to ensure his visit was unobserved.

When it started, every time he left his Whangarei home or his Wellington taxpayer-funded accommodation, activists recorded everywhere he went and broadcast the footage on social media sites. It was decidedly unpleasant. From his point of view, what these people, Marks included, didn't understand was that the technology protected them. It didn't invade their privacy the way they were invading his, it was outrageous. The police were useless. They said they couldn't arrest people walking on public streets unless they were committing a crime.

Cantwell blew out a quiet breath, the morning's chill making it resemble a vape cloud. Stepping onto the street, he looked around. The neighbourhood appeared asleep, but as his eyes grew accustomed to the light, he picked out a strange object next to the no-parking sign the residents had put on an orange traffic cone. Stepping closer to get a better view, he stopped in shock. Sitting on a camp chair was a figure dressed in black recording him on a phone. As he stared, the figure – he couldn't tell if they were male or female – pointed further down the street. Cantwell saw another black-clad figure sitting on the ground next to a letterbox, also capturing the scene.

Gritting his teeth, Cantwell strode over to the figure in the camp chair. 'Give me that phone,' he hissed as loudly as he dared.

A calm and recognisably female voice said, 'Fuck off. And if you touch me, we'll call the police. Get them here with their flashing lights and wailing sirens. Let them sort it out.'

Cantwell stood motionless, unsure what to do next. What would he have done if she had given him her phone? Smashed it? Kept it? All that would have achieved was getting him charged with vandalism or theft. They were probably live-streaming or uploading the footage in real time anyway. He decided to bluff. 'You're invading my privacy, I'll be—'

The woman cut him off, this time raising her voice. 'You're not *in* private now, Cantwell.'

His eyes widened.

'Yes, we know who you are, Cantwell, list MP and general right-wing waste of oxygen.'

He gestured for her to lower her voice, but she ignored him.

'You're in public now and your party supports the widespread use of public surveillance. Imagine me as a fixed camera, recording twenty-four-seven. What's the difference? That's what you want, isn't it? Or do you think the cameras will be excluded from *Carl's* street?'

Cantwell stared, open mouthed.

'And before you threaten me, that information is in the public domain too.'

He heard footsteps getting closer. Her accomplice, still recording, was approaching slowly.

'Okay,' he whispered, 'you're right, but you've got it wrong. Security cameras will protect people, not invade their privacy.'

The woman leaned towards Cantwell. 'If you knew we were here, would you have visited your boyfriend?'

He paused; it was the very reason he had kept away. 'I get your point,' he said. 'But if I knew the information wouldn't be used, like you're going to use it to ruin my life, I would have.'

'How long can security camera footage be kept?'

'I don't know,' the MP snapped.

'It's unstated,' said the woman. 'In other words, it can be kept for ever. It's you and your right-wing gittish friends who don't get it. The state can keep the recor*dings*,' she stressed their plurality, 'of your affair for ever. You'll wait, as people do under totalitarian regimes, for the knock on the door that says it's blackmail time.'

Cantwell processed this information, staying quiet.

The woman pushed herself up, putting her phone in her back pocket and folding up her camp chair which she put under her arm.

'What are you going to do with the recording?' he asked.

'What recording? I was only pretending to record.'

Cantwell stood dumbly. 'Oh. Thanks,' he croaked.

'There's no need for thanks,' she said. 'Having the information would make us as dirty as the system. This way, no one needs to worry about what to do. Except of course when . . .'

'When what?'

'When they install the real cameras.'

The politician watched the woman walk away, hand in hand with her partner. He stared after them, unmoving. He had dodged a bullet. Thirty seconds later he heard a motorcycle burst into life and roar away, he still hadn't moved. If they circulated the images, his marriage and political career were over. And he wasn't breaking the law, he was being human.

Walking to his car he whispered to himself, 'I get it. I get it.' If they had taken pictures, and he had only their word they hadn't, they could knock on his door at any time or post them on the internet. Sure, they might be breaking the law, but his life would be ruined. Tracking people meant you forced them to not only obey the law but also to tread a moral tightrope. Or else.

Trevor Hunt's long-suffering English wife of thirty years knew when to stay quiet. She put the tea down on the mahogany table and waited patiently while her husband, a well-known politician and rich-lister, bellowed into his phone.

'It was flying over my fucking house. I refuse to be spied on.'

He snorted as a male voice tried to explain the legal position.

'What?' squawked a reddening Hunt. '*They've* complained to the police? They were flying a fucking drone over my house without my permission, that's illegal.'

His wife watched as Hunt pulled back a net curtain revealing a small group of people clustered around a battered people mover. She moved closer to get a better view.

'What was I meant to do? Hmm?'

Hunt stood impatiently listening. 'Make a complaint to the Civil Aviation Authority? No wonder this country is going to the pack. How long would it take for them to investigate? Months. In the meantime, they can spy on me with gay fucking abandon.'

The politician juggled his phone before angrily pushing the red button to terminate the call. 'God, I miss slamming down the receiver,' he said.

'I can imagine,' said his wife. 'You could use a cup of tea.'

She poured two cups.

Hunt turned away from the window. 'Thank you dear, you're a brick. That bloody lesbian, commie, whatever-she-is Marks has managed to stir up all the unkempt scarf-draggers.'

'She's a journalist.'

'Is she? Well, she should stick to that and keep out of politics. The bloody whip is telling me to be careful. It's unbelievable. I'm a member of Parliament, they can't hound me like a common criminal.'

'Sugar?' his wife asked, even though she knew better than he did how he liked his tea.

Hunt nodded.

The only sound for a minute was the clinking of spoons on china and Hunt slurping.

'You know those dole bludgers have complained to the police,' said the MP, breaking the silence.

'I did wonder,' she said.

'In the day, the boys and I, together with a few of the farm workers, would've beaten the crap out of them. It'd cost a few rounds at the police canteen, but it would have been bloody well worth it. Now they can ponce around, fly a drone over my house and, if I have the temerity to shoot it down, I'm in the wrong. The world's gone mad.'

'You can't go around beating people up and firing guns, it's not the 1970s. I can't imagine the police will be that bothered, though; it wasn't as if you were shooting at a plane.'

'I expect you're right,' he said, the tea seeming to calm him. 'I didn't know they could spy on us and all I can do is complain. It seems beyond ludicrous.'

Whenever her husband talked calmly, he developed the hint of a Prince Charles accent.

'I know you dislike the Marks woman . . .'

'Dislike, she's a danger to society. This isn't the first time she's kicked up a stink about nothing.'

His wife tilted her head, it was her way of showing her husband she disagreed. It was a gesture she had called on many times over the years. If the truth was known, although she loved her husband dearly, when it came to his political views, he was basically an arse. She had been amazed when he had decided to get into politics, flabbergasted when they accepted him as a candidate and given the safest of safe seats. Any strategically shaved primate could've held the seat.

'Making the wealthy contribute to society was a just cause.' Hunt went to speak but his wife held up her hand. 'We don't need to get into that again, and her cause this time is interesting.'

Her husband's eyes widened. 'Interesting?'

'Yes, dear, interesting,' she cut in crisply. 'Hear me out.'

He stiffened.

'Marks is making the point that surveilling society is dangerous. In the wrong hands, deadly. What she's doing is giving parliamentarians, and their families, a taste of what life might be like when we are surveilled twenty-four-seven. And it's not nice, is it?'

Hunt scowled as he considered his wife's view. 'But I've read the white papers on the issue. The purpose of the surveillance is to keep New Zealanders safe, not invade their privacy like this lot at the gate are doing. You don't want another mosque shot up, or worse.'

His wife tilted her head. She was usually able to soften her husband's antiquated thinking. 'If you replace the activists at the gate with a high-definition camera with a zoom lens, and allow drones to fly overhead to keep away burglars, do you think we're safer and our privacy will be protected?'

Hunt's scowl softened.

His wife continued. 'Don't you see, you can't have one without the other. If cameras watch us all day and night, our privacy is only as secure as those with access to the information. Yes, it might stop robbers, or catch them later, but desperate people are desperate. Catching them after the robbery has turned deadly is a bit of a Pyrrhic victory. Wouldn't the money be best spent on lowering the amount of desperation?'

'You've always made a lot of sense.' He laughed. 'From time to time I've thought you should be the one in Parliament.'

His wife smiled; she had always thought that.

Hunt turned his head as the unmistakable sound of a drone entered the lounge. He jumped to his feet, his strongest South Island, r-rolling accent banishing Prince Charles. 'Those layabout arrrseholes have found another drrrone. I'm fucking shooting this one down too.' He disappeared into his office, where he kept his guns on display, illegally.

Pouring herself another cup of tea, she drank it looking out the window. She could see the activists, one of whom was clearly controlling the drone, which sounded faint. They must be flying it high to make it hard to hit. As she watched, her husband armed with a shotgun ran onto the lawn looking up, trying to locate the drone. It would no doubt be capturing her husband's antics in HD. He would appear on the news later that evening, the images making him appear a moron, not for the first time.

What would she do if he tripped and fell on his own gun? There would be a vacant seat. Maybe she would take up politics.

Mahana Glen, Green Party MP, her hands fidgeting, said 'I want it to stop, we get the point.'

'You say we, who do you mean?' asked the interviewer.

'My colleagues and I.'

'In the Green Party or in Parliament?'

Glen weighed the question carefully. 'The Green Party has never been in favour of widespread surveillance.'

'You are part of the Government, sort of, what about your colleagues in caucus?'

Taking her time before answering, Glen said, 'I haven't spoken to them directly, but a number are upset at being scrutinised under a microscope.'

The interviewer tried a different tack. 'Tell us about your experience, under the microscope as you say.'

The MP closed her eyes and nodded resignedly. 'When the story first emerged, I was all for it. As I said, the Green Party doesn't support surveilling the population as a method of reducing terrorism or crime. We agree with the points Grace Marks raised, it's not the way to solve the problem and it's not the way we want to live. When people started following me, taking pictures, I encouraged them. It's civic action, citizens making a point.'

'How long ago was that?' asked the interviewer.

'About a week, it feels longer.'

The interviewer waited for the MP to continue.

'It upset my partner first. She'd previously been in an abusive relationship and the protestors seemed to her to be stalking us. She couldn't leave the house because they followed her too.'

'Were either of you threatened?'

'No, but it *feels* threatening. They always kept their distance, but it was the constant observation. We had to keep the blinds closed during the day.'

'You said at the beginning of the interview you understood their point. What's your understanding?'

The politician drew in a calming breath, creating a short period of dead air. 'Well . . . and this is my opinion, not a party statement. If we continue down the path towards mass surveillance, this will be everyday life except that the people watching will be invisible, but they'll be watching. Everything we do, everywhere we go, will be recorded and presumably analysed by computer algorithms looking for' – she waved her hands as she searched for an appropriate phrase – 'criminal or possibly deviant behaviour.'

'Who decides what's deviant?'

'That's the point, isn't it? If this technology had come along in the sixties or seventies or earlier, I imagine there would have been a mass arrest of homosexuals. As we know because we are now living in a slightly enlightened age, this wouldn't have made any difference to the number of homosexuals, but it would have driven them further underground. Look at Russia or Belarus.'

The interviewer leaned closer. 'Does that make Parliament the arbiter of morals?'

'I suppose it does.'

'Is that bad?' asked the interviewer. 'In some regards, haven't our elected officials always been cast in that role?'

'They have, but don't you see that the danger is in locking in the morals of today.'

The interviewer squinted. 'I'm not sure I follow you.'

'As I said, if this technology had come along in the sixties, it could have locked in the thinking, and morals, of the sixties. Racism, sexism, homophobia, religious intolerance, political suppression. You name it and the government of the day could have suppressed it. The status quo becomes reified . . . made concrete.'

'Okay, but we have overcome many of those issues.'

Glen laughed. 'Have we? Or are they lurking under the surface, looking to make a comeback? What about Trump's "Make America White Again" attitude? Or the horror we see around the world every day? Even in Aotearoa, are we free from *isms*? Teenagers driving cut-down cars still find it funny to yell "lesbian" at women with short hair.'

The interviewer remained quiet.

'The key point, and what the last week has confirmed for me, is that mass surveillance will limit society's ability to evolve. We look back at the attitudes of previous societies, for example when slavery was common, marvelling at how backward they were. But at the same time, the societies themselves considered themselves enlightened. Future societies are going to look at us as backward. That's if we don't freeze society at this backward point in time.'

'Interesting views. Where to from here?'

'Well, I can assure those watching that my whanau and I get it. I'll be working to keep surveillance in check. In the meantime, please leave us alone.'

CHAPTER 30

Marla sat in the second-hand, blue 2004 Toyota Corolla she had bought earlier that morning from a car dealer in central Wellington. Dressed in her butch biker-chick clothes, she had told the young dealer she needed the cheapest most reliable car in the yard. He had taken her straight to the blue Corolla.

Normally Marla would simply pay the asking price, but she needed to conserve cash, at least in the short-term. Locking eyes with the dealer, she leaned closer, speaking slowly. 'You need to know three things: I've recently moved into the area, I've a long memory, and I hate being ripped off. Now tell me, is that too much to pay for this car?'

The dealer squirmed before saying, 'A bit.'

After paying in cash, she had driven the two hours to Palmerston North where Grace Marks lived. The car purred the whole way. She parked a block away from the journalist's house and, using the telescopic lens of the camera that she had also bought second-hand for cash, staked out the house. The first action occurred after 4pm when Grace arrived home in her red Ford. One minute later a white BMW drove past the house, parking fifty metres down the street.

'Goddammit,' said Marla. She was under surveillance, but by who? That complicated her plans. She couldn't let them see her, at any cost.

A little after 4.30pm, Grace left in her car driving towards Marla's position. Marla casually put the camera on the passenger seat, put her sunglasses on and held her phone to her ear. As Grace passed, Marla nodded as though she was agreeing with whoever was on the other end of the phone. She carried on mimicking the conversation until the white BMW had also driven past.

Grace was wearing a hoodie, so she was likely heading to the gym – her SIS file documented numerous gym visits. Marla didn't recognise the driver of the BMW, a suited male in sunglasses. It wasn't Tom or Jerry, who operated as a team, so it was likely a New Zealand agent. But why would the local SIS be watching Marks?

At 5.30pm Grace returned home, followed one minute later by the white BMW. They would have both driven past Marla except she had moved to the opposite end of the street. After the red Ford had disappeared up the driveway, and her tail resumed his patient vigil, Marla drove the long way back to her previous position. She wasn't concerned Grace would register her presence, but the agent should.

At 5.45pm, a Toyota Starlet parked on the street outside Grace's house. Two young people with backpacks, one male one female, disappeared up the driveway. Marla didn't need to take their photo, she recognised Grace's children from pictures she had seen.

The final action for the evening occurred ten minutes later when an older model sedan arrived. Marla captured the driver's profile, partially obscured by a smiling dog sitting in the passenger seat. An inspection of the photo confirmed the man was Grace's partner, a local lawyer.

An hour later, with night drawing in, Marla watched the white BMW drive away. The agent was calling it a night. Marla agreed, nothing else would happen tonight. On her phone she looked at the map and chose two small towns near Palmerston North, Woodville and Feilding, and flipped a coin.

Performing a neat U-turn, she headed for Woodville.

CHAPTER 31

'Hey,' Grace's children called out as they dumped their bags, keys, devices and shoes on any flat surface. They didn't stop for an answer, heading straight into the kitchen.

'Dinner's not far away,' Grace lied, sitting outside in the cooling evening enjoying a glass of chardonnay.

Grace heard the fridge and cupboards being opened and closed multiple times. When her children had ransacked the kitchen, they disappeared with their spoils.

The gym session had been a tough one and, although she had wanted to abstain, she felt she deserved a wine. Sean was coming over any minute, she would start dinner after he had arrived. But for now, she was relaxing and catching up with the latest developments her story had caused.

Ten minutes later, Roxy bounded onto the deck signalling Sean's arrival. Grace heard the thump of Sean's bag hitting the floor, Sean filling Roxy's bowl, Roxy emptying her bowl and Sean opening a beer.

After they had caught up about each other's day, Sean, indicating Grace's laptop open to the main NewsNZ site, asked, 'How's your call to arms going?'

'Fantastic,' said Grace. 'MPs covering the political spectrum are bitterly complaining about being followed, photographed and filmed. A small group of right-wing tosspots led by . . .' Grace looked expectantly at Sean.

'Hunt?'

Grace nodded. 'They're adamant the activists are breaching their civil liberties and they want the police to arrest *me* as the instigator.'

'Jesus, really? What have the police said?'

'That encouraging citizens to engage in lawful activity could not in any way be construed as illegal.'

'That's exactly right,' said Sean. 'Politicians are happy enough to throw citizens' rights under the surveillance bus, but not their own. Can't they recognise the ironic corner they've painted themselves into?'

'I know,' said Grace.

'How's the media treating you?'

Grace sniffed. 'Not bad. The police's stance has helped.'

'So it should. If what you suggested is illegal, organising protest marches would be treason.'

Grace smiled her agreement. 'Cantwell's become a surprise ally.'

'Cantwell?'

'He's a backbencher who hadn't said boo in the house, but now he's one of the most vocal, saying it's the state's duty to protect individual rights and privacy. He's part of New ACT and he's getting serious air time.'

New ACT formed after an embarrassing public schism had split the ACT party. Grace had covered the story for NewsNZ, dubbing it the battle of the teeny-righters and the weeny-righters.

'New ACT? They'd love a police state,' said Sean.

'They so would,' said Grace. 'Cantwell's created more ructions for them but, to be honest, both ACT parties are on life support.'

'Have you been keeping an eye on the dark side?'

'You know I've sworn off social media, and I'm glad. Trolls prefer to throw shit anonymously. The only way people can give me their opinion is by shirtfronting me. I received enough rape threats to last a lifetime when I challenged the wealthy's right to freeload off the tax system. And how many people did the police charge? Blot.'

'I would abandon it too,' he said. 'It gives a tiny proportion of the population a dirty great megaphone.'

'I take it I'm not receiving favourable comment on Iceberg's tool?' asked Grace.

'Iceberg?'

She shrugged. 'Everything about him reminds me of a lettuce.'

Sean burst out laughing. 'That's good and no you're not. But by not responding, the tirades die quickly. It ends up being morons agreeing with bigger morons.'

They sipped their drinks. Grace sensed Sean had something to say so she gave him space.

'You should know you're being portrayed as anti-Muslim and pro-terrorist.'

'I know,' said Grace. 'There's been coverage of it in the legitimate media. Some of it was balanced, but most was just click-bait. Controversy sells advertising space and much of the legitimate media is driven by profit, not journalistic integrity.'

'Not NewsNZ anyway,' he said.

'Exactly, and their model might be transferrable.'

'Go on,' he said, throwing a ball for Roxy who flew after it like a greyhound.

'It's counter-intuitive isn't it,' said Grace, sitting up. 'A state-owned news agency as a vehicle for independent news.'

'True,' said Sean. 'The term "state-owned" usually implies the mouthpiece of whatever regime is in power. Russia's the obvious example.'

'Except we're lucky enough to live in a country where governments value an independent media, despite what dribbling conspiracy theorists think. The western model uses both state and private but over the past decades we've lurched like drunks towards profit.'

'We have,' he agreed.

'The pressure to make money,' she continued, 'means the focus is on titillation, not providing balanced news. Remember Fox in the final throws of the Trump fiasco. They became a mouthpiece for his narcissistic ramblings because it made money. It's not journalism, it's what I've started calling "earnalism".'

'Earnalism?'

'Yeah, writing and running anything just to make money.'

'Nice.' He absent-mindedly threw Roxy's ball. 'So where does that leave everything? State-owned leans toward government mouthpiece. Competition heads us back to the page three girls.'

Grace chuckled. 'Christ, it wasn't that long ago.'

'Anyway,' he said. 'I guess the question is, how do you protect state-run news agencies from *ever* becoming the mouthpiece of the government?'

Grace held up her wine, surveying the pale-gold liquid in the sun. 'The hard answer is you can't. Currently the NewsNZ charter protects its independence and allows it to operate commercial-free, but the next government could change the legislation. It's not foolproof, but it's sound. So why not use it as a blueprint for surveillance?'

'You've lost me.'

'Right. NewsNZ's role is to provide balanced independent news. Why? Because society, democracy, can't function properly without it. It's too important left to the wealthy's mindless devotion to market forces. With surveillance, we want the benefits of stopping terrorists, or at least making it hard for them, without monitoring the population like the fucking Stasi. An independent agency could act as a counterbalance to the GCSB, SIS and our Five Eyes mates who are currently treating the public as experimental rats in a maze.'

'Okay,' said Sean slowly. 'I'm not sure how it would work in practice but the concept's good.'

'The spooks would hate it,' she said. 'They want the ability to poke around wherever and whenever they fancy. It would make them – drumroll please – accountable to someone other than themselves.'

'What would you call the organisation?'

'ThemisNZ.'

His face screwed tightly. 'Themis?'

'She's the Greek goddess of divine justice,' said Grace. 'She's the one holding the scales for every Ministry of Justice.'

'I like the concept,' he said, 'but the name . . . it's a bit clumsy.'

'Arsehole,' she said, laughing.

Sean laughed too. 'You know, Grace, it is possible to be too clever.'

CHAPTER 32

Brandon Cantwell, the New ACT Party list MP, silently closed the front door of his lover's Wellington house, anxious not to wake his neighbours. Cardigan Way was quiet, though at 5am it should be quiet. Since his run-in with the activists, and his subsequent vocal calls for a public inquiry, they had left him alone. They had stopped their crusade, at least for him, and he had resumed his extra-marital affair in secrecy.

Still, he remained alert, making sure he covered his steps thoroughly. Aware security cameras covered parts of his journey, he now parked in an area where they were absent. That was more difficult than he'd thought, more difficult than he'd hoped. They were popping up everywhere and it meant a ten-minute walk to and from his car.

Stepping onto the street, he looked around. Everything was still. The vegetation was uninhabited and there were no activists with cameras this morning. Inhaling the cool morning air, he put on a cap and tossed his Thule laptop bag over his shoulder. There were no street-facing security cameras in Cardigan Way – he had spent an hour looking for them under the cover of darkness. The odd one appeared on his ten-minute walk but, at least for now, the footage would remain private. And if he had his way, no person or system would ever be able to interrogate the footage.

It was a pleasant morning and having enjoyed a pre-dawn romp he had a decided spring in his step. His pace quickened as he bounded down the steep street. But as he rounded the final corner, he slowed. There was something wrong with the picture, something out of place. As he carried on cautiously, he saw through the window of the bus shelter that someone was waiting for the bus. It was odd, the buses didn't start running for at least an hour. Concluding it was likely one of the homeless, he let his pace quicken.

At the bottom of Cardigan Way, he came to an abrupt halt. The person had stood up and was leaning on the shelter. Backlit by an orange streetlight, he could see the man wasn't homeless, he was wearing a suit. The immediate impression Cantwell had was 'gangster'.

The man raised his eyebrows, confirming what Cantwell already suspected – he was waiting for him.

Looking around wildly, Cantwell assessed his options. He was alone, no cars were driving past, there was just him and this gangster. Although he sensed there was an inevitability about what was coming, avoiding it seemed the logical step. Walking briskly back up Cardigan Way, he looked over his shoulder. The suited gangster didn't follow, just put his hands in his pockets and watched.

Unsure what he was going to do, he rounded the corner back to Carl's house and came to a second abrupt stop, a gasp caught in his throat. Standing under a lone streetlight was the suited gangster. Cantwell's brain couldn't comprehend the situation. It felt as if he was in the twilight zone. Then the obvious conclusion hit him – there were two of them. He almost laughed but his relief was fleeting. He looked around for a second escape route. In the dim pre-dawn light, both sides of the street appeared covered with impenetrable vegetation.

The suited gangster in front of him lit a cigarette. Through a vast noxious cloud of smoke he said, 'Back the way you came, please. Let's make this painless and quiet. If you'd prefer, we can visit you at your family home in Wong-a-ray. I'm sure the right honourable Mr Cantwell doesn't believe in secrets.'

Cantwell stood frozen. In two sentences the gangster communicated that he knew who he was, where he lived, that he had a family and that he was having an affair. The gangster walked slowly towards him, a trail of smoke billowing behind giving the scene a Jack-the-Ripper feel.

'Let's go, Mr Cantwell. The quicker we get this done, the quicker you can get back into your closet.'

Cantwell closed his eyes but when he opened them again the image hadn't changed. As the gangster neared, Cantwell turned obediently and plodded heavily down the street.

The first gangster wasn't by the bus stop, he was now sitting on a bench in the adjacent children's playground. The scene was utterly incongruous.

'Go and sit down,' said the gangster behind him.

The grass surrounding the playground needed mowing. Cantwell tried to pick his way through keeping his shoes dry. As he neared the bench, the seated gangster showily checked his watch. 'Chop fucking chop, Cantwell.' He looked and sounded like a caricature of the psychotic Mr White from the film *Reservoir Dogs*. 'We don't want to be here when the world wakes up, do we? We've other people to visit.' In the garish orange light, his leer was ghoulish as he patted the bench.

Cantwell stopped in front of him. 'You can't do this,' he said, his voice coming out as an ill Kermit the Frog.

'Can't do what?' said Mr White. 'We're having a chat, that's all. You're free to go, we're not going to stop you. But you need to see it from our perspective. Our orders are to have this chat and we can't disobey orders, that's not a possibility. If you don't want to have it now, we'll have it later . . . but we will have it.'

Cantwell slumped onto the bench, breathing out heavily, 'For God's sake.'

'For anyone's sake you like.'

The second gangster sat gingerly, wriggling closer until he had wedged Cantwell tightly between them. Smells assaulted Cantwell's nostrils, on one side cheap aftershave, on the other cigarettes and sour male sweat. Men only sat this close if they were gay or wanted to scare the shit out of you. They weren't gay.

'This is nice,' said Mr White as he casually gave Cantwell's leg what amounted to an affectionate squeeze. Cantwell's spine went rigid, and he stared straight ahead to avoid looking at either of them. The replica Mr White took his phone out of his jacket pocket.

'We're going to play a selection of home movies. We're not experts, we're probably not even very good, but you'll find them interesting, won't he Reg?'

Reg grinned as he lit another cigarette. The early-morning stillness allowed the cloying atmosphere to envelope the trio like a cloak.

The images started predictably. Cantwell driving, parking and walking to and from Carl's house. The shot changed to Cantwell and his wife in their garden, they must have parked across the street. The shot changed again, this time it was Carl opening his Cuba Street adult supplies store. That was how they had met. He was browsing in the shop for items to 'jazz up' his sober marital sex life. Instead, he ended up arranging to meet Carl for a drink. The rest, as they say, was history. Except it wasn't history.

The screen went blank. Thinking the display was over, Cantwell started to let out his breath but stopped, his eyes widening, when the screen displayed a dimly-lit shot of Carl's bedroom, focused on the king-sized bed. The camera was at eye level, they must have hidden it among the myriad of knick-knacks adorning every flat space of Carl's bedroom. Although the shot was grainy, the camera had enough light to capture what was happening, and who was doing what.

'Do you know, Reg, this was illegal in most countries until recently. It still is in many. A hanging offence in some. Barbarians.'

Reg chuckled, causing a ragged plume of smoke to swirl around them.

'All right,' said Cantwell, 'that's enough.'

'Okay, boss, if you've had enough reminiscing.' Mr White pressed a button and the screen went mercifully blank. He returned the phone to his jacket pocket and they sat in silence, apart from the occasional hiss and pop from Reg's cigarette.

'What do you want from me? I'm not rich, but you must know that.'

Mr White put on a hurt look. 'Do we look like common blackmailers? Do we Reg?'

'Nope,' said Reg, flicking his cigarette onto the grass where it smouldered, the morning dew insufficient to fully extinguish it. It amazed Cantwell that, given the situation, the littering of a cigarette butt in a children's playground could still irritate him.

'Nothing like that Mr Cantwell, New ACT Party MP.'

Cantwell closed his eyes, knowing where they were taking the conversation.

The replica Mr White smirked as he started what Cantwell knew was a prepared speech. 'We've been asked to let you know that the noise about surveillance isn't necessary. Surveillance is for the good of the country. If you've got nothing to hide, you've got nothing to fear.'

His voice dropped an octave. 'And you've got something to hide haven't you, Cantwell, so you should be fucking fearful. Normally we don't fuck around with warnings and please-keep-your-mouth-shut. Normally we'd fuck you up. The fact that you don't want the world to know you're an adulterous, sodomising cunt would be the least of your problems.'

The words impacted with a physicality that made Cantwell, even with his eyes closed, wince.

Mr White's voice returned to normal. 'So please, shut the fuck up. Even better, if you don't want another chat . . . in private, change your stance. Be supportive of the efforts to keep your country safe from terrorists.'

Cantwell sat still, feeling a mix of shock and asphyxia from the smoke.

'Are we clear?' asked Reg.

Cantwell nodded.

'I'd prefer to hear an answer, Mr Cantwell,' said Reg.

'We're clear,' Cantwell croaked.

The two gangsters looked at each other before getting up, stretching and walking away as though they were strolling on the beach. Once back in their black BMW, they drove away sedately. When they were gone, Cantwell waved his arms around madly to clear the air. Looking around, he was alone. It was as though it never happened, but it had. He trudged back to his car, the spring in his step a distant memory.

At his car, he gritted his teeth and cursed. 'This shit doesn't happen in Aotearoa. Not in fucking New Zealand.'

But, as he had just discovered, it did.

CHAPTER 33

Grace ordered a coffee and chose a round table in the back, where she could see the entire café, including the entrance. She was twenty minutes early, as planned, and the café was steadily filling as lunchtime approached. A colourfully dressed woman took a table near Grace and immediately started reading a book.

Her coffee arrived as Grace was replaying the events since she had received the phone call. Few people knew her mobile number, she guarded it carefully, and the call came through 'Caller ID Blocked'. She let it go to voicemail. The caller, male with an American accent, left a message that he would ring every fifteen minutes until she answered. He emphasised she needed to answer or they, not he, would find an alternative way to get her attention.

Grace recognised he was a spook of some description. It was the same mix of passive-aggressive cockiness she had encountered when they tried to bully her away from investigating how the wealthy avoided tax. It must be part of the training, although the selection process would naturally favour arrogant wankers.

When her phone rang exactly fifteen minutes later, she again let it go to voicemail. Fifteen minutes after that, she answered. They weren't going to take no for an answer, and she wasn't keen on finding out about his alternative methods.

'Why didn't you answer the second call, Grace?' It was same American accent.

Far from fearing spooks, she said, 'I was having a shit.'

The rest of the conversation had been brief. Meet at the café where she was now sitting at midday. Come alone, they had information they needed to share with her. The spook waited, presumably for her to ask questions such as 'Who are you?' and 'What do you want with me?' All Grace said was 'Fine' and terminated the call.

It was 11.58am. They would arrive late – it was how spooks liked to roll. Closing her eyes, she tried to relax. She may have sounded tough on the phone, and she wanted to come across that way, but she was nervous. Spooks tended not to play nicely and liked to get their own way. They were grown-up sandpit bullies.

Turning on the recording app on her phone, she put it in her inside jacket pocket. Promptly five minutes late, two thinly disguised thugs in suits and sunglasses strutted into the café. They stopped inside the door and, like twins, simultaneously took off their sunglasses.

'Cocks,' Grace muttered. She didn't wave out; they would know what she looked like. One headed to the counter while the other stalked towards her, past the colourful woman who was holding up her coffee while she took stupid selfies to bore her friends with.

The thug smirked as he sat down. 'Ace Marks in the flesh. The talented investigative reporter. This is a privilege.' His accent confirmed he had made the calls. Leaning in close, he said in a low voice, 'I hope you had a good shit.'

Given that the other thug was ordering, Grace assumed the American thug was in charge. She took her time answering, trying to look bored rather than revealing that she was close to shitting herself. 'Let's cut to the chase. This is as far from a social occasion as imaginable. I want it over as fast as possible.'

He grinned, seemingly enjoying the exchange. 'Can do, Ace, I'm sure your time is valuable. If you don't mind, I'll wait for my colleague. And while we're waiting, can you kindly switch off your phone.'

'Why?'

'Because this conversation is off the record and I find journalists hard to trust.'

Grace pouted before taking her phone out of her bag.

'Tidy looking iPhone,' he said, 'you must be doing better than what your files say.' He leaned over in the same conspiratorial manner. 'I hope you're not fiddling your tax, Ace. The public would be disappointed.'

'What about your phone?' she asked.

The American shrugged half-heartedly. 'We could, but we know what we're going to say. There's no need for us to record the conversation.'

She shrugged an equally half-hearted okay. He was right, only she had an interest in recording the conversation. Grace switched off her phone, putting it on the table. They sat in silence until the second thug arrived, sitting down gingerly as though he had recently been at the bottom of a ruck.

'What did you order, Reg?' The American asked.

'Smoothies. Passionfruit.'

His accent was hard to place.

'Good choice.' The American pointed at Grace's coffee. 'I find it hard to sleep if I have coffee after ten in the morning.'

'I'm surprised you sleep at all with what must weigh on your conscience.'

Both thugs chuckled.

She rolled her eyes. 'Can we speed this along please. You mentioned information.'

The American cleared his throat. 'Sure.' He was about to start when their smoothies arrived in takeaway cups, he held up his hands in a what-can-you-do gesture. The takeaway cups meant, thankfully, they weren't planning on a long meeting.

Grace watched emotionlessly as they took long drinks before discussing the flavour and texture of the smoothies. She stared at them as they grinned. 'You guys have watched *Pulp Fiction* too many times. Is it part of your training?'

A wave of annoyance flitted across the American's face. 'Okay. The problem is, Ace, and please bear in mind we are only the messengers, a lot of people believe increased surveillance is in the New Zealand public's best interest. I'm sure we can agree, none of us want another Christchurch and your journalism is naïve – at best.'

She automatically went to reply, but what was the point of debating with the messengers. She let her breath slide back out calmly.

The American paused, eyebrows raised, but when Grace didn't take the bait, he carried on. 'The people we represent suggest you let the story go because you're acting counter to New Zealand's best interests.'

'Best interests as decided by who?' she asked.

'Let's say the international community.'

Grace snorted but stayed quiet.

'What do you say, Ace? There are plenty of other issues of vital importance you can focus on.'

Grace knew how to play games too. 'Sure,' she said laconically.

The thugs exchanged a look.

'We must be done,' she said. 'See you, fellas. I'd say it's been nice, but I've had more intelligent conversations with my vacuum cleaner.'

The men didn't move.

The American's eyes narrowed. 'How can we be sure you're going to keep—'

'Oh, for fuck's sake,' hissed Grace. 'Stop pretending you're clever and get to the fucking point. Journalists don't get warned off in this country, so obviously you're about to threaten me with something.'

They both stared at her.

'Are you following this?' she asked.

'We were being polite,' said Reg.

Grace touched her phone to check the time, forgetting they had made her switch it off. She grunted in frustration. 'I switch this on in two minutes – and I start taking photos. We could do a selfie.'

The American sat up straighter. 'We aren't warning you off, Ace. You're right, that doesn't happen in New Zealand. We're appealing to your values and . . .' Slowly he took a folded A4 envelope out of his jacket, placing it theatrically on the table. From it he took two photos, turning them for Grace to see.

Grace looked at the images, unsure what to expect. After the phone call, she had racked her brains for what they could possibly have on her. As she lived a typical boring life, she was intrigued what they might have dug up – or manufactured. After looking at the images twice, she looked up confused. 'You're joking?'

'Oh, it's no joke. She's very cute. A bit young if you ask me – at least for you.' He turned to Reg. 'It's like being in San Fran. Who knew homosexuality was rampant in A-a-tea-a-rower?'

'Must be something in the water,' said a deadpan Reg.

The first photo was of Grace and Elle, the domestic violence victim she'd been working with on a story, holding hands. The second was of them hugging and laughing. Both photos had been taken when they had been trying to enrage Elle's angry stalking ex. Grace had meant her comment literally; they must be joking because the photos weren't threatening or incendiary. The thugs had, thankfully, adopted a different interpretation.

To buy herself time she took a slow drink from her coffee, finishing it. If this was all they had, she wanted them to leave with the impression she desperately wanted it kept secret. To do that, she needed to play her cards well.

She shrugged. 'What does it matter? It's not a crime.'

'I agree,' said the American, his confidence returned. 'Reg and I both appreciate a bit of girl-on-girl action, don't we Reg?'

The other man grinned like a schoolboy.

'But it is an affair,' he continued. 'Sean won't like it, though maybe he'll be in boots 'n all as they say. Then there's the journalist coming out of the closet angle. That shouldn't diminish your star quality. You'll be back in the spotlight and, if you're honest with yourself Ace, that's how you love to roll.'

Her mind raced. She picked up her coffee but it was empty, so she leaned over and took Reg's smoothie. 'You don't have Covid, do you?'

Reg glared at her.

Grace dropped his straw on the floor and took a long drink. 'Not bad.' Picking the straw off the floor, she stuck it back in the smoothie before pushing it back to a seriously pissed off Reg. The American put a calming hand on Reg's arm as Grace put the thirty seconds she had gained to good use.

'If I find another story, you destroy the photos?'

'Close,' he said. 'You drop the story and we'll sit on the photos. For ever, if you're a good girl.'

Grace's teeth clenched. Calling a woman over fifty a 'good girl' was beyond misogynistic. 'And you can pull the photos whenever you want?'

'You're a quick learner.'

She carried on the debate, not wanting to look like she had rolled too easily. 'But don't you see, that's the problem with surveillance, it exists for ever. The state can silence people, you two included. What if your next boss looks at the world differently? You could spend the rest of your lives in prison.'

'Are you worried, Reg?'

A glaring Reg shook his head.

'Your problem, Ace,' he continued, 'is you've seen too many

apocalyptic movies. Surveillance is there to protect the public, to help us catch the bad guys. Remember that fucker who murdered Grace Millane? If it wasn't for surveillance, he might have walked free.'

'You don't get it, do you?' she said.

'Get what?'

'Surveillance has its place, nobody's arguing to get rid of it. What we're arguing is it shouldn't be in the hands of people who'll pervert it.' She shoved the two photos across the table. 'You're the bad guys in this scenario. You and your employers need to be kept on a short fucking leash.'

Tilting his head as though he was considering her point, he glanced at Reg, who pushed his smoothie away with a look of disgust that bordered on hatred. Grace shrugged. They stood and put their sunglasses on simultaneously.

Grace waited for them to have the last word. The American didn't disappoint.

'Find a new story and we'll never have to meet again. Disappoint our employers and we'll have no choice but to let the public know about the real Grace Marks. We'll have to have another chat, of course, but we'll have that one in private so we can bounce off each other, as they say.'

He waited for a reply, but she just stared at them. They turned and left.

Suddenly realising how tense she was, Grace huffed out a breath as she watched them leave. Those two were nasty fuckers impersonating human beings. They hadn't killed Will, but their sort, maybe a colleague of theirs, had. Grace had bought herself time but she would need to use it wisely. She wasn't letting two thugs warn her off this story, this was a career maker. But she also never wanted to see them again – unless they were in the dock.

Picking up the photos, her laugh drew the attention of the woman who'd been intently reading. She stared at Grace, who waved an apology. The woman eyed Grace, packed up, and hurried out of the café.

Grace said quietly to herself, 'What's her problem? It's a café, not a library.'

If they made these images public, Grace could have a lot of fun. She took out her phone, her old phone, from the pocket of her jacket. Stopping the recording, she replayed a little to check the audio quality. She heard, in a clear American accent, 'I hope you had a good shit.'

Excellent.

CHAPTER 34

In an anonymous mirror-glassed office building in Wellington's CBD, in a meeting room devoid of corporate art, Jenna and an SIS colleague, dressed uniformly in black pants, a white shirt and a black jacket, sat waiting at a boardroom table.

The door opened and their identically dressed boss, the woman they referred to as Anne, took her place at the head of the table. 'Status?' she asked, not needing to add any context. They all knew why they were meeting.

Jenna, her laptop open, said, 'Nothing concrete, but bits don't add up. The police have come up with blanks and, because they've unofficially heard the killer has left the country, they're not using too much resource. Marks' story has ruffled a number of politician's feathers.'

'You don't have to tell me,' Anne cut in. 'I'm feeling the heat though I keep telling them it's a police matter.'

'It's not even a police matter,' said Jenna's colleague. 'Marks was clever, no one's broken the law.'

Anne scowled. 'Any intel through Five Eyes signals?'

The male agent shook his head. 'Very quiet.'

Anne snorted. 'They think it's done and dusted, don't they? What about the op itself? What do we know about that?'

'Everyone's denying it exists,' he said. 'From what I've manage to pry out of my sources, it's related to a new technology.'

'Why wouldn't they keep us in the loop?'

'I don't know, and nobody's talking,' he said. 'Officially there is no pilot, which means it's not under the CIA or the NSA. Whatever's going down, it must breach our mandate, or maybe the law. If we knew about it, we'd have to report it to the government.'

'Who would naturally quash it,' said Anne, 'because once it's on record, on their watch, they have a ticking political bomb. So, our US *colleagues*,' she spat the word out with distaste, 'have decided they can use us as their testing ground. If they're successful, they'll sell it back to us at an exorbitant price.'

Jenna watched her boss mentally run through their options, the woman's rhythmic wheeze was the only sound as she and her colleague stayed quiet. Anne went to stand, seemingly about to call the meeting to an end, but then she sat down. Fixing her gaze on Jenna, she asked, 'What bits don't add up?'

Jenna smiled. 'I've been checking a few angles, but it's speculative.'

'Tell me about your angles.'

'Okay. The story they've given us is sketchy, but it could be true. The agent or merc lands in Aotearoa, conducts the hit and they whisk her away. They alter the records, like only they can, and there's no evidence she was ever here. Hard for the police to track and catch a phantom. On the surface, fucked up, but, as you said, done and dusted.'

Anne's face was unreadable.

'Now for the bits that don't add up.' Jenna opened a file. 'The health authorities have been contact-tracing what they're calling the Bethel Woods cluster.'

'Makes it sound like they've sponsored it,' said her colleague.

'I know,' said Jenna. 'A contact told me they took a positive test from a person in MIQ who doesn't exist. It's been classified as a data collection error.'

Anne's eyes widened. 'Are you saying she caught Covid?'

'No. We know she spent time at Bethel Woods, probably twice.'

Anne added, 'She moves in and out of MIQ but catches Covid, conducts the hit and they extract her. No?'

Jenna was shaking her head forcefully as she waited for Anne to finish. 'I don't think so. The orphan Covid sample was taken on Wednesday, two days before the hit. If it was her, she's already infected. I think she's the missing patient zero.'

'Okay,' said Anne. 'What does it change materially?'

Jenna sat forward. 'A police tech tested positive for Covid. He's linked to the Bethel Woods cluster but he'd never been in the bar.'

Anne's face conveyed she couldn't see the relevance.

Jenna carried on. 'The only link to the tech is Manilow's laptops, both accessed by the woman. We knew she had access in the office, but when the tech checked the laptop from his home it had been reset to its factory settings.'

'When did she do that?'

'The police say it could have been any time from Friday through to Sunday, but I think it was before the murder, before she was in Manilow's office.'

Anne frowned. 'Why?'

'The laptops were clean but the police found a document on the printer in Manilow's office. It was a photo of an event log which showed that Manilow had stopped using his work laptop at four minutes past four. I made them keep that out of the police report.'

Anne's frown intensified. 'Why?'

'I don't think she killed Manilow.'

'What?' Her superior's frown turned to a look of annoyance.

Jenna held up a hand. 'I kept it out of the report because I didn't want all our cards on the table for everyone to see. The woman had to have taken the photo, no other scenario is possible. Manilow stopped using his laptop fourteen minutes *before* she arrived. He could have stopped because he was about to leave but . . .'

'He may have been interrupted by the killer,' said Anne. 'But the security footage didn't show anyone entering apart from the killer' – Anne rolled her eyes – 'the *suspected* killer after the receptionist left at four.'

'If they can erase MIQ records,' said Jenna, 'altering security footage in an office building can't be harder. Also, the footage shows the receptionist leaving at four without locking the door. The woman arrives at four eighteen and *unlocks* the door. Why would Manilow lock himself in if he's planning to head out in fifteen minutes?'

Her colleague asked, 'If they did tamper with the footage, and JP's right in saying that it's child's play, why didn't they remove the footage of the woman?'

'It's a good question,' said Anne. 'Equally, why would she leave a printout pointing to her innocence, at least of the murder?'

'It must have turned to custard,' he said. 'She's saying "I didn't do it". They're making it look like she did. Whoever had Manilow killed is happy to frame her – but why bother if they've extracted her? Why not leave it a mystery? And who killed Manilow?'

They looked at each other and back again with resigned nods.

'Different agents, same team,' said Jenna. 'It's the only scenario I can make work.'

'Jesus,' said Anne. 'This is turning into a nightmare.'

'It doesn't get any better,' said Jenna as she opened a document on her laptop. 'One of the Covid cases linked to the Bethel Woods cluster is a man who works in a second-hand shop in Newtown, Opportunities for Animals. He lives in Masterton and helps out on Saturdays.'

Her superior's face was expressionless.

Jenna ignored her. 'If the woman is patient zero, as the timeframe indicates, we know she was in Manilow's office and in his home, leaving

Covid on his laptops which infected the police tech. She also had to be in Newtown on Saturday, infecting the man in the second-hand shop. There isn't enough time for anyone who caught the virus from her to become contagious. This variant takes two days before someone can pass it on.'

'Right,' said Anne. 'According to our colleagues' – this time she said the word normally – 'she's left the country.'

'According to our colleagues,' said Jenna, 'she killed Manilow. I need to check, to make sure the virus transmission confirms my suspicion. But if she was in a second-hand shop in Newtown, it's doubtful she's expanding her wardrobe before they extract her.'

Everyone, including Jenna, mentally pondered the logic of this.

Jenna's colleague broke the silence. 'JP's spot on. That's why the woman had to have been in Manilow's house before she visited his office, afterwards she's gone to ground. That means she's now hiding out in . . . I was going to say Wellington, but she could be anywhere.'

'But she's only been in New Zealand for three days,' said Jenna. 'She can't have set up anything in that time and she can't use anything they've set up. Buying clothes from an op shop indicates to me that she's winging it.'

Anne added, 'And, as our American colleagues are involved, they must have known this because she's disappeared off the radar. They'll be keen to find her to tidy up loose ends.'

'I've come up with two scenarios,' said Jenna. 'One, she's decided to get out of the game alive. Aotearoa's an attractive option.'

'But if that was her plan,' interrupted Anne, 'why go through with the assignment? She could have bolted the instant they got her out of MIQ.'

'Agreed,' said Jenna. 'Which leaves impulsive flight. The custard scenario.'

'It fits,' said her colleague. 'She's working in a world where getting burnt is an occupational hazard. She may not have had a plan specifically for this, but she would've had some plans.'

'I would,' agreed Jenna. 'If she has access to money, she can buy whatever she needs for disappearing; clothes, disguises, accommodation, transport, tech.'

'Fuck,' said Anne. Jenna's eyes widened slightly – her superior seldom swore. 'If she's off the radar, she'll be impossible to track down.'

'There's another gap,' said Jenna, breaking the short silence.

Anne slumped a little. 'Go on.'

'According to the security cameras, she was in Manilow's office for fifty minutes. Once she'd finished with Manilow's laptop, what did she do? I doubt she read the porno mags in the receptionist's drawer.'

Anne's head tilted.

'The receptionist was very embarrassed,' Jenna said, with a snicker. 'Plus, our missing woman had been at Manilow's house for god knows how long. If I put myself in her shoes and I find a dead body maybe I don't expect to find, I use the time to my advantage. I print out a log file to point to my innocence. There were boxes of flash drives in the office, copying Manilow's files might give me a bargaining chip. The receptionist had no idea if any were missing – they'd been giving them out at conferences.'

Dropping her head into her hands, their superior massaged her temples. 'Sum up for me where we are, please JP.'

Jenna closed her laptop. 'The official story is that the killer, a rogue woman agent, has left the country. It could be true. The Americans know for sure and they're not talking. If we believe the science, which Americans struggle with, she was in Newtown buying second-hand clothes the day after the hit. She had time to access both Manilow's files and her own organisation's resources, so she may have sensitive information.'

Her colleague added, 'They haven't the resources to track her down, not in New Zealand, and as they've given us a bullshit story, they can't get help from us.'

Anne pressed her fingertips together. 'Let's assume you're right, what would you do if you were her? You're wanted for murder, rightly or wrongly. You're infected with Covid. You're a liability to your employer and let's assume you have sensitive information.'

The room descended into a heavy silence. Anne waited.

Jenna's colleague was the first to speak. 'Assuming I have access to money, in the short-term I'd hide out in a medium-sized holiday town. Only bad luck would give me away. When the time was right, I'd fly off to a foreign country.'

Anne looked to Jenna.

'I agree, except I'd go to ground after I'd handed over the information, to fuck over my former employer and hopefully clear my involvement. My best chance for long-term survival is to weaken their presence here.'

'She can't go to the police,' said Anne. 'They'll arrest her on sight and all the evidence points to her. She can't trust us because she's a problem from every angle we'd gladly hand back. That leaves . . .'

'A journalist,' said Jenna, finishing the sentence. She had reached that conclusion already. 'And which journalist was lunching with Manilow the day before he was killed?'

'That woman's the living dead,' said Anne. 'You think you've finished with her and she shuffles back into the frame.' Anne turned to the male agent. 'What's the latest on Marks?'

He tapped on his laptop. 'Not much. She's at the supermarket, not exactly James Bond stuff. Shall I tell them to watch out for the woman?'

'No! I don't want anyone else to know what we know, or what we surmise. Let's act as though our files are compromised, add nothing until we've cleared this up. If this woman does pay Marks a visit—'

'Or has already paid her a visit,' cut in Jenna.

'Indeed. I want to know. And if Manilow was killed for what he knew, that's the key. JP, Marks knows who you are,' Jenna reddened, but her boss carried straight on. 'But we can use it to our advantage. Pay her a visit. Find out whether she's been contacted.'

Pleased that the subject of her previous blunder when Marks had caught her tailing her wasn't dwelt on, Jenna said, 'I'll pretend that we know she has been contacted, see if I can make her squirm. I owe her some discomfort. What about the woman, the merc?'

'Let's leave that problem to our US colleagues,' said Anne. 'Given she's most likely a highly trained agent who doesn't like the idea of being burnt, she'll be hard to track down. My gut feeling is she'll do what you said: disappear. And if she does have sensitive information, she'll use it. I bloody well would.'

CHAPTER 35

It had just gone seven and Marla was sitting in a dimly-lit café-cum-bar on Palmerston North's George Street, where she was meeting an accountant called Damien. Having spent the previous night in a run-down motel in Woodville, she had decided to use her preferred method of finding anonymous accommodation: a short-term romance. While recovering from Covid, she had created profiles on two dating websites using the name Norma Smith. On the first she was a woman seeking a man, on the second a woman seeking a woman. It would have been simpler to identify as bi but, in her experience, that option attracted scores of dribbling men who expected to play out their pornography-inspired fantasies.

This was her second potential hook-up for the evening. The first with Erica hadn't given Marla the right vibe. Erica, a university tutor, was pretty but she came across as intense and needy, traits that could create difficulties while Marla stayed and complications when she abruptly left. They parted with a promise to catch up soon, which wouldn't happen.

Damien, if the messages they had been exchanging were a guide, seemed a better prospect. If he wasn't suitable, she had chosen to stay at a pub hotel in Longburn, a small satellite town.

Marla recognised Damien when he entered, a good sign. It meant the photo he used was current. He had no trouble recognising her either, as she had taken a photo of herself in the motel dressed as a middle-class struggling single teacher. She was wearing that outfit now but had flirted it up a couple of notches.

'Norma, you look wonderful,' said Damien as he came over.

'Likewise,' said Marla. Dressed as though he had come from the office, Damien was slightly taller than Marla, attractive with a warm, welcoming face. His photo didn't do him justice.

They hugged and Damien ordered drinks, insisting that he would be buying dinner. After they ordered, Damien asked the standard first-date question. 'Tell me a little about yourself?'

Marla beamed as she wove her real life in with back stories she had used previously. 'Grew up in Chagrin Falls, Ohio. I had a shit childhood that I escaped by joining the army. After I left the army, I ran a café for a while but when my relationship fell apart, I decided to see the world. I was in New Zealand when the pandemic hit, fell in love with the country and the people, and I've decided to stay. How about you, Damien?'

'Wow, you packed a lot into so few sentences. Me, I'm more a what-you-see-is-what-you-get person. Grew up in Wellington but went to uni here. Graduated as an accountant, landed a job in an accounting firm, still an accountant. But' – he leaned towards her smiling – 'don't let that fool you, I'm a racing car driver trapped in an accountant's body.'

They both chuckled.

'Married?' asked Marla.

'Divorced, two children. My daughter's followed in my footsteps; she's working in Auckland. My son wants to be a poet; he's a uni student in Dunedin.'

'A poet, that's so cool,' said Marla.

'I know. I'm not one of those parents who wants to enslave their children in the workforce. A poet would be awesome, forget the money, he'll get half of mine one day.'

Their food arrived and Marla, who was starving, tucked in.

'Are you looking to settle in Palmerston North?' asked Damien.

She laughed. 'Um, not yet. My plan is to see New Zealand first, let life work that out later.'

'And that's what you've been doing?'

'Yep. My army service means money won't be a problem, for a while.'

'I wish I could float like you,' said Damien.

'What's stopping you?'

He put down his fork. 'That's a good question.' He looked at Marla, who remained quiet. Finally, he said, 'Nope, I can't think of a single reason.'

'It's a tough question,' she said. 'You've spent your life getting to where you are, but if you want more . . .' She finished her sentence with a shrug.

Damien frowned.

'Don't get me wrong,' said Marla. 'I wouldn't be here if the carpet hadn't been ripped out from underneath me, for damn sure.'

'That might have helped,' he said. 'When you've no choice, you have to act.'

'You do,' she said, with a brief iciness in her voice that she quickly suppressed. 'Most people have no choice. Your problem, Damien, is that you're a victim of your own success.'

They ate and chatted amiably. Damien was ideal. Living alone in his own house – it was perfect camouflage. The bonus was that he was good-looking and interesting, a rare combination for an accountant.

Over coffee, he asked, 'Where are you staying?'

'Last night was a motel in Woodville, before that, Wellington. Tonight, maybe Longburn.'

'Is that how you travel around? Motel to motel?'

'If there's no better option,' she said, raising an eyebrow.

His eyes narrowed.

'Cards on the table time,' said Marla, leaning closer. 'What I prefer is to discover nice people and places.' She whispered, 'It's the best way to see the country and make friends.'

'That makes sense,' he said.

'It's way cheaper too. Instead of paying for a box of a room, I can spend the money on food, refreshments and dining out as a thank you.'

Damien looked serious. She sensed he wanted to tread carefully, to make sure he wasn't misunderstanding the offer she was making.

'I'll be straight up,' she said. 'You seem nice, does that sound interesting to you?'

'It does,' he said. 'It's just . . . unexpected.'

'I'm a good judge of character, and besides, I have my army training in case I get it wrong. I haven't so far. As long as you know it's not a forever thing and that I'll be moving on in a few days or weeks.'

He leaned towards her. 'I'm in.'

CHAPTER 36

Wellington's weather had delivered up a bleak day. It had rained non-stop since Otaki, slowing Grace's journey to a crawl. It was still bucketing down when she pulled into the empty Whenua Tapu Cemetery car park. She was early, Corin would be amazed. She had allowed an extra thirty minutes but had needed only twenty-five.

While she waited, she opened the NewsNZ app on her phone to check the latest news updates. She wanted more detail about a story that had broken yesterday, *Surveillance technology thwarts possible terrorists*. Police had raided two Dunedin properties under the Terrorism Suppression Act, arresting four individuals who, they alleged, were preparing a terrorist-style attack.

The police credited new surveillance technology with allowing them to track the movements of the suspects. The police acted after the group had purchased a range of chemicals and implements from local hardware stores. The commissioner was quoted as saying, 'Surveillance technology has developed to the stage where we can focus on crime prevention, not just on catching criminals after the fact. This technology means we aren't potentially dealing with the aftermath of a serious attack.'

Grace flicked her screen, causing the story to disappear, it hadn't been updated. The arrests looked too convenient, but was she thinking like a conspiracy theorist? And what about Cantwell, the vocal MP railing against surveillance who had disappeared from the public eye. No sound bites, no television appearances, that he obviously loved, and he wasn't returning her emails or calls. Minor MPs like Cantwell would sell their soul in exchange for the publicity he was getting; now he was hiding under a rock. The dogs weren't barking, they were howling.

In her rear-view mirror she saw Corin's car arrive. Parking next to her, he jumped out with two coffees. With the rain pelting down, she opened the door and he passed the coffees to her before levering his tall frame inside.

'What a fucking miserable day,' he said, accepting his coffee back. 'I assume you're over Covid?'

'I was negative. Thanks for the coffee. I see your colleagues thwarted a group of terrorists yesterday.'

'No foreplay today? No, how are you going, CT? How's your love life?'

Grace chuckled. 'Sorry, a lot's been happening. How is your love life?'

'As lousy as the weather. Fancy helping me change that?'

'Sorry, I'm happily settled. You need to move in new circles. Take up bridge, I hear it's a good pick-up hobby.'

He looked blankly at her. 'Thanks for the advice but I'm not seventy.'

'Enough foreplay?'

'More than enough. The terrorist bust or Covid outbreak?'

'Hmm.' Grace had organised the meet because of the terrorist bust and her encounter with the two thugs, but the Covid outbreak was a related puzzle. 'Covid outbreak – your cryptic text said a police tech caught it. Had he been in the bar?'

Corin shook his head. 'Never been near the place, hardly drinks. Manilow's laptop was the vector.'

'What? Are you saying the killer had Covid? Did she catch it in the bar?'

'Not catch, spread,' he said. 'There wasn't the time for her to catch it in the bar and transfer it to the laptop.'

'That explains the confusion,' said Grace. 'They first said patient zero was in quarantine. Two days later they didn't know who patient zero was. But that means . . .'

'That means,' continued Corin, 'that she flew into the country and stayed in MIQ. Except she didn't stay in MIQ, the people who flew her in had the ability to move her in and out of the hotel. It's the only scenario that makes sense.'

Grace sipped her coffee. 'Hang on. If she's patient zero, I wasn't at the bar on Friday, I met Will on Thursday. Why was I a close contact?'

'She was in the bar Thursday lunchtime when you were schmoozing Manilow. They're not a hundred per cent sure, but a similar woman, careful to avoid the security cameras, was there. The waitress catches Covid from her, you're a close contact of the waitress.'

'That works. But why was she in the bar on Thursday?'

Corin made a don't-look-at-me gesture. 'Reconnaissance? Only she knows.'

'Okay. And the health authorities will be dazed because their confirmed patient zero has disappeared.'

'She's left the country. The records have been sanitised.'

Grace scowled. 'Can they really sweep it under the carpet? Will Manilow was murdered.'

'You know they can,' he said. 'They almost swept you under the same carpet. They have a positive Covid test from Mr or Mrs Nobody, so it's been recorded as a data collection error.'

'And we want to cuddle up with these people? No thank you.'

They drank their coffees in silence allowing her time to calm down.

'I'm not meaning to get at you, CT, but it's frightening the police can know what happened, but can't act on their knowledge.'

'I know,' he agreed. 'But even if we could investigate, we're chasing a ghost. We can't prove anything. Added to that, nobody wants a scandal, especially the government. The carpet may be lumpy as fuck, but they'll always make room for another body.'

'They sure will.'

'I don't want to throw oil onto the fire, but did you want to discuss the terrorist bust?'

Grace sighed. 'Yep. According to the press release, it's thanks to new surveillance technology we've only just heard about. Did you know about it?'

He shook his head. 'It's not surprising, though; they have quite a few trials running on what they call "emergent technology". Like you, we find out about the projects when they're in the news.'

'Gut feel about this bust?'

'It feels off, but that's because I know that dodgy shit is going down.'

Grace massaged her temples.

'You mentioned you might need my help,' he said.

'Your brain, as always,' she said, 'but the police too, though it's hard to work out which side you're on.'

He went to speak but she held up a hand and took him through her 'coffee date' with the two thugs, playing part of the recorded conversation. He listened intently, occasionally shaking his head. When the American mentioned the images, Grace handed him the two photos. She stopped the recording while Corin studied the images.

'Fuck,' he said matter-of-factly. 'Where to start.'

'Those images are of me, and a woman called Elle,' said Grace. 'I see her from time to time about a story I'm writing on domestic violence. She's being stalked by her very unpleasant ex. On that day he had turned up again, so we put on a special show for him. Those two spooks think they have this over me, I played along.'

'Right. I didn't suspect you were a switch hitter. Had I known—'

Grace cut him off. 'Don't go there, CT, you're better than that.'

'Am I?' He raised his eyebrows. 'I'm always up for new experiences.'

She combined a shake of her head with an eye roll, thinking that this must be the commonest male sexual fantasy. She wanted his mind back on the problem. 'Back to the spooks if you don't mind. Any thoughts?'

'Right, assuming you want to keep going.' Before she could protest, he added, 'I'm on your side, Ace, but there's already one dead body.'

Grace paused; he was right. Freedom of speech was a noble value, but to enjoy it you needed to be breathing. 'This is New Zealand. We can't let them go around killing people and threatening journalists. Where will it end?'

As soon as the words were out of her mouth, she knew the answer to her own question. It might take years, generations even, but eventually surveillance would be weaponised: human history guaranteed it. Those in power would use surveillance to identify dissenting voices, forcing obedience. They would round up opposing voices, a la Hong Kong, and silence them. Then 1984 would have truly arrived.

She glanced left and right before flicking on the rear windscreen wiper to check their rear to make sure they were alone, which they were. 'We should stop meeting, CT. I must be under surveillance, so it's only a matter of time before they spot you and who knows what they'll do.'

'I doubt they'd threaten me,' he said. 'Too risky to take on a detective, but it'd take them two minutes to get me transferred or fired. And anyway, what *are* we going to do? The recording is highly suggestive, but it's no smoking gun. You don't know who they are, and they chose their words carefully. In a perfect world, you'd lay a complaint and we'd try and track them down to bring them in for questioning. In this world, if you lay a complaint that'll tell them you're not playing ball.'

Grace watched the rain run in veinlike patterns down the windscreen. 'I agree. I can't go to the police officially, not yet. I've a slight advantage in that what they have is comical, not ruinous. But I get one chance to use it before . . .' She didn't need to complete the sentence.

'The irony is that we, the police, are excellent once a crime's been committed,' said Corin. 'Surveillance technology would help us prevent crime, but the cost would be high.'

'Way too high. We need an independent agency between the law and the public to control access to surveillance information.'

He stroked his smooth chin. 'Watching the watchers. We wouldn't care, if we could access the information to catch crims and track known fuckheads. The SIS and co would hate it. You'd be pissing over their territory with a huge hose.'

Grace let out a short snort-like laugh. 'If the SIS hate it, I must be on the right lines. Ideally, we want a society that doesn't need the SIS. Right?'

'That would be a society without humans,' he said. 'We're no different to any other species on the planet. Human nature is a nice term for blind, maniacal, ruthless competition.'

'Not all humans have those traits.'

'It doesn't matter,' he said. 'You only need one despot. If you could keep the maniacs from power, it would be fine. But democracy doesn't seem able to do that consistently.'

'The only way to work towards an objective is to work towards an objective,' said Grace. 'Heading off in the other direction is a dumb idea.'

'Who said that?'

'No idea, but it makes sense. If we want a society without the need for the SIS, giving them unbridled power is definitely the fucking wrong direction.'

He nodded. 'What are you going to do?'

'I'm working on it,' she said. 'The public are being sold the virtues of surveillance. No terrorists, no crime, a beautiful utopian society. Bit by bit democracy is weakened, but people don't notice because we're all grinning inanely, dribbling out the side of our mouth looking where they want us to look.'

'Misdirection,' said Corin. 'It's what magicians do. Get people looking at a handkerchief while they steal your watch.'

'That's how Will Manilow put it,' Grace said sadly. 'We need to focus people on the real issues.'

'We?'

'We! You're a public servant and I'm a member of the public.'

'If only it was like that,' he said with a short, bitter laugh. 'I'm working with these arseholes, not trying to stop them.'

She looked at him sideways. 'I know you are. I've been a guest of the state before.' The SIS once made her wait for hours in a tiny interview room under the Wellington Police Station to break her down psychologically.

'Back to the point,' said Corin. 'The police do as we're directed. You need the politicians to change the law.'

'And politicians only change laws when people are marching in the street. But people won't march in the street to stop something that hasn't happened.'

'Sorry?'

'The problem wasn't having an East German police force, the Stasi; the problem was how they operated. But people couldn't have known in advance that they'd become a ruthless force of oppression. They didn't have a crystal ball.'

'I'm with you,' he said. 'And by the time they knew . . .'

'It was too late.'

Corin checked his watch. 'I better get back. I don't think I've helped.'

'It's been super helpful,' she said. 'And I don't expect you to risk your career helping a known satanic, lesbian, Marxist journalist.'

He smiled, but not happily.

'People won't march in the streets and so politicians won't act,' said Grace. 'Having politicians hounded was working, now I need to have them hounded over a cliff.'

'Good luck, and if you need me, or the police, call. We can sort out whatever later.'

She leaned over and kissed him on the cheek. 'I will, thanks CT.'

'Right, back to fucking work.' He dived out of the car and hustled back into his mufti car. Seconds later, she was alone in the carpark with the rain.

'Push politicians over the edge,' she said, starting her car. A plan was forming.

Later that evening Grace was in a cautious but buoyant mood. The spectre of the thugs hovered over her like a threatening cloud, but after her meeting with Corin she felt the excitement of closing in on a major story. Taking the groceries, mainly wine and cheese, out of the boot, she was looking forward to a relaxing evening watching the news channels and spending time plotting what to do next. She was still a firm believer in the maxim 'Hope is not a strategy'.

Meandering up her front path, she breathed in the scents from her immaculate garden. The roses were blooming, native plants were thriving and there wasn't a weed in sight. It might sound pretentious, but employing a gardener was the best investment she had ever made. It didn't cost a fortune, and it removed the burden of finding time to do a job at which she was incompetent. A gardener was Zen yoga mixed into a chardonnay.

In the lounge she went to pick up the remote from the coffee table. But instead, she froze, her mouth open, her hand centimetres from the remote.

'Relax, Grace,' said Marla. 'I'm not here to kill you.'

Grace straightened, her mouth staying open. Sitting calmly at her dining room table was a woman with jet black, close-cropped hair. She had sunglasses on the top of her head, a leather motorcycle jacket over a plain grey t-shirt, jeans and red motorcycle boots adorned with a large letter S. On the table was a large bag and a plain black motorcycle helmet. Grace knew exactly who she was, but she looked like a petite version of the Terminator.

The woman indicated the supermarket bag Grace was holding, 'You didn't buy wine, did you? Your house gave me the impression you'd have a well-stocked wine rack but . . .' She gave a go-figure gesture.

Grace blinked hard, bringing her back from the surreality of the scene to its reality. 'Yes, I bought wine.' She spoke in a monosyllabic tone. 'I try not to keep it around. Remove temptation.'

'Very wise. May I have a glass?'

'Okay.' She backed towards the kitchen.

The woman stood, her hands palm down in a calming gesture. 'I get that you're wary. But as I said, I'm not here to kill you. I'm a contracted agent, but I'm also an IT specialist, at least I was. And I'm not a psycho – I kill only as a last resort or in self-defence.'

'It didn't look like Will Manilow attacked you,' said Grace, her mouth dry.

'Manilow was dead when I arrived. It was two of my former colleagues.'

Grace tried to swallow, staying quiet.

'I'm here to give you information that will help. I read your story. You were on the right lines. And I know you'd been in contact with Manilow.'

Grace stayed quiet.

'You're quiet for a journalist. If you want, I'll go. Or you can run from the house, call the police. I won't stop you. I'm not armed. But I need to warn you, you don't want the wrong people to know I've been here. I think you know who that is.'

'Okay,' said Grace. 'Normally I'm good at taking things in my stride, but this, this is way out there.' She went into the kitchen and put the groceries on the bench. Opening the chilled chardonnay, she poured two glasses. She went to put the bottle in the fridge but stopped, turning to look at the woman, who was standing in the middle of the lounge watching her.

The woman shrugged. 'It was an educated guess from your file. Besides, it seemed rude to arrive empty handed.'

In the fridge was an unopened bottle of the same chardonnay. Grace waited for a beat but didn't wake up from what was turning into a trippy episode of *The Twilight Zone*. Handing a glass to the woman, she indicated they should sit at the table.

'Cheers,' said the agent, raising her glass as they sat facing each other.

'My children might come home any time,' said Grace, her eyes widening.

'Nobody's getting hurt. I'm hoping I'll be gone before anyone else arrives, but if they do, I'm a journalist acquaintance who's popped over for a wine and a catch up.'

'Okay,' said Grace. 'You seem to know a lot about me' – she held up her wine – 'but apart from the fact you killed Will, at least everyone thinks you killed Will, and you're meant to be out of the country, I don't know even know your name.'

'Call me Marla,' the woman said, taking a sip of wine and nodding appreciatively. 'Where's it from?'

'Where's what from?'

'The wine.'

'Oh – Marlborough.'

Marla looked upwards. 'Top of the South Island. I need to visit Marlborough.'

Grace took a large drink. 'Right, I'm coming around to the fact this isn't a weird dream. You're involved in Will's death' – her face suddenly screwed up – 'and you've got Covid.'

'Had Covid,' she corrected. 'I'm fine now, though you'll have to take my word for it. I can't exactly get a test.'

Grace made a mental note to get another Covid test – if she survived the evening. And yet what this woman, Marla, said rang true. Whether she killed Will or not, if she wanted to kill her, she would have been dead five minutes ago. 'Okay, so why are you here? Why haven't you left the country?'

'Good questions.' The agent sipped her wine, seemingly trying to collate her thoughts. 'I was meant to leave, but the plan changed. My employers decided it would be best if I left the planet.'

'Like Will?'

'The same two who killed Manilow tried to kill me,' she said. 'They'll have classified me "rogue", meaning I can be justifiably terminated. If they catch me that is – my plan is to make sure they don't.'

'Who's they? And who do you work for?'

'To tell the truth, I don't really know. I have my suspicions but there's a spider's web of companies that work for Uncle Sam when Uncle Sam can't be involved.'

'So why come here? Why not disappear?'

'I'm about to disappear, but while I laid low recovering from Covid I had time to consider my options. My assignment was to wipe Manilow's laptop and sanitise a specific document from all physical drives and the cloud. Finding Manilow's body made me question my employer's intentions, so I kept a copy of the document. Manilow thought you should have it.'

'How do you know that *Will*,' Grace emphasised his first name, 'wanted me to have the document?'

'*Will*,' Marla parroted, 'wrote your name on it. It's the smoking gun they want buried. That's why Tom and Jerry encouraged you to "find a new story to write about".'

'Tom and Jerry?' Grace squinted. 'The two at the café, one was called Reg—'

'The lead agent goes by the name Tom,' interrupted Marla, 'so Reg is known as Jerry. Tom and Jerry, the cartoon characters.'

Grace nodded. 'But . . . were you at the café?' Grace recalled images from that day. 'You *were* there. You sat near me and read the whole time.'

'I followed you to the café. I considered approaching you there, but it wasn't right. They've painted me as a murderer so in public you may have freaked out. And anyway, I could tell you were anxious. Few people secretly record meetings, so I watched.' A chuckle escaped Marla. 'I must admit, when those two turned up, that made me anxious. If I was a different person, I would have shot them where they sat.'

Grace's eyes widened.

'I would've been doing the world a favour, believe me.'

Grace swallowed as though her wine was the consistency of soup. 'Are Tom and Jerry as nasty as they seem?'

Marla nodded.

'What document?' asked Grace.

Marla took a stapled A4 document and flash drive out of her bag, sliding them over to Grace. 'There are no electronic copies of this document. I'd wiped Will's laptop before I knew what was going down.

If you scan it, I'd call the file *My holiday snaps*, not *B-Star*, which might set off alarms. The flash drive has some files you'll find interesting too.'

'What are they about?'

'You'll see. Some are hard watching, unless you're into gay porn.' Grace was about to ask the obvious question, but Marla held up a hand. 'You'll see.'

Grace picked up the flash drive, inspecting it cautiously. 'This is from Will's office.' She held up the flash drive to Marla, the Erebus Optics brand clearly readable.

'They had boxes of them. They must use them for marketing. I took a few from an open box. It's untraceable but I get your concern.'

'Will what's on this get me killed?'

Marla pursed her lips into a Billy Idol-esque sneer. 'I'd say you're in no more danger now than you're already in. If they knew I'd visited, that you had a copy of that document, for sure. Do you have a stand-alone computer?'

'I do,' said Grace. 'I use it when I write stories I don't want anyone to know I'm writing. Experience has taught me a dose of paranoia is healthy.'

'It is these days. Use that. I would assume we – they,' Marla corrected herself, 'can see your online activity because they usually can.'

'What about Will? He didn't deserve to die. He was doing the right thing. Shouldn't those two be locked up? Shouldn't I let the police know who you are, what you're doing?'

Marla stared at Grace, though not aggressively – more contemplatively.

'They should and it's up to you,' she said after a pause. 'My former employer will ensure every piece of evidence points at me, not them, and you've no idea who I am and what I'm doing next.' Marla pursed her lips, her voice rising slightly. 'And you're right and you're wrong. I agree, those responsible should pay, but who's responsible? The gun they used, is that responsible? The agents? They're assets deployed exactly like the gun.' She leaned closer. 'Tell me, if they use a drone to drop a bomb, is the drone responsible?'

'Obviously not.'

'Is the person who controlled the drone, the pilot sitting safely hundreds of miles away, responsible?'

Grace could see where the woman's logic was heading. She tapped her lip but didn't answer.

Marla continued. 'No, they can't be. Otherwise, whoever flew the planes over Hiroshima and Nagasaki would be responsible. It's the people who decided to drop the bomb, or to send in agents to protect their plans. Sure, if they catch me, they'll throw me in jail for ever while those responsible will be free to watch the sunrise. They'll find new assets.'

It was a compelling argument.

'I'm not excusing what happened,' said Marla, her voice sounding colder. 'I'm certainly not excusing Tom and Jerry. I know killing is wrong, but most *assets*' – she underlined the word icily – 'aren't like me. The training removes that, it makes us unquestioning, seeing the target as solely a target. Most assignments are righteous, scumbags of humanity who need disposing of like garbage.'

Grace didn't know what to say, so she retrieved the wine from the fridge and topped up their glasses. Marla smiled a thanks and took a slow sip.

'What now?' Grace asked.

The agent sat up straighter, her voice returning to normal. 'What now? I disappear. You'll never see me again. You're exactly where you were half an hour ago, except that information has dropped into your lap.'

Grace stared at the document while Marla took out a handkerchief and wiped the table, her glass and the flash drive.

'Habit,' she said. 'You can't be too cautious.' She stood, picked up her helmet and tapped her wine. 'Marlborough, here I come,' she said with a wink. 'I can see myself out, but you need to do us both a favour first.'

'What's that?' asked Grace.

'You need to go back to the supermarket and buy whatever it is you've forgotten.'

She looked blankly at Marla.

'The agent who's tailing you will follow, and I can leave unobserved.'

'I'm being tailed?'

'I've been watching them watching you.'

'Is it,' Grace gulped involuntarily, 'Tom and Jerry?'

'Thankfully no. I doubt they're ours, they must be yours.'

Grace harrumphed, remembering the SIS agent who had tailed her around Wellington. 'Haven't they got bigger fish than journalists?'

'You were discussing surveillance with Will over lunch the day before the hit. As they think I did it, I might be the biggest fish but you're a close second.'

Grace harrumphed again as she took her keys off one of the hooks by the front door. She stopped, her hand on the front door handle. 'I'll take my time, but when I get back, I'll have to call the police.'

'It's your call, but I wouldn't.'

'Why?' Facing Marla, she saw why the police suspected her. Height and build-wise, they could've been twins.

'It's not Tom and Jerry,' said Marla. 'But if you ring the police, they'll find out. It's what they do. They'll be curious why I visited.'

'Right,' said Grace, the situation dawning on her.

'That's why I wouldn't get a Covid test either,' said Marla, 'which you're thinking of doing. I'm clear, but if I wasn't, and I gave it to you, the epidemiology will link us. Believe me, it's best if the world never suspects we've met.'

Grace stayed silent.

'When you come back from the supermarket, if you found a document and flash drive on the dining room table, would you call the police?'

Grace grinned. 'No, one of the children would have left them there.'

The agent grinned back.

Grace opened the door. 'If one day you want to tell your story, get in touch with me first.'

A brief chuckle escaped Marla. 'Sure, you're at the top of a very short list.'

CHAPTER 38

Through the window next to the door, Marla watched Grace take a shopping bag out of her car and walk calmly down the street without a backward glance. That was a bonus, she expected Grace to take her car. Three minutes later, a white BMW driven by the suited man in sunglasses purred after Grace. Marla chuckled – they might as well have written 'spy' on their car.

She watched the street for a few minutes, looking for differences or unexpected movement. The street was quiet. She took a small black GPS bug, about the size of a key fob, out of her bag. Looking at it she said to herself, 'Hopefully you won't need my help, Grace, but I've got time.'

Checking to make sure she was leaving only the document, flash drive and wine behind, she locked the front door and went to Grace's car. Hidden from the road, she lay on her back and wriggled under the car like a mechanic. Her first surprise was the discovery of an identical GPS bug. The question was, whose was it? The New Zealand SIS or Tom and Jerry? Wriggling further under the car, she placed her bug in a secluded spot.

As she was about to shuffle back out, she picked off the foreign bug. If it was the local SIS, why were they keeping eyes on Grace? That didn't make sense. It left Tom and Jerry, who had been in Palmerston North. They could have planted the bug while Grace was waiting in the café. She tossed the bug into nearby bushes. It would appear to them that

Grace was spending time at home. They would get suspicious but not for a day or two. Hopefully that's all the time Grace needed.

As she was about to exit from under the car, the sound of a car pulling up and two car doors opening and closing made her lie motionless. Her bag, with the Sig inside that she had lied to Grace about, was out of reach. Bending her head to an awkward angle, she saw two pairs of shoes enter the driveway. She closed her eyes and exhaled noiselessly as two pairs of funky trainers, shoes Tom and Jerry would never wear, wandered past on their way inside. She watched Grace's children's shoes disappear before the front door opened and closed.

Spinning 180 degrees, Marla recovered her bag and helmet and squirmed out from the far side of the car. Seconds later she was standing on the street, casually brushing herself down. She looked left and right; it was quiet. She set off towards her car, checking the tracking app on her phone. A blue dot pulsed over Grace's house.

Around the corner, twenty metres from a busy fish and chip shop, was Marla's car. It was a place where people would take no notice of cars coming and going. She tossed her helmet onto the passenger seat, then sedately drove away, taking a planned route to a large children's play area where comings and goings would also go unnoticed.

It was a fine evening and the park was full of children burning off any remaining energy they had left after school. Worried-looking parents kept a watchful eye, hoping to get home for a pre-dinner drink or three. The parents were an eclectic mix of races, ages and, by the look of their clothes, occupations. There were even two clearly gay couples, one male one female. That was still rare where she came from. Although it looked an idyllic scene, it was foreign to her.

Changing out of her biker clothes, she put on a colourful crochet beanie, changed her sunglasses to a pair of John Lennon inspired ones with purple lenses, her riding boots to flats, took off her motorcycle jacket and wound down both front windows to let the breeze cool her. The biker look had been hot and uncomfortable but, if Grace did elect to call the police, they and anyone else would be looking for a female motorcyclist in leathers, not a hippy in a blue Toyota Corolla.

Now that Grace had the document she could disappear, her conscience a little clearer. Grace could, if she wanted, blow the lid off the story while Marla disappeared into the South Island. For both of them, it seemed like the smart move.

As she watched, children swarmed over the playground while older children shot hoops. She grew up in a town smaller than this, in Kansas. It was a cookie-cutter small mid-western town full of people with small minds. She didn't have parents who acted like these parents, and she never considered this type of life was an option, not for her. In the town she grew up in, being a lesbian or bi was a sin – according to the god-fearing rapists in charge.

A small child, having lost confidence, stood howling at the top of a long slide. A grinning dad, looking like a superhero, jogged towards her. Marla wound up the windows, quietening the little girl's howls and the playground chatter.

Why was Manilow killed? Marla sensed Grace wanted an explanation, but she didn't have one, not one easily understood. If Grace hadn't had lunch with Manilow, he might still be alive. But what sort of explanation is bad luck.

During her time with Grace, it had become clear to Marla she couldn't let the journalist end up like Manilow. Even though this wasn't of her making, she could influence the outcome. She had no doubt Grace wouldn't let a couple of mobsters warn her off and, as soon as her former colleagues figured that out, they would move to neutralise the threat. That's how it worked in their world.

And that was the problem. The American agent's conscience wasn't clear, and she couldn't disappear until it was. It wouldn't make up for Manilow's death, but it would help. She didn't know how long it would take, but now that she had deep cover in suburban Palmerston North, she had time.

CHAPTER 39

Back in her lounge, Grace let the tension drain away. On her way back from the supermarket, after buying more wine, she saw her son's car parked outside the house. She speed-walked home finding her unaware children in their rooms and no Marla. After pouring a large and much-deserved glass of wine, she collapsed onto her couch.

Calling the police was an option, but Marla was right. The police, the two heavies and maybe the SIS would want to know what they had discussed. What other motive could Marla have for visiting Grace apart from passing information? She would be painting herself as a problem, and these people were ruthless when it came to problem solving.

If it came out later, Grace's story of finding the document and flash drive was sound. She could claim she didn't try to investigate where they came from because clearly the source wanted to remain anonymous. Journalists respected their sources' desire for anonymity. If Marla remained at large, it was a story Grace would never need to tell.

In the fridge Grace found the unopened bottle of chardonnay, the only other sign Marla had visited. Paranoia made her wipe it down, but she was confident the authorities couldn't yet detect who had bought the wine. In the rapidly approaching camera-dominated future they might. Shops already existed that used a multitude of cameras to track customers so they could avoid using a checkout and the company could avoid paying a salary. Although it was a warm evening, Grace shivered.

It wasn't a society she wanted her children, and future grandchildren, to live in. Topping up her wine glass, she went to the office and her stand-alone computer.

Leaving the printed document for last, and after making sure her stand-alone computer was indeed off the grid, Grace plugged in the flash drive. She wasn't sure if she was nervous-worried or nervous-excited. The journalist part of her couldn't wait to expose the truth; the self-preserving part, the mother-to-my-children part, was scolding her to leave well enough alone. 'Who do you think you are, Grace Marks?' her nagging other self was fond of asking.

The flash drive contained an image named *Manilow mind map* and three folders labelled respectively, 'Marks-NZ', 'Selfies' and 'Cantwell'. Grace copied the folders on to her computer so she could dispose of the Erebus Optics branded flash drive. She was taking a slight risk keeping a copy of the files in her house; the SIS had invaded her home previously to copy her files.

The *Manilow mind map* was a photo taken at 4.38pm on the Friday of Will's murder. Marla must have taken it while she was in his office. Will had created his mind map on a large piece of branded stationary. Lines and arrows connected numerous boxes labelled with words such as 'Clearview AI', 'vehicle tracking', 'facial recognition' and 'phones'. In the middle was a circle labelled 'B-Star', the word underlined in red. From this circle Will had drawn a large arrow, which he had coloured in for emphasis, pointing to the phrase 'UPS & cash'.

From her conversation with Will and her research, she mostly understood the diagram he had created. Combine the vast database of images scraped from the internet with live images streaming from security cameras and channel them through sophisticated software. The result Will had labelled 'UPS & Cash'. Cash was obvious and Grace knew she would soon find out what UPS meant.

Grace next opened the 'Marks-NZ' folder. Grace knew the SIS would have a file on her, but what she found was ridiculous. There was an embarrassing amount of information in the form of documents, receipts, videos and photos: hundreds of photos. Opening files at random, she read and saw what she had been doing and who she had been doing it with.

The images and videos captured her life in minute, boring detail. Most were from security cameras, but some were clearly taken by a photographer. Having coffee with Sean. Checking for mail. Exercising at the gym. Sitting in various press conferences. Holding hands with Sean. Gardening, and numerous shots of her outside Elle's house collecting evidence for the domestic violence story. They had even taken one outside her house with Sean's hand on her arse. What a waste of taxpayer money.

Grace fumed. She was a journalist, not a fucking spy. And, most galling, how come she hadn't spotted these people?

A separate subfolder contained an eclectic mix of receipts, bills, bank statements and letters. Grace shook her head; they must be collecting her recycling. What was it called? Dumpster diving. That's how Marla knew what wine to buy – it featured on her supermarket receipts.

Puffing out a breath, she closed the folder. Although it rankled that a journalist could be a legitimate SIS target, she needed to focus on the now. She would use this information later to create a story that painted the SIS as the equivalent of peeping Toms, but she needed to get to the future first.

She next opened the folder labelled 'Cantwell'. There were over fifty photos and a dozen movies, the time stamps indicating they were recent. The first image she opened was of Cantwell laughing as he walked with a woman, presumably his wife.

'Brandon Cantwell,' she said. 'The New ACT Party MP who was leading the charge against surveillance – until recently.' She browsed through the images, suspecting what she would find. She was right and it made her half sad, half angry. This was why Cantwell had disappeared from public view.

The images were a mix of family photos and photos of a man who Cantwell was obviously having an extra-marital gay affair with. The first video Grace watched confirmed this in graphic detail, she now understood what Marla had meant. Whatever people did in the privacy of their own home was consensual sex; watched as a video, it was pure pornography.

She spent the next few minutes checking every video in *her* file. Thankfully none were of her and Sean's lovemaking. That sort of privacy invasion would have crossed a line.

They had Cantwell, on the other hand, cinematically by the balls. A married man with children, a pillar of the community who campaigned on a return to a moral New Zealand. And here he was, having an athletic affair with a man. It would be the end of Cantwell's political career. Not because he was gay, bi or whatever, New Zealand had MPs of diverse genders and tastes. It was because they had caught him red-faced in a lie. They could expose him as a fraud who deceived those who voted for him. That was unsurvivable for anyone bar Trump.

Grace swivelled in her chair and opened her main connected-to-the-world laptop. She checked her emails, deleting the majority as she didn't need a quack Covid remedy, a survival knife or a penis enlargement. She started an email to Cantwell, rubbing her temples as she mentally penned the words. She needed to get the message right, to let him know she knew what was happening and that she wanted to help.

But she suddenly halted, deleting the email. The GCSB couldn't legally read his or her emails without a type 1 warrant, but the rest of Five Eyes could. She couldn't risk alerting Tom and Jerry. The only way to contact Cantwell was to surprise him in his parliamentary office. She would travel to Wellington, and with her prized hard-won parliamentary press pass she would knock on his door.

The folder labelled 'Selfies' held two images. Opening the first caused her to laugh out loud. Dominating the image was a cross-eyed Marla holding her coffee up for a selfie. Over her shoulder she had captured Tom and Jerry after they had taken off their sunglasses. Grace guessed correctly, the second image was an enlarged and sharpened picture of the thugs; she printed two copies.

Finally, and with a small rush of adrenalin, Grace picked up the document 'B-Star Pilot – UPS Operational Strategy'. On the front Will had written 'For Ace' in red pen. If he had given it to her at lunch, she could have been in grave danger.

Making herself comfortable, she started to read.

CHAPTER 40

Grace was sweating hard. She was fifteen minutes into a thirty-minute treadmill run at the local university gym.

Last night she had read the document twice. It was indeed the smoking gun that had shot Will. Alongside their successful commercial software, A-Star, the Erebus Group were piloting a system they called B-Star, which was designed to monitor an entire population. Using piping – an IT term that equated to diverting public and private security camera feeds through an AI engine – their goal was to demonstrate they could deliver UPS – Universal Population Surveillance – in real time. It was part of a plan to corner the surveillance market, which would be hugely profitable in terms of money and intelligence gathering.

That was bad enough, but the involvement of the SCS, the Special Collection Service, linked the operation to the US government. There was scant information available about the SCS, a shadowy organisation rumoured to be part NSA, part CIA, though the US Government denied it even existed. Unofficially its expertise was capturing difficult-to-access information, though clearly it had expanded its focus.

After ringing Sean for his advice, she finished the evening with wine and a rubbish reality TV show featuring minor celebrities trying to shaft each other on a tropical island. It was the sort of mindless distraction she needed to help her sleep on what she had learned.

It hadn't been a good night's sleep – she blamed the wine – and at 6.30am after two coffees had failed to perk her up, she decided a gym session might do the trick. She left her semi-adult children dreaming, she would be back before either of them surfaced. Then she could work out the best way to blow the lid off the story without ending up like Will.

The local university gym, where she was a member, was almost deserted. So given that nine of the ten treadmills lined up next to each other were free, Grace found it odd that a woman elected to hop on the treadmill right next to the one she was currently labouring on. It didn't bother her, she usually exercised when it was hard to find a vacant treadmill. It was just odd.

Grace was running virtually around Nepal, which helped distract her from the agonisingly slow clock counting off the minutes. In her peripheral vision, she noticed the woman next to her was running at a furious pace, double Grace's speed. It wasn't a competition, but Grace increased her speed to demonstrate that she too had higher gears.

Two minutes later, a struggling Grace dropped her speed back to a comfortable, lumbering jog. The woman continued to belt out a hectic pace. Glancing at the woman, wanting to confirm she was decades younger, she did a double take when she recognised the female SIS agent who had been on her case throughout her investigation into tax. The double take caused Grace to lose focus and she stepped half on the treadmill belt, half on the metal frame. Physics took over. She managed a strident 'Oh fuck' before crashing onto the treadmill, which spat her backwards. She landed with a dull thud and the delicacy of a sack of potatoes.

Grace lay on the floor, her heart thumping as she waited for her body to provide a damage report. She tested her limbs, which confirmed that only her ego had been damaged. The woman had stopped and now stood over her.

'You don't know how much I enjoyed that, e hoa,' said Jenna. 'I wish I'd recorded it. A few colleagues would've loved it too.'

She offered her hand as Grace sat up gingerly.

'Piss off,' said Grace, not looking at her.

The agent left her hand outstretched. 'Are you okay? Anything broken?'

Grace looked up darkly before accepting the woman's helping hand. Once she was back on her feet, their height difference making her feel like she was back at school talking to a teacher, she said quietly, 'Thanks, now piss off.'

A gym staff member wearing a black t-shirt decorated with the helpful word 'Staff' came rushing over. 'Are you hurt?' she asked, her eyes wide.

'She's fine,' said the SIS agent. 'She's as tough as old boots.'

Grace, ignoring her, smiled at the staff member. 'I'm fine. I lost my balance when I realised the gym allowed in undesirables.'

'Phew,' said the staff member, who looked younger than Grace's sixteen-year-old daughter. 'The amount of paperwork we have to fill out for an accident is mega.'

After the staff member retreated to her counter, Grace turned to the woman who towered over her. 'What the fuck do you want? If this is your idea of tailing me, it's about as subtle as last time.'

The agent rolled her eyes. 'Whatever. I just want a little korero. You know, an off the record chat.'

Grace stared intently, her mind racing. Did she know Marla had visited? Or about the document? Had they caught Marla? Grace bought herself some time by using the interview tactic of repeating back the question. 'You want an off the record chat? Why?'

'We want to make sure you're safe.'

Grace mentally stepped through her encounter with Marla the previous evening. The agent had been confident no one knew she was there. Grace had inspected the information offline. Marla had left after the tail was gone. The chance they knew of her visit was unlikely in the extreme. This was a fishing expedition.

'When have you lot been concerned about my safety?'

'Our role is to protect and serve.'

'It is, but you don't stipulate who you're protecting and serving. The last time we caught up it was the rich.'

Jenna's eyes rolled again. 'Jesus, you're annoying. As I said at our last chat, that's above my pay grade.'

Grace's eyes narrowed. That chat had been over a video link after they had kept her in a room the size of a broom closet for five hours. 'I remember, but not fondly.'

A smirk briefly flickered over the agent's face. 'Let's have a coffee this time, my buy. You've managed to get yourself involved with some unsavoury characters. We want to make sure you know what you've got yourself into.'

Grace sighed resignedly, or rather she tried to sound resigned. 'Okay. And too bloody right you're buying. I don't know your name either, who are you?'

'You can call me JP.'

'Okay JP.' Grace checked the clock on the wall. 'Let's meet in The Square at two. I'll be near the chequerboard.'

'I'll find it.'

'Mine's a tall, non-fat latte with caramel drizzle,' said Grace with a smirk.

'Sounds a bit wussy, but fine.'

'Now,' said Grace, 'if you don't mind, I'm going to finish my workout, preferably in peace.'

The agent retrieved her towel from the treadmill. 'Have fun. Try not to get the speed wobbles again.' She gave Grace a theatrical wink. 'You could do yourself serious damage . . . at your age.'

Grace made a face at her back as she left. It was the second time in a matter of days that a spook had taken a crack at her age.

CHAPTER 41

It was a cloudy afternoon but not cold and, dressed in jeans and her go-to black jacket, Grace arrived fifteen minutes early for her meet with Jenna. As she walked towards The Square, a small park in the middle of Palmerston North's city centre, she let out a grunt. A tall figure in sunglasses was already sitting on the park bench near the chequerboard; it could only be one person.

Grace sat next to her, leaving as large a gap as possible.

'Kia ora, here's your coffee.'

Grace accepted the takeaway cup unsmiling. 'I was only joking. I don't drink lattes with or without caramel drizzle.'

'I know,' said Jenna. 'It's your usual, an Americano.'

Grace took a confirming sip. 'Thanks, but it's not comforting you know how I like my coffee.'

The agent shrugged.

They sat in silence for a minute, sipping their coffees as ducks wandered over to check them out for food. Jenna waved a foot at them, sending them scurrying away.

'You don't always have to be a bully,' said Grace. 'Anyway, tell me why you're concerned for my safety?'

Jenna pouted for a second. 'Why don't we start with you telling me what you know about Manilow.'

This meeting was going to be like playing chess thought Grace. 'Okay, though you'll know most of this. *Will,*' Grace stressing his first name, 'was

CEO of Erebus Optics. The company's owned by Americans and it was doing well. I tracked him down as part of my research into the increase in street crime. He was concerned a hidden agenda existed to introduce mass surveillance by stealth. He hinted he'd found inflammatory information that he was willing to share when he was ready. But he never got the chance. What do you know about him?'

The agent paused before answering. 'We obviously know a lot about his background, we checked after he was killed. The only relevant event was selling his company to Erebus for shitloads. It sounds like you know more about why he was killed than we do. The suspected killer wiped his laptop and backups. Whatever he found may have been the reason he was killed.'

'What about the killer?' asked Grace. The agent's use of the word 'suspected' indicated the SIS may have doubts that Marla was the killer.

Jenna held up a finger. 'It's my turn to ask a question. Has anyone been in contact with you about Manilow, sorry, Will?'

Grace took her time. 'Yes. My turn for a question now?'

'Don't be a dick.'

Grace chuckled.

'Who contacted you?'

Grace bit her nail. 'At first I thought they were colleagues of yours. They were spooks or ex-spooks. They wanted to meet and share information.'

Grace watched her body language intently. The other woman frowned.

'We met in a café,' said Grace, 'but it turned out they didn't want to share information, they wanted me to back off the surveillance story. They tried to warn me off.'

'They?'

'You don't know about this, do you,' said Grace. 'Two men, one with a strong American accent who did all the talking.' Jenna nodded imperceptibly at this news as Grace took out a phone and, raising her eyebrows, said, 'I secretly recorded the meeting.'

Grace played a short segment, the part when they showed her the images.

'What pictures do they have?'

Grace laughed. 'They think I'm having a lesbian affair, which I'm not. They took photos of me with a friend pissing off her stalking fucker of an ex.'

'Nice,' said Jenna. 'I don't suppose you'd let me have a copy of the audio?'

Her surprise was obvious when Grace said, 'Sure. Get out your phone, I'll airdrop it.'

Grace had already worked out that this might work in her favour. In this way she might get the SIS working to find the two murdering thugs and reign them in. It took a couple of minutes to get the airdrop to work, but eventually the process started.

As the file zipped across thin air to Jenna's phone, Grace asked, 'Tell me, who are they? How are they connected to the suspected killer?'

Jenna didn't answer immediately. 'We're not sure how they're connected. We think they were part of the same team.'

Her answer told Grace that while the agent might not know exactly what was happening, her use of the word 'were', rather than 'are', meant she suspected they were no longer on the same team. That stacked up with what Marla had told her – 'The same two who killed Manilow tried to kill me'.

'Now, I've played ball,' said Grace. 'Tell me what you know about the woman who everyone thinks killed Will.'

'Everyone, but not you? Okay, some of this is fact, some speculation,' said Jenna. 'She flew in, probably from the US, with Covid. She conducted the hit and then, we were told, she was whisked out of the country. The story we were given was she's a merc.'

Grace listened intently. 'Is that what you think happened?'

Jenna snorted. 'Some of it. Our working assumption is it turned to custard after the hit, forcing her to go to ground.'

'She's still in the country?' said Grace, trying to put on a surprised look. The problem with acting is it's too easy to over-act. Grace knew she had delivered that line as though she was starring in a pantomime – *she's behind you.*

'Don't go on the stage, Grace. You know she hasn't left the country.'

The conversation was like balancing on a trapeze wire. Grace decided to play it if not straight then a little straighter. 'From what I'd heard, it seemed dubious.'

The agent stared at her before asking, 'Has she contacted you?'

'Why would she contact me?' said Grace, sounding credible by dodging the question. Emboldened, she added, 'And with you lot tailing me twenty-four-seven, how could she?'

'Okay. We think she might contact you.'

'Why?'

'Most likely to give you information, less likely to kill you.'

Grace tried to look a combination of confused and concerned.

'When or if she does, you need to let us know. It's important we get to her before her former colleagues.'

'Okay,' said Grace. 'I have information to add, but I need to know I can trust you.' Before the other woman could speak, she continued. 'What I tell you mustn't get back to the two from the café. That would make my life dangerous.'

Jenna snorted. 'We know how to keep secrets.'

'Yes, and you know how to ferret out secrets and throw people under buses.'

They stared at each other.

Grace was unsure how to proceed. Should she give the SIS the flash drive in her pocket? She had added a scanned copy of the document and left a few of the photos of Cantwell. She wasn't going to give the SIS gay porn; they would probably arrest her. If possible, she was going to erase Cantwell's videos off the face of the earth.

Choosing her words carefully, she said, 'When I came home last night, I saw a flash drive on my dining table. I figured it was the children's at first, but when I went to tidy it away so we could eat I saw it was branded Erebus Optics.'

She watched Jenna's interest flare.

'She stayed longer than she needed to in his office,' said Jenna. 'I kept that out of the police report. What was on the flash drive?'

Grace licked her lips, deciding not to mention the printed document. 'Evidence that they're blackmailing an MP. *And* a copy of your file on me.'

'Our file on you?'

'You know, where you put the trivial shit you collect about me. Christ, you have copies of my supermarket receipts. I can't believe you employ people to go through my recycling.'

'Don't be thick,' said the agent. 'We're not living in the eighties. We get that out of the supermarket systems, they're electronic replicas.'

'That's not fucking reassuring.'

'Neither is you getting hold of a file that's meant to be impossible for you to get. Which MP's getting blackmailed? There's been chatter around Cantwell?'

Grace played her poker face. 'I need to confirm it first myself. Ideally, I'd like to get the material they're using destroyed.'

'Tricky if it's electronic. Was the information on the flash drive the reason Manilow was killed?'

Grace shook her head, not exactly lying. Staring at the chequerboard, it was as she had predicted, the conversation was imitating a game of chess and if felt like Jenna had just put her in check.

The agent squinted at her. 'I'm not trying to beat you to a scoop, Grace, I'm trying to keep you alive. If she took a copy of what they killed Manilow for, and now you have it . . .' Grace remained silent as Jenna pressed on. 'The only reason you're alive is that they can't know you have Manilow's information.'

Grace raised her voice. 'Okay, I get it. The problem I have, the problem every journalist has, is trusting you and your organisation. The last time our paths crossed, you tried to set me up. As far as I know, you're on the same side. A big-old Five Eyes jamboree in lederhosen.'

Jenna huffed.

Having bluffed her way out of check, Grace countered. 'Why should I give you the document? It needs to be out in the open, not buried beneath a mountain of GCSB bullshit.'

'I'm not asking you to sit on the information,' said Jenna. 'But if we have the information too, we can work out what's going on and do what we're meant to – keep Aotearoa and New Zealanders safe.'

Grace abruptly stood. It was a stalemate. 'I need time to think.'

'Okay, but I'm not asking you to stop. Write your story, publish the information. Whatever. But let me do my job too.'

Grace folded her arms. 'Do you have a number or an email I can reach you on?'

Jenna stood slowly and took a card out of her jacket pocket. 'I don't give these out often.'

Grace took the card and without looking at it put it in her jacket pocket. Staring up at Jenna, she didn't know what to say. In the end she gave a curt nod and headed to her car.

As she drove home, she swore multiple times. Jenna was right, the SIS should have the document. She would give it to them at the same time she filed her story. That meant she needed to finish it as soon as possible, and that meant confirming it was Tom and Jerry who were blackmailing Cantwell. In New Zealand, blackmailing an MP over his sexual orientation would be as explosive as the surveillance plot.

Sitting in a car on the other side of The Square, Marla watched Grace in discussion with another woman through the telescopic lens of her camera. The car wasn't her second-hand blue Toyota Corolla, it was Damien's near-new Nissan Leaf. Her car, she lied, was temperamental and he didn't mind her using his car if she dropped him at work and picked him up later. She could have used her car, but if B-Star was active, Damien's car wouldn't raise any flags.

Marla photographed the meeting, initially assuming it was a journalist colleague – but the body language wasn't right. There was obvious tension between the two women that made it possible the woman was with police or the SIS, but she couldn't check. They would have blocked her access and trying to sign in would have set off all manner of alarms.

After their meeting finished, Marla watched Grace's car via the tracking app on her phone as Grace drove back to her house. The bug made keeping an eye on Grace easy. Marla drove to a nearby park, close to where Grace lived. Opening a Robert Harris novel she'd bought from the second-hand store in Wellington, she left the tracking app running where she could see it.

By 4.50pm the locator arrow was still gently pulsing over Grace's house. She figured that with children to feed Grace wouldn't be heading anywhere now, and she needed to pick up Damien. She would keep an eye on the tracking app, but it looked as if she was in for a treat, a quiet night in. As she drove away, she thought of Lucas and hoped he was okay.

CHAPTER 42

In an anonymous mirror-glassed office building in Wellington's CBD, in a meeting room devoid of corporate art, Jenna and an SIS colleague, dressed uniformly in black pants, a white shirt and a black jacket, sat waiting at a boardroom table. Jenna, having met Grace, had organised an urgent meeting.

The door opened and their boss, Anne, dressed almost identically in a black skirt, white shirt and black jacket, took her place at the head of the table. She looked at Jenna. 'What's new?'

Jenna took them through her meeting with the journalist. Her crashing off the treadmill, which provided the only moment of levity during the meeting, Tom and Jerry warning off Grace, the audio recording which she played part of and an MP, likely Cantwell, was being blackmailed. She finished with Grace letting slip she had a document of Manilow's that was likely the reason he was killed.

Her superior sat frowning throughout Jenna's report. 'I would have said warning off a journalist was a big step, but it pales compared to murder and blackmailing an MP. If Marks *is* in possession of Manilow's files, they can't know. Has she met this agent – or merc?'

Jenna frowned. 'I don't know. Surveillance hasn't picked up anyone but . . .'

'She's an agent, she's trained to avoid surveillance.'

'Exactly.'

'They must consider the information has been sanitised,' said Anne, 'but the first inkling they have that it isn't, they'll act. None of this can go in our files until we've mitigated the danger. JP, you'll need to keep the audio recording safe but away from our servers. Clear?'

Both agents nodded in unison.

Anne turned to Jenna's colleague. 'What's the NSA saying?'

'It's strange,' he said. 'If you asked me to speculate . . .'

Anne nodded.

'I'd say they don't know that much. They're out of the loop too. The CIA maintain their agents are observers, so we'd need more than that recording to twist their arm.'

Anne turned back to Jenna. 'Will Marks send you the document?'

'If I press her, maybe, but she'll publish at the same time. It'll create a shitstorm, but as soon as it's published the document isn't life threatening. If she sent it to me, what would we do with it?'

Anne drummed her fingers slowly. 'Why wouldn't *we* leak it? Throw whoever's pulling the strings under the bus, it's all they deserve. Don't get me wrong, the story will be hell for us too.'

'What's the best end game?' asked Jenna. 'Assuming we can't put the genie back in the bottle.'

'Marks will publish, and everyone will distance themselves from the operation, which will be terminated. It'll be like the police's facial recognition pilot that hit the headlines, only ten times worse. The US will come under backroom pressure to give up the killer but, as they don't have her and she probably didn't do it, it will be quietly shelved. No one wants the public to know what really happened.'

'What about Marks?' asked Jenna's colleague. 'Does she know what really happened?'

'She knows the woman didn't kill Manilow,' said Jenna.

Anne looked at Jenna. 'She may well know but without evidence it's speculation. It'll be easy to make her sound crazy. Do you think the document is as explosive as it seems?'

'It was explosive enough to have Manilow killed,' said Jenna.

'And do we want the genie back in the bottle?' asked her colleague. 'That would mean Marks has been silenced. That'd create its own shitstorm and their op would still be running. We need it quietly stopped.'

'I agree,' said Anne with a sigh. 'All options will require damage control. Best case, Marks gives us the document in advance of publishing so we can move on whoever we need to. Worst case, they eliminate Marks and neutralise the document. I'll need to brief my superiors. A black op in our backyard or a dead journalist, I know what they'll think is worse.'

CHAPTER 43

The alarm went off at 6am, but Marla was already awake. She tested the water with Damien, who groaned sleepily and rolled away. Shrugging, she headed to the shower.

Dressing in her hippy look – John Lennon sunglasses, a green paisley-inspired long-sleeve top and patchwork shorts – she checked Damien's fridge for food. As they had been dining out each night, and he never ate breakfast, his fridge contained nothing but condiments and alcohol. Before she left to find coffee, she checked the tracking app. The blue location marker pulsed softly over Grace's house. Her plan was to shadow Grace and, if needed, run interference to keep Tom and Jerry at bay until the story was out. Then she would need to disappear fast.

Twenty minutes later she was back with coffee and pastries. She called out, 'Rise and shine, handsome, I've bought breakfast.'

Five minutes later Damien emerged in a dressing gown, looking all his fifty years. She handed him a coffee.

'What are you, a giant lark?' he said, giving her a hug then turning on the news.

Marla set up her laptop on the breakfast bar. If she was honest, she found the prospect of a new life both exciting and chilling. It would be one far removed from her current life, but she also doubted her past would let her go easily. Her employer would view her as a ticking bomb, one they must defuse.

Financially she didn't need to work, but she was a realist. Two days lying in the sun reading was all she could take without going crazy. When she settled, she would take up art again, although she would need a new medium so that no parallel with her 'No Rules' art could ever be drawn. Then there was Lucas – she missed him and his funny ways. Maybe she could return one day, but the political climate would need to alter. Entering the US now wouldn't just be sticking her head above the parapet – it would be jumping up and down in a clown suit.

The first decision was which identity to use. As a precaution, she owned three solid, untraceable identities each with solid bona fides. The one she preferred, the one she had partly used for Damien, was Alice Green. Born in Chagrin Falls, Ohio, she was a thirty-five-year-old ex-marine who had made her money running a successful café. When her marriage collapsed (she never spoke about her marriage or her ex) she decided to see the world and was in New Zealand when the pandemic hit. Falling in love with the country and the people, Alice had decided to stay.

She confirmed her decision with a grin. She would become Alice Green.

Next, where to live. Marla had decided on the South Island – it was remote, and the wine seemed good. She had little else on which to base a decision. 'Have you travelled much in the South Island?' she asked Damien.

'Yeah, it's great. The kids and I have done a few roadies; one time we ended up on Stewart Island.'

She looked at the map, locating Stewart Island below the South Island. 'Wow, that would've been cool. What places should I see?'

Damien looked thoughtful. 'Do you like space or crowds?'

'Definitely space, but not too isolated.'

'Okay, keep clear of Queenstown, Christchurch and Dunedin. They're fun to visit but they're like any other city. There are loads of nice towns: Oamaru, Cromwell was nice, Invercargill. Take your pick.'

She browsed the towns at random but selecting a place to live without visiting was an impossible task. She decided to spend time touring until she discovered a town that felt right. Touring, an extended roadie, would be fun and would smooth her transition from quasi-government agent to regular citizen.

'I was thinking of getting a dog,' she said. 'You know, a travelling companion who doesn't talk.'

Damien frowned. 'Dogs are great but it might cramp your style. I miss having a dog, but it's like looking after a child.'

'True.'

'Did you have a dog as a kid?' asked Damien.

'My . . . father hated dogs and there's no place in the army for pets.'

'It's your call, but I'd wait until you put down at least one root.'

She nodded; he was right.

As Damien went back to the news, the last step Marla needed to organise was transferring sufficient money into New Zealand. The car, technology, camera and running around had left her with just a few thousand in cash. She needed to move a chunk of her wealth into a New Zealand bank account. Her Alice Green documentation was bullet proof, so it should be straightforward to create an account. She wouldn't even have to visit a bank – her contacts could organise the transactions remotely.

She finished her coffee, flipped on the kettle to make another and checked the tracking app. She did an instant double take.

'Son of a bitch.'

'What's up?' asked Damien.

The blue locator arrow wasn't blinking at Grace's house, or at the gym. It was edging through Shannon. 'Son of a bitch,' she said again, this time under her breath. She remembered Shannon from her trip to Palmerston North – it had reminded her of run-down Midwest towns.

Grace was heading to Wellington, probably to meet Cantwell, and she had a thirty-minute head start.

'I forgot, I have to go to Wellington today to sign immigration forms,' she lied.

'You can take my car if you want.'

'Thanks, but you'll need it today. Mine will be fine.'

Marla calmly considered her options. She needed to follow Grace but she didn't need to keep her in sight, not with her GPS bug in play. She also needed to avoid the agent in the BMW who would be dutifully tailing Grace. The smart move was to head to Wellington, aiming to arrive ten minutes behind Grace. That meant she wouldn't need to speed – much – and would avoid Grace's tail.

'I'll see you tonight,' she said, giving him a kiss on the cheek. 'I'll get dinner, we can eat in for a change. Put our feet up with some crisp South Island wine.'

'Sounds perfect. Drive carefully. If your car doesn't make it, give me a ring.'

Two minutes later she was on the road to Wellington. She plugged her phone in, perching it where she could keep an eye on the tracking app. Grace was nearing Levin. Marla sped up, settling at ten kilometres per hour over the speed limit. If the police pulled her over, she had an international driver's licence; in fact, she had four.

With a selection of her favourite songs blasting, drinking coffee with the front windows down, Marla could taste her coming freedom.

CHAPTER 44

Grace flashed her Press Gallery membership pass, hoping to wander straight in, but since the occupation at Parliament, security was tight. The security guard checked her credentials closely before letting her through. For obvious reasons, MPs' office locations aren't public knowledge. Rather than wandering around aimlessly, looking suspicious, she asked the security guard the location of Brandon Cantwell's office. He took out a clipboard and told her, in effect, that Cantwell wasn't senior enough to have an office in the Beehive. His was in a nearby building that had been recently earthquake-strengthened.

It took her fifteen minutes to negotiate her way through a second set of security checks before she tapped lightly on Cantwell's door.

'Just a minute,' a muffled voice called out.

She heard the rapid clicking of a computer mouse and the scraping of a chair. The door opened and the easily recognisable figure of Cantwell appeared framed in the doorway. He looked as though he had leapt straight out of his public relations material. The generic blue suit, white shirt and striped tie, manicured beard and fashionable glasses. It was all there – except the beaming, vote-for-me, teeth-unnaturally-white smile. In fact, Cantwell looked like he hadn't slept for days.

'Hi. I wasn't expecting anyone.'

Wearing her standard consulting attire of black shoes, skirt and jacket, but with a red shirt because she hadn't done the washing for a while, Grace didn't resemble her 'jeans and a t-shirt' media image.

Offering her hand, she said, 'I doubt you were expecting me. I'm Grace Marks.'

Cantwell shook her hand, his thin welcome fading as his brain filled in the blanks. 'Grace Marks – the journalist.'

'That's right,' she said. 'We've been in contact about surveillance.'

'Yes, but I'm terribly busy now.' He spoke rapidly. 'I simply don't have time to dedicate to that issue. I'm sure you understand.'

He started to close the door, but Grace stepped forward. She hadn't come all this way to let Cantwell brush her off at the door.

'I don't need much of your time. Can I come in?'

Cantwell held onto the door, his politeness fighting with his desire to slam it. 'I don't have anything to say about surveillance. You're best—'

Speaking softly, Grace leaned towards him, cutting him off. 'I've seen the pictures and videos. It's best if we discuss this in your office.'

The MP's mouth opened but he couldn't find the right words, or any words. He finally settled for an apprehensive 'Okay.'

Retreating into his office, he slumped into his chair. Grace followed, closing the door behind her. Cantwell looked the sort of man who would usually organise his guest a chair and offer refreshments, but today he sat and watched her draw up a chair to the opposite side of his desk.

'Before you leap to any conclusions,' she said, 'I'm on your side. And I'm sorry this has happened.'

Cantwell snorted. '*You're* sorry. I'm ruined. Now the media has the . . .' He left the sentence unfinished. 'I'll be on the front page of every paper. My life's ruined.'

'Hold on,' said Grace. 'Before you jump, the media don't have the materials, I do. I can't tell you how I got it, but I can assure you I'm the only one, apart from the people who took the . . . home movies' – she shrugged an apology – 'who knows what's on them.'

Cantwell slumped further into his chair, now looking a world away from his PR image.

'I'll never use it,' she said, 'and I'm sure as hell not here to blackmail you. I'm here to find out who's behind it and if we can expose them. Maybe they can be . . . blunted.'

The politician sat up slightly.

'How did it happen?' she asked.

Cantwell's eyes flashed. 'Your story started it.'

Grace sat calmly.

His anger was fleeting, and he let out a long, agonised groan. He took her through the two activists who pretended to capture his actions, how that demonstrated to him the danger of what was happening. It was the catalyst for his support of the campaign to limit surveillance and for a public inquiry. That was before the two gangsters accosted him early one morning.

'They made it clear,' he said. 'Drop the issue, even become pro-surveillance, and they'll *sit* on the home movies. They also made it clear that next time they wouldn't be so nice.' A laugh escaped him that made him sound unhinged. 'I understood the dangers but now it's too late. They can keep the material for ever; whenever they want me to jump, they only need to knock on the door. If I resist, they'll publish and beat the shit out me. My life is so fucked.'

Grace took out the image of the two men Marla had photographed over her shoulder.

'Were these the two?'

Cantwell looked at the image, seeming to stiffen as he nodded.

'They didn't accost me like you,' she said. 'I met them in a café, and they made it clear I should stay away from the surveillance story. They tried the same blackmail tactic on me, showed me images they figured I'd want kept hidden.'

'You're fucked too.'

Grace shook her head. 'The images they have of me aren't compromising.'

He frowned.

'They think they're compromising,' she explained, 'but they're harmless.'

'That's good, at least for you,' said Cantwell. 'I don't see how I can help. It's not my battle now.'

'It may not be your battle, but if we accept that politicians and journalists can be silenced by force, where exactly are we living?'

Cantwell leaned forward; his face flushed. 'I know, but what the hell can I do? I don't want my life ruined.' His voice cracking, he looked on the verge of tears. 'I've worked so hard to balance life and stay sane. To not hurt my wife and children. I know what's fucking right and wrong, but I can't always do what's right.'

Grace stared at him. 'Okay,' she said. 'I'm not here to force you to act. I'm only here to confirm it's the same two thugs.'

'Why don't you act?'

'I'm going to.' She decided he didn't need to know the SIS were involved. And he certainly didn't need to know the two who were blackmailing him likely killed Will Manilow less than five hundred metres from where they were sitting. Without that knowledge he was already on the ledge.

'Fair enough. Do you know who they are?'

Grace shook her head. 'My best guess is agents, or ex-agents.'

He leaned forward, indicating the taller agent. 'He had an American accent. I didn't recognise the other one's accent.'

The discussion appeared to have come to a natural conclusion. Grace looked around, spying a water cooler. Pointing at it, she asked, 'Do you mind?'

'No, please help yourself. It was rude of me not to offer. I'm not quite myself.'

She smiled as she filled a glass.

'Is there any chance you'll be able to destroy the files?' he asked.

'That, as you know Brandon, is at the heart of the problem. Not only can they hold the information for ever, it's the ability to have it replicated. It's likely on backup systems over the world. Your information could be in Utah, Iceland and Timbuk-fucking-tu.'

The MP slumped back. 'I'm fucked.'

She softened her tone. 'I wouldn't give up hope, not yet. As I said, I am about to act. Do you read Lee Child?'

'Sorry?' The sudden change in the direction of the conversation made him look at Grace as though she had asked him if he knew the price of Brent crude on the New York stock exchange.

'You know, the Jack Reacher books.'

He frowned. 'Occasionally.'

As Grace moved towards the door, she said, 'In every book he says, "Hope for the best, prepare for the worst." In your situation, that's solid advice. You know what could happen so at the very least you shouldn't be taken by surprise.'

She tried to look encouraging while also recognising that it wasn't her best philosophical pep talk. Cantwell stared blankly at her as she shut the door.

CHAPTER 45

The trip to Wellington passed without police intervention. Marla took the same route as Grace, by-passing Levin and arriving in Wellington, as anticipated, ten minutes behind the journalist.

Taking the motorway off-ramp onto The Terrace, she decided to park. Looking around, she felt a mix of emotions. She had been here not long ago, but she was an agent on assignment then, an assignment that led to the death of an innocent businessman. Forcing that line of thinking from her head, she focused on putting her skills to use. When this was over, then there would be time to philosophise.

The tracking app showed that Grace's car had stopped on Molesworth Street near the Beehive, part of New Zealand's Parliament Buildings. It was what Marla had expected, she was visiting Cantwell. While she did that, Marla had other plans.

Using Google maps, she drove the five-minute journey to Katherine Mansfield Memorial Park, reverse parking on Hobson Street. She didn't usually reverse park, but she wanted the ability to get away quickly, left or right.

The warm morning had encouraged mothers, and the odd father, to take their children to the park. With her camera slung over her shoulder, Marla wandered along a path running parallel to Fitzherbert Terrace. As she neared the end of the park she moved onto the grass until she had a clear view of what she was interested in, the back entrance of the US Embassy. She moved as far away as possible keeping the entrance in sight, finding the perfect spot on a small grassy knoll. The irony was delicious.

From her vantage point she had a clear view of the gate, but large trees kept her hidden from the abundant security cameras that were eyeing the street suspiciously. She didn't need her telescopic lens to see when the gate moved – she needed it to read licence plate numbers. Tom and Jerry didn't drive an over-priced, over-hyped Tesla; they had been driving a black BMW without diplomatic plates. Marla knew this because that was the car they had been driving when they tried to kill her and intimidate Grace at the café. The intel that Grace was at Parliament would reach Tom and Jerry. They would come out to see what's what because their GPS bug was telling them that Grace was at home.

It was after 11am and she settled herself to wait. The tracking app confirmed Grace was still at Parliament. Embassy traffic was light; one car had arrived, not Tom and Jerry, and none had left. The odd person strolled by her position, often sharing a smile. She was pleased her career had ended in a country like New Zealand rather than in an impoverished, war-torn hellhole.

At 11.38am the embassy gates smoothly opened. Picking up her camera casually, Marla watched a black BMW edge into the street. The plate number matched, though one look at the two mobsters in the front seats was enough to confirm it was them. Packing quickly but calmly, Marla walked briskly back to her car, hidden from the BMW by a continuous hedge. As she neared her car, the BMW cruised past, slowed and turned right. Less than thirty seconds later, she was on their tail.

Tom and Jerry drove unhurriedly. A few minutes later, seemingly without a care in the world, they parked behind Grace's car outside the High Court on Molesworth Street. Marla drove past before looping back, parking on the other side of the steep one-way street. Tom was standing on the street vaping; a minute later Jerry bobbed up from between the two cars. Grace's car had just been rebugged.

Marla watched them saunter uphill, disappearing into a bar. A glance at the tracking app confirmed they hadn't found her bug, which was still pulsing outside the High Court, not in the bar. She surveyed the environment. The view from the bar would let them see Grace coming from Parliament, but not the cars. Putting on a face mask, Marla crossed the road into the blind spot. Slowing as she drew opposite their car, she clumsily dropped her bag. To anyone looking, she was having difficulty retrieving an item that had frustratingly rolled under the black BMW.

When she had placed the bug, Marla turned and walked away still hidden from the bar where Tom and Jerry would be perched. She took a circuitous route back to her car via the Wellington Train Station. It was probably overkill, but now was not the time to make a mistake. Back in her car she refreshed the tracking app. Two locator arrows overlapped on Molesworth Street. Pleased with her morning's work, she paid for two hours parking, put on her backpack and joined the people streaming through a narrow security gate into Parliament's park-like grounds.

Posing as a visitor, she strolled through the grounds before sitting in the sun on the parliamentary steps. The parliamentary grounds were swarming with people eating their lunch, ambling visitors taking photos, and smoothly-dressed minions with interesting hair styles walking purposefully and looking important. She surveyed the grounds for a vantage point where she could see the cars and the bar's entrance. The spot she selected was on the grass near a children's playground. Women sitting near playgrounds are invisible, men look dodgy as hell.

At 1.15pm Marla spied Grace eating as she walked back to her car. With sunglasses on, dressed in corporate attire, she blended nicely with Wellington's corporate-cum-bureaucrat pedestrian traffic. If Tom and Jerry were on their game, they would see Grace, though with their bug in place they could sit tight. Through her telescopic lens she watched Grace take a laptop bag from her car, add time to the parking meter, then walk up Molesworth Street towards the bar, towards Tom and Jerry.

Tossing on her backpack, she paralleled Grace as she assessed the options. Grace had been eating, and anyone who limits the amount of wine they keep around is unlikely to frequent a bar at lunchtime. The chances she would go in were slim, but not zero. Marla watched with a measure of relief as Grace walked past the bar without breaking stride.

Marla casually stepped onto the large, manicured lawn and sat down among the lunchtime crowd to wait. Unless Tom and Jerry were asleep, they would soon emerge. Through a gap in the trees, she trained her camera on the bar's front doors. Seconds later they emerged, looked around as they put on their sunglasses simultaneously, and sauntered after Grace.

Letting them get sufficiently ahead so they would have to turn right around to see her, she started tracking them on a parallel footpath. A stark choice was coming, coinciding with the end of Parliament's grounds. If she wanted to keep following, she would have to double back to the security gate, break cover and follow them on the street. It was risky. Tom and Jerry may be dullards, but they were professionals.

To her relief, as she neared the end of the grounds, she could see that Tom and Jerry were standing in conversation outside the National Library. Grace must have gone in to research or write. Hidden in the shade of a clump of large trees, Marla watched them head back to their car.

After they had driven away, she sat on a bench watching them drive back to the embassy on her tracking app. With Grace safe and busy, Marla bought lunch. She toyed with the idea of returning to Palmerston North; Grace would be returning at some stage, but she decided against it. It didn't hurt to stay around.

With time to kill, she drove to the top of Mount Victoria, where she took photos of Wellington to show Damien. Then she took a two-minute walk to Manilow's house on Lookout Road. Depending on your perspective, it was either a gorgeous home or a monument to extravagance. He had occupied such a small footprint in the house that she couldn't imagine he felt on top of the world, even if he literally was. Heading back to her car, she reminded herself it still wasn't time for philosophy.

CHAPTER 46

The Vice President of International Operations at Erebus Group, Webb Fowler, put down his neat bourbon and banged his fist on the glass-topped boardroom table. 'I had a bad feeling about this project Bill, New Zealand was always too far away to control. And why didn't they silence the journalist the same time as Manilow? Jesus H Christ, if they decided to kill Manilow . . .'

The only other person in the room was the Group's Head of Security, Bill Paxon. 'Couldn't do it,' he said. 'Our asset was compromised.'

'How?' demanded Fowler. 'From the reports I've seen, there's been no trace of him.'

The briefest of smirks crossed Paxon's face 'There were complications with Covid,' he said. 'A decision was made to extract *her* immediately.'

Fowler felt his face redden. He knew they gave him only part of the intelligence briefings. '*She* caught Covid?' he asked.

'Actually, she had it before she left,' said Paxon, 'Time was a factor so she was told the test was negative, we needed her to carry out the assignment. We planned to have her in and out of the country before she was tested again but flight delays meant a test was unavoidable.'

'No wonder you didn't tell her. And, from what I've read,' said Fowler with his own brief smirk, 'she's disappeared.'

Paxon's face remained impassive. 'It appears she had contingency plans.'

Fowler waited but knew he wouldn't get any more out of Paxon. 'What's the status on the document?'

'Before she disappeared, she reported it had been successfully sanitised and she had reset his personal laptop. A New Zealand police report confirmed they found no information on his laptop or in the cloud. The document's been contained.'

'Do you think she took a copy?'

Paxon shook his head. 'It was only after she'd sanitised the loose copies of the document that her situation altered.'

'Good,' said Fowler. 'And if Manilow had given a copy to the journalist, it would have been front and centre in her story. The bitch would have delighted in bending us over the table.' Fowler suddenly frowned. 'Hang on. She whacks Manilow, sanitises the document, then disappears. That doesn't add up.'

Paxon paused, his tongue running over his teeth. 'She'd tested positive for Covid, we couldn't risk her staying the fourteen days in quarantine. New Zealand's contact tracers would link her to what they're calling the Bethel Woods cluster. That would have presented us with difficulties.'

'I can guess the rest,' said Fowler. 'Whatever plan we had to "extract" her, it didn't work, and she's gone to ground . . . alive. She could pop up anywhere. This is bad.'

'She can't pop up anywhere.' said Paxon. 'She would've had an escape plan, she's a pro, but she's naked. She'll hide for as long as she can, but she has no leverage. I've had our IT team all over it, they've confirmed all copies of the document have been sanitised. Plus, she's wanted for murder. If she does surface, we can abduct her, trade her, extradite her or let her rot in a New Zealand jail. And if she does hide, one day she'll appear on a security camera, B-Star will alert us, we'll track her down, and she'll have an unfortunate accident.'

Fowler considered this for a long moment. 'Okay, that brings us back to the journalist and her story. What damage is that doing?'

Paxon provided a summary. The story had encouraged activists to follow MPs, and many were now complaining loudly and publicly about the invasion of privacy. The pressure was impacting on political opinion and there was a growing call for a public inquiry into surveillance.

Fowler closed his eyes. 'A public inquiry, shit. That'll slow things down.'

Paxon nodded. 'We need to alter the course of the narrative in New Zealand.'

'What about discrediting Marks?' suggested Fowler. 'Paint her anti-Muslim, her principles more important than innocent lives.'

'Trolls are all over it,' said Paxon as he pulled over the keyboard that operated the large screen on the wall. 'We've also encouraged her to keep quiet. People don't like their family and friends to become collateral damage from their personal crusades.'

Fowler took time to digest what Paxon was saying. 'We're putting the squeeze on a journalist? That sounds risky.'

'The risk is manageable. We've become adept at intimidating public figures without giving them the ability to broadcast their problems. Outspoken politicians and journalists aren't unique to New Zealand.'

Fowler nodded along with the logic.

'We've become subtle over the years,' continued Paxon. 'Five Eyes have kept Marks in their sights ever since she came to prominence during a previous scandal. A sniffer programme identified a call she made to a security company CEO. It wasn't to Manilow, but it appears to have led her to him. We've tracked her since, online and the old-fashioned way. And it appears she's having an affair.'

Paxon displayed an image on the screen, it was of a laughing Grace holding hands with a smiling younger woman.

Fowler chuckled.

'She's in a relationship with this woman,' said Paxon. 'New Zealand's SIS have previously photographed her hanging around mornings and nights. We've been subtle and we're monitoring what she does. So far she's toed the line but, if we need to, we can come down harder. She has two adult children.'

Fowler didn't need it explained further. 'That will work great on social media too,' said Fowler. 'We can feed it to the trolls alongside the anti-Muslim stuff.'

'As soon as it gets out,' said Paxon, shaking his head, 'the threat vanishes. It's the fear of exposure which keeps people in line.'

Paxon changed the image. 'The other person who's decided to help us is this man.'

'Who's he?'

'He's a minor member of New Zealand's Parliament. The question we wondered was why would an insignificant politician break with his party's policy and become the leading voice for a public inquiry into surveillance?'

Fowler shrugged. Paxon's smile reminded him of teachers he had suffered through, smugly waiting for the obvious answer that wasn't obvious.

'What happened that suddenly made him earn his salary?' asked Paxon rhetorically. 'Marks' story encouraged activists to follow politicians and record their movements. On the assumption they caught Cantwell doing something he shouldn't, we kept an eye on him. We were able to convince him to change his tune, soon he'll be publicly backtracking his position though I understand we'll need to lean on him again. I sense our team on the ground are looking forward to that.'

'Good work,' said Fowler. 'And as I understand it, New Zealand has had some success with their surveillance?'

Paxon nodded. 'We employed the "post nine eleven" playbook. Make people think they're under attack and they'll let you do what you want. Back then we found sleeper cells of Islamists hiding out in bumfuck-nowhere places to help justify invading countries we didn't like.'

'I remember,' said Fowler. 'The charges were quietly dropped after a year or two.'

'Exactly. This time the New Zealand authorities found some miscreants through the surveillance technology. The public will soon forget their concerns, they'll want security cameras everywhere so they can sleep safely in their beds, thanks to the new technology.'

Fowler picked up his bourbon and held it up smiling. 'To B-Star.'

After leaving Cantwell, Grace spent the next hour in a café plotting the outline of her story in detail. She decided the best approach was an all-out exposé. Dump the entire story into the public domain. This should ignite public outrage.

As a story, it was huge, having all the elements of a cold war thriller. An American company linked to the US Government was involved in a clandestine operation to track New Zealand citizens – the assassination of Will Manilow, who had discovered their intentions, blackmailing a politician and a journalist. Grace intended to release the inflammatory document alongside the story. Without it, much of the plot would read as supposition, and in an age where fake news and conspiracy theories proliferated it would be easy to discredit.

On the way back to her car she bought a filled roll which she ate as she walked. After adding time to her parking meter, she headed up Molesworth Street with her laptop. She loved to work in the old-world environment that was the National Library. Surrounded by books, she would spend the afternoon writing the story.

Grace was still furiously tapping on her laptop when a voice announced the library would be closing in fifteen minutes. It was nearly 5pm, she had lost track of the time. That meant she would find a large parking ticket waiting for her. Not that she cared – what she was doing was why journalists were vital to democracies. As she had written, 'Aotearoa New Zealand society was under covert attack and the public needed to know what rights and freedoms they were about to lose'.

Before she packed up, she sent an email to the NewsNZ editor, letting him know to hold Monday's front page. Over the weekend, she told him, she would be filing a story with a document that would shake New Zealand. She stretched, clicked her neck and her yawn drew concerned looks from library patrons. She walked stiffly, letting her muscles come slowly back to life. She had been sitting for nearly five hours.

Back in her car, Grace texted Sean, inviting herself and her children for dinner. He replied with a thumbs-up emoji. Opting for music on the drive home, she let Spotify do the selecting. Her brain needed time off.

As Grace was leaving the National Library, 14,000 kilometres away in a windowless room in Beltsville, Maryland, a computer operator read Grace's email. Pursing his lips, he considered its content before activating an alert flag on the message.

Seconds later an alert pinged on Bill Paxon's phone. After reading the alert he closed his eyes and looked down, uttering a single 'Fuck.'

He sent a one-line message over an encrypted communications circuit before calling Fowler.

'I saw it,' said Fowler. 'What in Jesus H Christ is going on now?'

'We have a problem,' said Paxon. 'A big problem.'

Five minutes later, the back gate of the US Embassy slid open allowing a black BMW to ease into the Wellington evening.

CHAPTER 48

After filling her car with petrol, Marla parked at a supermarket in Paremata. Her position gave her a clear view of the highway and all traffic heading north would drive past her location at a sedate fifty kilometres per hour. After Grace had driven past, Marla planned to photograph the driver of the white BMW, in case it was necessary to identify him, before joining the leisurely convoy back to Palmerston North.

She got out of her car, stretched and yawned. After the morning's surprise of Grace heading to Wellington, the world was back spinning smoothly. It was nearly five o'clock and according to their website that's when the National Library closed. As she watched, the locator arrow marking the position of Grace's car started inching up Molesworth Street. She smiled to herself. It would take Grace roughly thirty minutes to reach Paremata, plenty of time in which to buy dinner and treats to share with Damien as she had promised.

Twenty-five minutes later, armed with a selection of fruit, cheeses, cold meats and two bottles of Marlborough wine, she was back in her car. For the second time that day she did a double take after checking the tracking app.

'Son of a bitch!'

The locator arrow showed Grace past Porirua, moving smoothly towards Marla's position, as expected. It was the second locator arrow that caused her double take. It had been stationary at the US Embassy, where it should be, but it too was approaching Porirua. Tom and Jerry were following Grace.

Several scenarios ran through Marla's head as she impatiently waited. Two minutes later Grace drove past, apparently singing. Less than a minute later, the white BMW sailed past. The other locator arrow showed that Tom and Jerry were two minutes away, hanging back and out of sight.

Marla put herself in Tom and Jerry's shoes. *Why would I need to follow the journalist? She visited Cantwell but he is no threat. She had spent a few hours at the National Library and was heading back to Palmerston North. I didn't need to be in Palmerston North last night, why tonight?*

As the traffic flowed on past, Marla came to the logical conclusion. Something had changed.

Making a snap decision, her tyres screeched as she hustled the Toyota to the carpark's exit. The traffic was dense, but she barged her way in, earning a barrage of annoyed honks. She wanted to put herself between Grace and Tom and Jerry. There weren't many reasons agents would tail a bugged car, none of them were good.

As the traffic snaked its way around the bend towards Plimmerton, the tracking app showed Grace a kilometre up the road and moving quickly. Marla's car, using the phone's GPS, appeared as a blue dot moving slowly around the bend. The unbugged white BMW didn't appear on the tracking app but was between Grace and Marla. Behind Marla was the predatory red arrow of Tom and Jerry.

Flipping over her bag on the passenger seat, Marla opened the discreet panel containing the Sig. She didn't need to check; it was fully loaded minus the bullet that had killed Manilow. Taking in a centring breath, she was as ready as she could be for whatever might happen. And she had the advantage of surprise. No one knew she was part of the convoy.

CHAPTER 49

Fowler paced nervously listening to Paxon's phone call. Paxon was standing near the window in his thirty-third-floor office, Boston spread out before him like a banquet.

'With all due respect,' said Paxon, 'that approach will create as much damage as the document's release.'

Paxon listened to the reply, eyes closed nodding slightly. 'I'll organise it.' Putting his phone on his desk, he ran a hand through his hair.

'Well?' asked Fowler.

Paxon spoke slowly. 'They've decided the document must be sanitised – at any cost.'

'But that will—'

Paxon cut him off. 'I know, but the document identifies the SCS's role in the project. That would make the system unsaleable and cause a political earthquake on both sides of the Pacific.'

'Fuck,' said Fowler. 'How did she get a copy? I thought it had been sanitised.'

'There's only one possibility, Simmons gave it to her. She not only manged to stay alive, she managed to make a copy of the document.'

'Why? What's in it for her?'

Paxon shrugged. 'Leverage? Revenge? We underestimated her, I can accept that, but I can't forgive her for giving it to the journalist. The fallout from that act will be messy and Simmons will pay for her betrayal.'

Fowler nodded. 'What now?'

'I have to send two encrypted messages,' said Paxon, as he sat at his desk and logged in to his computer. 'The first to our in-play agents.' He spoke as he typed. 'Document must be sanitised asap.' Once it was on its way, he started a second message. 'This one's to our contact in New Zealand's SIS. Pull the tail off Marks. Time critical.'

'Now I guess we hope,' said Fowler.

'Are you a religious man, Webb?'

He shrugged half-heartedly. 'When there's time.'

'I'm not either, but now's the time to pray,' said Paxon. 'The agents are professionals, but no matter what they do or how they do it, the New Zealand authorities will be all over it. The shit's going to hit the fan, Webb, one way or another. We have a few hours to make sure we duck.'

Despite the uneventful nature of the journey, Marla remained on edge. The tracking app continued to show Grace driving towards Palmerston North, Marla's car behind, Tom and Jerry further back. Traffic thinned the further they drove from Wellington, allowing her to keep the white BMW in view.

The arrow of Grace's car turned right to bypass a town called Levin. Marla expected this, it was the same route that Grace had taken going down to Wellington. What Marla didn't expect was that the white BMW would miss the turn and keep heading towards Levin.

'What the actual fuck?'

She watched in disbelief. The agent couldn't have missed Grace's turn, it wasn't possible. It was dusk but Grace's headlights stood out like beacons. As Marla turned to follow Grace, she watched the white BMW's headlights bouncing over the uneven road. He had abandoned the tail.

Two minutes later she watched Tom and Jerry's red arrow take the bypass. The road was long and straight and in her rear-view mirror she could see their headlights.

The evening was drawing in and Marla, like an old-fashioned Rolodex, flipped through the options, starting with the worst-case scenario, a hit. If it was her, waiting until Grace was home was too risky. She might not go home, and if she did there might be other people at her house including her children. The arseholes who ordered the hit wouldn't want the attention the obvious murder of a journalist would bring.

The best-case scenario had them tailing Grace as a precautionary move. Marla scoffed. It would be an unlikely but pleasant surprise. She continued to consider all options as the convoy travelled in lockstep. She was a minute behind Grace, Tom and Jerry were two minutes further back.

At an intersection in the middle of nowhere, Grace chose to take state highway fifty-seven. As Marla approached the same intersection, she noticed that the red arrow of Tom and Jerry was closing the gap. They weren't trying to catch up to her, they wanted to catch up to Grace. They were going to do what she would have done, take out Grace on the road. Marla sped up but not noticeably. She wanted to get as close to Grace as possible. The red arrow was closing fast and, on a marginal straight, the black BMW screamed silently past.

'Fuck.'

Marla gently increased her speed, but she had to let them disappear. At the speed they were travelling, it would be obvious if she kept pace.

Marla grabbed her phone and dialled 911. She didn't know if the number worked in New Zealand, but she was pleased it did.

'Which service do you require?' asked the operator.

'Police.'

'Hold the line.' The operator's voice was calm, unhurried.

A second operator asked, 'What's your emergency?'

'There's been a crash near' – Marla switched back to the tracking app – 'Toe-co-mar-you.' She pronounced the unfamiliar name slowly, adding 'near Palmerston North'.

'Tokomaru,' the operator said perfectly. 'Are there any injuries?'

'I don't know, it looks bad.'

'Can I have your name please?'

Marla terminated the call. On the tracking app, she watched the red arrow rapidly catching the blue arrow as it innocently meandered towards Palmerston North. As Grace neared Tokomaru, Tom and Jerry were right behind her.

CHAPTER 51

The road ahead kinked gently right, the small town's sole impact on the state highway. Grace let her old, reliable but in-need-of-a-service radiant-red Ford Mondeo coast up the small rise before Tokomaru, the small town with the gentle kink near Palmerston North and home. She glanced at the dashboard: it was almost seven o'clock.

'Whatever will be, will be . . .'

She sang along to the song Spotify had selected for her. She had Googled Doris Day recently when researching a story, clearly security cameras weren't the only devices monitoring people day and night.

Grace buzzed down the window, letting the warm evening air rush over her. Tokomaru had never looked so good. She was in a rare mood because she had a story, and not just any story, a scoop. For a semi-salaried journalist that was the equivalent of finding an oasis in the desert. It wouldn't change her life, but success equalled money and money kept the financial wolves kennelled.

'The future's not ours to see . . .'

As her car took the kink, Grace rolled her shoulders and clicked her neck. She had been up since half five and was too mentally drained to put the polish on her story tonight, not that it needed much. It was Saturday tomorrow, and as getting up before her teenage children surfaced was no contest, she could finish the story in peace. Once she had filed it, along with the document that had caused all the trouble, she would feel safe.

'Que sera, sera . . .'

The headlights of the car behind her blazed brightly as the driver failed to observe the reduced speed limit. With the light blinding in her rear-view mirrors, the car raced up behind her and sat on her bumper.

'*What will be* . . . Fucking dickheads,' Grace muttered. Kiwis were mostly good drivers but there were a few morons with a death wish.

Leaving the town limits, she slowly increased her speed. The car following stayed glued to her bumper. Now pissed off, she took her foot off the accelerator as she took the next corner, a gentle left-hand bend. With a sudden mix of insight and alarm, she realised it wasn't a typical moron tailgater. And at that instant the car behind rammed into her.

Grace instinctively braked. The combined forces jolted her forwards, the seatbelt saving her from damage. In the rear-view mirror she could see Tom and Jerry, the two thugs masquerading as agents who had tried to warn her off the story. Bathed in the red of her brake lights, the scene was hellish. The agents with predator-wide eyes and excited leers.

There wasn't time for rational decision making. When they dropped back a few metres, Grace accelerated, but her car was no match for whatever they were driving. It ploughed into her for a second time.

'Fuck you!' she yelled.

Speeding up wasn't going to work. Stopping was likely to be a death sentence.

With no plan in mind, she slowed as they approached another left-hand bend, bracing herself. This time the blow was less severe, but well-aimed. The car hit her left back panel and, as the thug who was driving accelerated hard, the back of Grace's car started to slide to the right.

Time slowed. Grace saw her speed was eighty and, unhelpfully given the circumstances, that she needed petrol. There were no headlights from oncoming vehicles – that was good. They had the road to themselves – that was bad. And ironically there were no security cameras to capture the action.

She felt the car sliding out of control. A rally driver would have counter steered and taken their foot off the brake. Grace wasn't a rally driver. Her instinct was to steer left and brake.

As physics took over, Grace swore quietly. As Doris sang sweetly on, she closed her eyes. Turning left had accentuated the skid. That, combined with the force of the car behind, made losing control an inevitability.

As her car yawed further sideways, the tyres could no longer keep turning. The speed of the car meant that it was equally inevitable that the car would roll. Time slowed.

'Will I be happy, will I be rich . . .'

Grace screamed as her car tilted, slowly at first, before it reached the point of no return. With the acceleration of a roller coaster, it went into a violent roll. She was in the equivalent of a spin dryer. Her car rolled five times across the road, crashing through a fence before landing the right way up on a side road.

Unaware if she was alive, dead, unharmed or badly injured, she found it incredible the world could be so silent after the cacophony of the crash. Even Doris had stopped. The only sound she could hear was the ticking of her engine as the metal cooled. If she was dead, or about to die, she knew with a comforting certainty her children would be okay. They were old enough to look after themselves; for all her worries and doubts as a single parent, she had done well.

She stayed conscious long enough to hear the screeching of tyres as Tom and Jerry rushed back to the scene. She was still alive, though the odds they were coming to help keep her that way were low.

She tried to unbuckle her seatbelt but her arm wouldn't move. She needed to get out of the car, to get away, but she couldn't stop herself slipping into the inky darkness.

CHAPTER 52

Marla flew through Tokomaru, her car protesting as she took the kink at a hundred and fifty. The two cars had disappeared around the next corner. On her tracking app, the two arrows had become one. She trod harder on the accelerator, but her Toyota was already at its limit. Keeping one eye on the road, she watched the arrows take a bend before the blue arrow disappeared. It was as though Grace had driven off the planet. The red arrow was stopping.

She eased back to a hundred, wanting to approach with caution. Around the next corner, the last of the sun illuminated a small dust cloud in the distance, reminding her of mist on a tranquil Nebraskan spring morning. Slowing as she drew closer, the tracking app indicated Tom and Jerry were somewhere in the middle of the cloud. Confirming this, she saw their headlights as she approached the scene.

Dropping her speed further, Marla arrived in the manner of a cautious motorist wondering if their assistance was needed. The light breeze was dissipating the dust and Marla saw the driver getting out of the black BMW, pulling on an orange high-vis jacket. The other mobster was still in the car. She couldn't see Grace's car, which meant it was well off the road.

She slowed to thirty. The BMW's hazard lights started flashing. Fifty metres from the scene she recognised it was Jerry in the high-vis jacket, he was waving her on. Behind him she could see Tom getting out of the car. Anyone arriving at the scene of an accident waved on by a high-vis jacket wearer would feel immense relief and drive on. Marla saw the lights of an oncoming car cautiously approaching the scene. She cursed and stopped in the middle of the road; there was no one behind her.

After Jerry had waved through the on-coming car, he walked towards her, smiling and waving her through. Marla moved forward at a walking pace then, when he had no chance to run, she hit the accelerator. A flicker of recognition crossed his face as she ploughed into him. He had tried unsuccessfully to jump over the car thundering towards him, but the Toyota hit his body with a dull thud before he disappeared, reappearing in Marla's rear-view mirror as an unmoving heap in the road.

His eyes as large as saucers, Tom was reaching into his jacket, but seeing Jerry run down had delayed his reaction. Time was now against him. Marla, accelerator still floored, aimed at the rear panel of the BMW. She ricocheted off, but the force spun the BMW violently, hitting the man like a giant pinball bumper bar. She watched him fly into the fence.

Stopping past the accident site, Marla put on her hazard lights. Holding the Sig in both hands out in front of her, she ran towards Tom who was slumped at the base of the fence. It was hard to judge how badly injured he was, not that she cared, but he wasn't moving and wasn't likely to without help. He was no immediate threat. She threw the gun he hadn't managed to draw into a paddock, which was when she saw Grace's car, it's headlights on, sitting the right way up on a side road. It looked as though a couple of teenagers had parked out of sight for a frantic rumble.

Before she could check on Grace, Marla needed to secure her position. She approached Jerry cautiously. He was groaning softly, one leg at an unnatural angle. Ejecting the magazine from her Sig and putting it in her pocket, she carefully wiped away her fingerprints before swapping it for his fully loaded Glock 19. The murder weapon was back in the hands of the murderers.

Satisfied the two men were no threat, Marla rushed to Grace's car. Opening the front door cautiously, she found her slumped at the wheel, still in her seatbelt. Marla put her fingers on her neck to check for a pulse, but when she touched her, Grace snapped awake. Not easily surprised, Marla jumped backwards.

Grace looked at her with obviously confused eyes. 'Why?'

'Ace, it's Marla. I'm going to send your story to the media.' Grace looked concussed and her left arm was broken although it wasn't bleeding heavily. Apart from that, considering the state of the car, she looked okay. Marla heard a car approaching, people coming to help. She didn't have long.

Grace tilted her head, her eyes flickering. 'It's in the boot, but not finished. Typos.'

'I'll fix them,' said Marla, almost laughing.

'It's Marla.'

'It is.'

'No, the password,' said Grace.

'Right. Hold on, help's coming.'

Grace tried to reach into her jacket, but pain stopped her. 'In my jacket pocket.'

Marla leaned in and, as gently as she could, took a business card out of Grace's pocket. 'Jenna Parrota. You met her in The Square.'

'Parata,' corrected Grace.

Marla half laughed. 'I do believe you're going to be okay.'

'She's SIS, send her the document too,' Grace said weakly.

'Sure. If you trust her.'

Grace's eyes closed and she slumped forwards.

Marla yelled out, 'Over here, she's alive,' as she went to the back of the car. Amazingly, the boot was still locked, but after one well-aimed kick it popped open. She grabbed Grace's laptop bag and made for the road.

Two people were rushing towards Grace's car, one with a small first aid kit, the other with a blanket.

'Don't move her,' Marla called to them. 'I called the police, let them get her out.'

Back on the road, people were applying first aid to Tom and Jerry. As much as Marla wanted to, kicking them a final time would, at a minimum, make her look somewhat unsympathetic.

Putting Grace's laptop on the back seat, she inspected her car. The right front was badly dented, and the impact had smashed the right headlight, but it was drivable.

'Are you okay, dear?' asked an elderly man, dressed as though he was off to the theatre, complete with bow tie.

Marla eyed the man carefully. 'I'm fine,' she said, quickly realising he was just a good Samaritan. 'It's an old dent,' she said, realising he was looking at her damaged car. 'I stopped to see if I could help, but I'm not needed.'

'Are you sure your car's okay to drive?'

The sound of sirens, weak but audible, drifted over the scene. They were a few minutes away.

'Sure is, it's never looked better,' she said winking.

She jumped into her car and drove slowly away. She lowered both front windows and listened for strange noises. Breaking down near the scene of the accident with a bashed-up car wouldn't be a good look. She patted the dashboard affectionately, it sounded normal.

As she drove towards Palmerston North, a series of police cars and ambulances flew by.

CHAPTER 53

'Hey,' said Damien, beaming. 'I'd given up on you. Thought you might have decided to stay in Wellington.'

Marla gently kicked the door closed behind her. 'I ran into some former colleagues,' she said poker-faced.

He frowned. 'I didn't think you knew anyone in New Zealand.'

'Neither did I, it's such a small world.' She held up the groceries to change the conversation. 'I've got dinner if you're still hungry.'

Damien leapt up, taking the bag and giving her a hug. 'Starved. I guess you noticed I don't keep much food around, not now the kids have gone. Drink?'

'Please,' said Marla.

He poured two wines, though Marla could tell he had already had a couple. That was handy, she had work to do later so the quicker he fell asleep the better. She was tired but happy as they ate, talked and drank. Damien had started off as convenient, but he was genuinely nice. She planned to make sure their last night together was memorable.

Later, with Damien snoring alarmingly, Marla went to his office where she had stored Grace's laptop. This was a cross-fingers moment, had the laptop survived? Pushing the on button, she listened to the pings and hisses of electronics firing up, but the screen remained stubbornly blank. As she was losing hope, the screen burst into life.

As Marla anticipated, Grace's laptop was password-protected. From her bag she retrieved her trusty 'Bootable password reset drive'. Five minutes later she was searching through Grace's files. After putting her own name into the password-required box, she read Grace's story. It was unquestionably a bombshell, and she couldn't find any typos. The story referred heavily to the document that had caused the trouble; she found it in the same folder. The title gave it away: *My holiday snaps.pdf.*

The combination of the story alongside the document was more than explosive, it was thermonuclear. They must have learned, or suspected, that Grace had a copy and had sent in Tom and Jerry. And if that was the case, they knew it had to have come from her. If they thought Manilow had given Grace the document earlier, the New Zealand police would have had two murders to solve. She laughed, but only briefly. A lethal document until it was in the public domain.

Marla leaned on the desk, her chin in her hands. Her former US employer was psychotic. If they knew she had given Grace the document, they would be . . . unhappy. She would have to make sure she disappeared without trace. The SCS ran a black budget which was the equivalent of a blank cheque.

She copied Grace's story and the document on to an Erebus Optics flash drive; she had taken five. On her own laptop, using one of her many untraceable email accounts 'LeighdeSchit@protonmail.com', she sent the files to the editor of NewsNZ with a message.

I'm sending you these on behalf of Grace Marks. She was in a car crash, I assume she's in Palmerston North Hospital, battered but okay. A friendly word of advice. The document is why they tried to kill her. I wouldn't sit on it for too long. Once it's in the public domain, the desire to kill anyone who has a copy will vanish.

She signed the message 'M'. Smiling slyly, she added, *PS: If the police don't make it public, the Sig Sauer P228 they used to murder Will Manilow was at the scene of the crash.* She copied in SIS agent Jenna Parata.

As she turned off both laptops, her yawn was so loud it competed with Damien's snoring. She would return Grace's laptop before she disappeared, but now she was going back to bed.

CHAPTER 54

Webb Fowler packed the last of his personal items into a square cardboard box. He would have liked to take his drinks cabinet with him, but it belonged to the Vice President International Operations, a role he had reluctantly resigned from two hours ago.

Not that he had any choice. The fallout from the botched operation was severe. If he insisted on staying, they would have sacrificed him and he would have ended up in prison. On the international stage, the US Government had to demonstrate to the world they were acting against what they were calling 'a rogue element within the umbrella of their security organisations'. His resignation meant they could relocate him to a far-flung foreign spot until the heat died down. His new role was as a civilian adviser to the Iraqi Security Forces. It was down a very long snake career-wise, but it was infinitely preferable to prison.

A knock on the door brought him back to the present.

'Yo.'

Bill Paxon, who was still Head of Security for the Erebus Group, entered. 'Just popped in to say good luck. You'll be back, Webb.'

The two men shook hands.

'Thanks Bill. Drink?'

'Sure, no point leaving it for the new guy, he's teetotal.'

'Jesus H Christ,' said Fowler, as he poured them both liberal bourbons. 'When are you off?'

'Two hours. They're ultra-keen to get me offshore.'

'What about your family?'

'They'll be fine. They hardly saw me anyway, but after this tour, after the heat's gone, I'd like a role where I can spend time with them. I'm sure not taking them near goddam Iraq. What about you, Bill? Any fallout?'

'A little. Most of the damage occurred at the local level. Simmons' handlers have been redeployed.'

Fowler took a large slug, wincing as he swallowed. 'I assume B-Star is dead.'

'For now, but the infrastructure is still in place. The New Zealand company will be rebranded. Erebus, it seems, isn't a lucky name in New Zealand. It'll be kept on the backburner while the public are outraged, but that won't last long. Politicians will create issues to distract them; Covid lockdowns, threatening wage freezes or tax hikes usually works.'

'What about the journalist?' asked Fowler.

'Marks? Untouchable. Besides, she was doing her job. We shouldn't have let ourselves get in the position of having to take out a journalist. Even if we were successful, it would have backfired as badly.'

Fowler downed the last of his bourbon. 'So New Zealand's done and dusted for you, at least for a while.'

'Almost,' said Paxon, finishing his bourbon too. 'I've one loose end that needs sanitising.'

CHAPTER 55

Marla drove her banged-up Toyota Corolla into a chaotic-looking wrecker's yard. She had chosen it because it looked the sort of establishment that liked to deal in cash and wouldn't ask questions. She explained it was too costly to repair to pass its insurance. The tall, bearded man in filthy dungarees, who had introduced himself as the owner, chewed gum which appeared to help him digest the information.

'Wof,' he said.

Marla tilted her head.

'In this country, it won't get no wof.'

She let her accent loose. 'Gotcha. Won't get no wof.'

'I'll give you a hundred for it.'

Lowering her sunglasses, she fixed her gaze on the now shuffling figure. 'Pardon?'

Continuing to shuffle, he said, 'Okay, okay. Four hundred.'

She winked and replaced her sunglasses. 'You give me *three* hundred, promise me this car will never be seen on the road again, and you've got yourself a deal, cowboy.'

The owner grinned. It was a great deal.

Marla again lowered her sunglasses and her voice. 'I mean it. If I hear this car is on the road, I'll be back. And you don't want to see me again, believe me.'

The owner gulped.

'Righto,' she said, reverting to her pleasant self. 'Let's get this deal done and I'll be long gone.'

Outside the wreckers she jumped into Damien's car, leaned across and kissed him. 'You've been so good to me. When I'm back this way, if you're still single, I'll be paying you a visit.'

He smiled sadly. 'I'm sorry you have to go. When the travelling bug's out of your system, I'll be here.'

'It's good to know. Now, let's catch that ferry.'

He gave her a wink while he revved the engine and they took off in a shower of stones.

Marla buzzed down the window and shrieked 'Yeeeehaaaaa.'

CHAPTER 56

'I'm fine to go home,' said Grace, sitting up.

'I think it's best to keep you under obs for another night. It was quite a blow you took,' said the tall, dark, smiling doctor.

She made an exasperated groaning noise as she lay back down.

'Thanks doc,' said Sean.

The doctor beamed. 'It's for the best.'

Sean waited until the doctor had gone before shaking his head in a parental fashion. 'You're a pain in the arse as a patient.'

'Don't you start,' she said. 'Honestly, I'm well enough to go home. And I'm bored shitless.'

'I know, but it's only one more night.' He smirked, stepped back and said, 'If you're a good girl.'

Grace went to hit him but a shooting pain in her arm made her instantly regret it.

'I'll come back later tonight,' he said, giving her a gentle kiss.

Alone, Grace harrumphed. Opening her laptop, she browsed to the NewsNZ homepage. Her story was still headline news; it had sent shock waves through governments and populations across the world. In New Zealand, the opposition, civic rights groups and the public were all demanding answers from the Government. The US Government had distanced itself from the company and the operation, condemning its actions.

As Grace basked in her journalistic glory, Jenna, dressed in jeans and a t-shirt, walked noiselessly into the room. Peering over Grace's shoulder, she said, 'Can't get enough of yourself, e hoa?'

Grace jumped which made her wince. 'Arsehole,' she said quietly.

The agent smirked. 'I brought grapes.' She upended the grapes on the bed, pulled up a chair and started eating them. 'They're not bad.'

Grace gave her a steely glare but ate a grape. 'Is there a reason for the visit? Or have you come to enjoy seeing me in pain?'

The woman paused before smiling. 'No official reason. I wanted to see how you are and thank you for getting the document sent through. The twenty-four hours' head start, thanks to you, helped unbelievably with damage control. And I thought I'd fill in a couple of gaps for you, maybe you could fill in a couple for me too. How's the body?'

'Not too bad, they tell me I was lucky. Broken arm and I'm having shocking headaches, but the drugs are working.'

Jenna nodded. 'To be expected. The crash inspectors tell me you rolled five times. Your seatbelt, and the fact that your old dunger is, or was, pretty solid, saved you.' She munched on a grape before asking, 'What can you remember?'

Grace frowned. 'I'm hazy. And I'm not sure if what people have told me, and what I've read, has become my memory.'

'That's common.'

'I remember visiting Cantwell and writing in the National Library. After that, it's fragmented. I can see the two spooks lit up in red in my rear-view mirror, talking to someone, being in an ambulance, then waking up here. And I can't get Doris Day's song "Que Sera" out of my head.'

'Who talked to you?'

Grace looked out the window. 'Marla.'

'Is that her name?'

Grace turned back. 'You didn't know?'

The agent half shrugged. 'It won't be her real name and how could we know? They erased all traces she was here and nobody's admitting she exists. The real question is, how do you know her name?'

Grace frowned.

'She gave you the document, didn't she?' said Jenna. 'I mean in person.'

Grace nodded.

'We figured that. And she was at the crash site, but why?'

'I guess she wanted to make sure the document got to the media. She knew publishing it removed the danger. She also gave me the files they used to blackmail Cantwell.'

'We've contacted him. We've got techs trying to track down and erase the images, and the . . . porn.'

Grace's face soured at the memory. 'Will they be able to?'

Jenna shook her head. 'It'd be best for him if he came out of the closet. When he figures that out, the material becomes harmless.'

'Maybe,' said Grace, 'but aren't you meant to stop that stuff happening? Blackmailing MPs? Whose side are you on?'

Jenna made a what-can-you-do face. 'Whoever's side we're told to be on. Shit answer, I know, but we're trained to act, not question.'

'We need to change that. A journalist should never be the enemy.'

'I agree, but how do we change it? You've more chance than me. If I kick up a fuss, I get relocated to traffic patrol outside a primary school.'

They sat in silence, eating grapes.

'What's the fallout for you?' asked Grace.

Jenna pondered. 'It hasn't made us look good. A bit like after the mosque attack, we look a bit clueless. Though in the corridors of power, everyone knows what the US is like, so the focus is on them, not us. No one believes that the NSA and CIA didn't know about the op, though they're sticking to the story that their agents were involved in a traffic accident.'

'Fill in the gaps for me,' said Grace. 'I was driving home, minding my own business.'

'Right, here's what we've pieced together. You're driving home with two GPS bugs on your car, neither of them ours.'

Grace's mouth opened.

'I know. The police found them when they searched your car. As soon as they found a gun at the crash site, it became a crime scene. We had you under surveillance, but you knew that, so one bug must have belonged to the CIA agents and the other to Marla. It's the only scenario that makes sense. To add to the mystery, the police found a bug on the BMW which we're assuming was hers too, it wasn't ours.' Jenna raised her eyebrows. 'Quite an effort to bug a car that lives inside the US Embassy.'

'Okay. I'm driving home followed by your agent, the thugs and Marla.'

'That's it, except our agent gets called off the tail. We're investigating how it happened but while you were duelling on the road, he was in Levin eating a burger.'

Grace gave Jenna a what-the-fuck look.

'I know,' said Jenna. 'The next morning the police and the crash team inspected the site. There were two crashed cars and three injured people but only your injuries and car fitted the evidence.'

Grace frowned.

'Your car rolled and landed on the side road. They found you in the car, unconscious with a broken arm. Tick, that all adds up. The BMW had damage in the front consistent with the damage to the back of your car, but they had also taken a massive whack to the right rear. It's not possible it happened in the collision with your car. Then there were the two agents. It looked like they'd been thrown from the BMW, but the crash team said no way. And there was a third set of tyre marks at the scene, that made it a three-car collision.'

'Marla can't have crashed,' said Grace.

'There were two collisions,' said Jenna.

'How?'

'I asked them to make up a scenario to match the evidence. Collision one. CIA agents spin you off the road, they come back and park. One puts on a high-vis jacket to do traffic control. The other was likely going to use the brand-new hammer the police found in the BMW. Make sure you died in the crash.'

Grace winced.

'Sorry,' said Jenna, 'but they weren't there to fuck spiders.'

'Where are they now?'

'Wellington hospital under police guard. They're claiming diplomatic immunity, it'll be a behind-closed-doors decision. My guess is that when they're better, they'll be whisked back to the States as though they were never here.'

'Fuckers,' said Grace. 'You know they killed Will, not Marla.'

The agent nodded. 'But all the evidence points to Marla. The police found the gun that killed Will on one of them, but it's obvious she swapped guns. What agent carries an empty Sig with a full Glock magazine?'

'She didn't do it, at least that's what she told me. And she was the cavalry.'

Jenna smirked. 'Agent for hire seamlessly pivots to caped crusader.'

'I hate that expression,' said Grace.

'Caped crusader?'

'No, seamlessly pivots. It's brainless management diarrhoea.'

Jenna chuckled. 'Good to know your brain's still working. Anyway, the crash team say the third car, Marla, approaches the scene from the same direction, which fits as she was following you. Agent in the high-vis jacket waves her on but she runs him over and slams into the BMW. That's collision two, which sends the one called Tom into the fence.'

Grace ate another grape. 'She gets my laptop and drives away.'

'She made sure you were okay first. Witnesses said she called out, made sure people knew you needed help. She even chatted to an elderly guy before driving away.'

'Any idea where she is now?'

'Not in custody that's for sure. She's off and gone. I doubt we'll find her, but we'll be looking.'

'She was here,' said Grace.

'Where? *Here?*'

'Hmm.' She tapped her laptop. 'Returned this.'

'Did you talk to her?'

Grace shook her head. 'I woke up and it was there. She left a note.' She winced as she retrieved a large yellow sticky note, handing it to Jenna who read it out.

'Great story, Grace. Jesus, bring me a bucket,' said Jenna, before continuing. 'You should be safe now. I'll let you know when I'm ready to have my life story told.' Jenna held up the note, 'She even drew you a smiley face, what a wuss.'

'You're a fucking hard-arse,' said Grace. 'You could check the hospital security cameras, see if you could track her. I mean, I owe her, but she did have a part in Will's death. She should probably pay.'

'Probably?' said Jenna.

'She was programmed like a drone, wasn't she?' said Grace. 'They aimed her at the problem and she did what they ordered her to do. What they trained her to do. It's what you're trained to do, isn't it?'

The other woman's face screwed up as she ate a grape. Grace waited but Jenna blew out a breath, clearing the unanswerable, maybe unthinkable, question.

'Tell me, Ace, what are you going to get out of your near-death experience?'

It was Grace's face that screwed up this time. 'That's a good question.

I'll get fifteen minutes of fuck all fame . . . *again*. Hopefully NewsNZ will put me on a full salary. It's funny. I was desperate for a story, you know, boost my career and pay some bills. I got it, nearly died and in two weeks I'll be desperate for another story.'

'NewsNZ should bump you up to a whopping salary.'

Grace chuckled. 'Yeah, right. Like you, I'll have to work until I can't.'

They ate more grapes, each lost in thought.

'You know who the real hero is, don't you?' asked Grace, not waiting for an answer. 'Will.'

'How?'

'He was loaded from selling his company, sure, but he was doing the right thing and he was murdered for doing it. He could have ignored what Erebus was doing. Wait until he could leave and live the high life in retirement.'

'He did what every citizen should do,' said Jenna.

'What, like rorting the tax system?'

'Jeez, Ace, are you still banging on that drum?'

They both laughed.

Jenna stood, looking thoughtful. 'I don't know much Ace, but I figure if money's the problem, it can't be the solution too.' She winked and said, 'Kia kaha.'

'Until next time JP,' said Grace with a broad grin.

Jenna's eyes rolled, but Grace could hear her chuckling as she walked away down the corridor.

END